THE LOVE SERIES

THE LOVE SERIES

A CHRISTIAN CONTEMPORARY ROMANCE SERIES

ELIZABETH MARIE

CONTENTS

LOVE UNDER INVESTIGATION I
Book One

LOVE NEVER LOST 73
Book Two

LOVE CALLED TO SERVE 145
Book Three

Free Excerpt from "Love After Trauma" 275
About the Author 279

LOVE UNDER INVESTIGATION

BOOK ONE

CHAPTER 1

Sara took a deep breath, stood up tall, and plastered a smile on her face. She moved towards a group of guests who were engrossed in conversation. The men were in 1920s-style suits with waistcoats and slicked-back hair, the women in flapper dresses adorned with sequins, pearls and feathers. Amongst the swaths of glittering gold fabric tablecloths, elegant floral centerpieces that towered above their heads, and the upbeat jazz music floating from the live band on stage, all under the warm glow of crystal chandeliers dripping from the ceiling, Sara could almost imagine she'd been transported back in time to the roaring twenties.

"Champagne?" Sara asked, extending the tray of glittering champagne flutes she held to each individual in the group. She admired how wealthy New Yorkers created an exclusive reality for themselves, with numerous balls and galas, and all for worthy causes like charity. *What a magical way to live*, she mused. Her life could use more magic. As an onlooker, she felt glamorous tonight, and perhaps some magic would rub off on her. The drop earrings she wore were fake, but no doubt the earrings she noted on the women she served were genuine diamonds. She blinked, the fake eyelash extensions irritating, but she knew she looked the part with her sparkling eyeshadow and red lipstick, although she had to continually resist the urge to tug her short, low cut ballerina style black and white cocktail waitress costume further down. She was no prude, and she'd left her Christianity behind in her teens, so she vaguely wondered why she felt so 'exposed' in this outfit. No doubt it was because it was quite clear the costume was from the wrong decade, judging by the slim-fitting, knee-length or below glittery costumes of the wealthy guests, but this was what she was handed when she arrived for work. Yes, that was surely it. She was just in the wrong decade.

The group she approached brushed her off with a wave of one of their regal hands and she moved on. "Drinks?" Sara asked another group of guests. A dark-haired man turned and Sara noticed his reaction to her. A honeyed smile oozed over his face as he gazed at her appreciatively. "Yes, please."

Sara attempted to ignore his eyes traveling up and down the length of her body as she passed out the glasses of champagne to the rest of the group, whose impatient hands were held out towards her. The tray was empty before the dark-haired man could take a drink.

"I'm sorry, sir, let me go back to the bar and get you one," Sara apologized, turning quickly toward the kitchen, where she intended to ask one of her co-workers to return with a drink for the overly friendly man.

"Hold on," the man blurted as he stopped her, grabbing her wrist. Sara looked down at his hand on her arm in mild shock, then back up at his face.

"Excuse me, you seem to have caught my wrist," she managed coolly, despite the rising heat in her face and fire in her eyes.

Sara had learned a lot while working for this exclusive event planning agency; the Marionette only took on elite New Yorkers as clients. Her primary lesson? Some clients believed they could do, or get, anything they wanted, and far too often, they did.

"I want you to stay with me for the rest of the night, sugar." He leaned in closer. Sara caught a whiff of his fetid alcohol-tinged breath, and held back the gag reflex she felt rising in her throat. "I'll make it worth your while."

Sara couldn't help the shiver that went down her spine. She jerked her hand from his grasp.

"Someone else will get you that drink," she growled through clenched teeth. The smile she usually held on her face had slipped away. She began to turn away again, but the man grabbed at her once more and knocked the tray out of her hand. It clattered to the floor. No one in the group even bothered to look up from their chatter as the man swayed toward Sara, and she noticed his unsteady stance.

"I like that you're playing hard to get, honey, but I'm getting impatient," he crooned and moved as though to put his arm around her waist. Sara darted toward the floor to avoid his grasp and grabbed her tray in a deft move.

Their exchange had now attracted the eyes of the other guests.

"I'm not your *honey*," Sara stated firmly, trying to keep her voice low and even. She took a step away toward the safety of the kitchen, but the drunken guest lunged at her, once again grabbing her by the arm. "Hey, wait up, baby...."

Sara didn't wait for him to finish speaking as she let her free hand swing hard to punch him in the face, her reflexes springing to life. All that self-defense training she'd done since coming to New York had apparently kicked in, and despite her pulse pounding in her ears and the throbbing in her hand, she felt surprisingly calm. The other guests gasped in horror as the stricken man stumbled backward, swearing loudly and covering his eye with one hand.

"That'll teach you," Sara muttered under her shaky breath and turned away. Ignoring the whispers and stares around her, she hoped to make a stealthy exit from this embarrassing scene. No such luck.

"You little piece of—"

Sara spun around at the sound of his voice, ready to fend off another attack, and managed to step aside just as his fist flew through the air. She winced at the sound of his fist slamming into an innocent man who had been standing behind her. The dark-haired man attempted to recover himself immediately, mumbling an apology to the tall blonde man he'd just punched in the side of the head, who turned to glare back at him.

"Hey, look—sorry about that... I—I didn't mean to hit you," he fumbled.

The other man, his blue eyes now boring fiercely into the stuttering guest's own, clenched and released his fists at his sides.

"No, you meant to hit a woman," he retorted, controlled anger evident in his tone.

The inebriated guest held his swelling eye with his hand but scoffed and began to shuffle away as he cackled, "So what? She's just a waitress...." He had barely finished speaking before the blonde man swung at him, sending him to the ground this time. Sara's eyes widened in shock. Oh, no. This was bad. Now a small cluster of guests had formed a sort of ring around the action, with Sara at the center of it. There was no escaping now. She would be fired for sure. She didn't have time to think about what to do next before she heard her name barked shrilly behind her.

"Sara!"

She recognized the thick French accent before she even turned around. Julien, her boss, had approached the scene, his thin face red and his nostrils flaring.

"Kitchen! Now!" he screeched, then immediately turned toward the two men to offer his personal apologies and assistance.

Sara marched towards the kitchen, relieved to find some refuge but prepared for the tongue lashing she was about to receive. She knew she was in serious trouble.

Sara sat at a small foldaway table in the kitchen where event staff would take their breaks a few minutes later, drumming her fingers and trying to calm herself with deep breaths. It wasn't working. Julien would fire her; she had no doubt. She had been a lousy employee from the start, she had to admit. Sara had found it practically impossible to keep silent when guests were rude, which happened far too regularly.

But with focused determination, she had found strategies to avoid those guests as much as possible, and had achieved positive reviews–and even a couple of encouraging comments from satisfied clients–over the past three months. Julien had actually even agreed to make her an assistant event planner as a trial on this gig, and she had poured herself into the task. She had been so proud of her work, and dared to hope that Julien might even consider her for a promotion if it went well. Working as a waitress for the Marionette paid so much better than any job she'd had previously in New York. But now... Now what would she do? She closed her eyes and groaned inwardly at the thought.

"Sara, I have no words!" Julien approached her with his hands raised, fingers pressed to his temples, and his eyes squinting almost shut. She shot to her feet immediately.

"Julien, I can explain. I didn't mean for it to escalate. The first guy had it coming, and the second one I—"

Julien raised a hand to stop her.

"Before you start running your mouth, like you always do, let me introduce you to—"

"The man who took the punch instead of me and knocked my assailant out cold," Sara interrupted before Julien could finish. She hadn't even noticed he was standing there until now but couldn't resist blurting out what he'd done.

The man smiled and tilted his head forward in a slight bow in Sara's direction. Suddenly it hit her that he was actually quite attractive. He was at least a few inches taller than she was, even in her high-heeled work shoes, and the bright kitchen lights reflected off the natural highlights in his slightly tousled sandy blonde hair. Something in his eyes, a unique shade of deep gray-blue, struck her as familiar, and she wondered briefly which movie she must have seen him in. He wouldn't be the first famous actor she'd encountered at a plush New York party during her job, but she rarely recalled celebrities' names until she had described them to her best friend, Debra, who seemed to know everyone. This handsome—no doubt arrogant—stranger was still grinning at her, but his gaze unsettled her for some reason. What *had* she seen him in? He obviously imagined he'd done her a great favor, clueless rich guy that he appeared to be. He was probably used to women fawning over him, she mused, and her irritation at his warm smile grew.

She shook the thought away and focused on her boss, who now stood with his hands on his hips, one eyebrow raised imperiously in a stern glare at her.

"Sara, this gentleman has agreed to handle any fall-out from tonight's *unfortunate* events, including any trouble that the first gentleman might wish to make. We are, of course, extremely grateful for his gracious offer. So, if you would kindly thank him—"

"Thank him? For what?" Sara burst out in reply without thinking. "Accidentally walking into a punch that I had already dodged, or knocking a creep out that I could have handled myself? Or perhaps for doing the decent thing and standing up for someone else? I wasn't aware that simply being a decent human being warranted special appreciation, but apparently, we average humans are supposed to grovel at the feet of the benevolent upper echelons."

Sara stood squarely facing the tall man, her eyebrow raised and her face flushed. His smile had faded into a look of slight confusion. *Okay, maybe I was overreacting a little*, she thought; this man didn't deserve the ire that had been building in her over the months that she had endured this job. But she was so sick and tired of famous, wealthy clients always getting what they wanted, seemingly just because they had the money to pay for it.

Julien's face paled, his jaw dropped. Sara had succeeded in making him truly speechless. Yup, she'd probably gone too far. Like her reflexive punch at the drunk man's head, her verbal tirade just flew out before she could think to stop it.

"Excuse me…" the handsome man finally spoke, but he didn't sound perturbed. If anything, he looked rather amused. Sara blushed as he smiled at her again, annoyed both at the realization of what she had just said to a client, and at the fact that she still couldn't place that attractive but gnawingly familiar grin.

"I am so sorry, sir. She is such a clown. Didn't you mean to say 'thank you?'" Julien awkwardly intervened. "I'm sure that she did."

"Look, it's totally fine, sir. I really wasn't fishing for gratitude," the man spoke up.

He wasn't fishing for gratitude? How cocky of him, Sara thought. Starring in his own private action drama. Ugh, these actors are all the same! Good looking and arrogant.

"Well, you are most certainly humble," she mumbled sarcastically. Her hand flew over her mouth. Oops, she hadn't meant to say that out loud. She really was on a roll tonight. What was it about this guy that she just couldn't seem to hold up her work façade?

Julien turned to her in shock and she averted her eyes from his disgusted gaze. She caught a hint of surprise in the gentleman's face in front of her, before a wide amused smile slowly took over his expression. She narrowed her eyes at him, not trusting his knowing look, when Julien's explosive tone captured both their attention.

" Sara Ward! You're fired!" Julian blasted at her.

"What? No!" Sara cried as the stranger interceded, "That isn't necessary."

"Necessary or not, I have had enough of your smart mouth. Excuse me," Julien huffed and stomped away.

Dang it, why am I such an idiot? Why couldn't I just shut up for once? Sara scolded herself silently. The angry, sarcastic words just seemed to stream out of her mouth like champagne from an uncorked bottle at times, and now she'd totally screwed up.

"Hey, I'm so sorry about this. Can I—" the gentleman started to say, but Sara didn't let him finish before groaning and walking away, her head in her hands. She would *not* let this irritating stranger see her cry.

Sara grabbed her bag from the shelf where the staff kept their belongings when Debra, her best friend, roommate, and now ex-colleague, hurried up to her.

"Sara! I saw the whole thing! I've warned you about not controlling your feelings and mouthing off! I don't need to remind you that this is your seventh job in two years! Ugh, you had been doing so great, and now this..."

"You came here to lecture me?" Sara could feel a hint of moisture increasing in her eyes. She swallowed and fished in her purse for her subway card.

Debra pulled Sara into a small alcove away from the bustle of the kitchen around them, placing her hands on Sara's shoulders and fixing her gaze with her own dark brown eyes. "No. I came here to tell you to go and apologize to Julien. I fought to get you this job, and if you would just hold it together, maybe I could get you a promotion to a position like mine, senior event planner. Or maybe you could eventually get a position doing something you are actually great at, like, I don't know—*public relations*?! But Sara, that won't happen if you keep pulling stunts like this."

Sara drew a ragged sigh and huffed it out. She knew Debra was right. They'd been over this before. She felt jealous that Debra seemed to have grown up so much in the past three years since they'd met, and Sara still felt like she was running in circles, like a silly puppy chasing its tail. Why couldn't she just learn from her mistakes, get a grip on her anger, and move on? She placed her bag back down on the shelf.

"Okay, fine. Just stop looking at me like you've just lost your best friend." Debra grinned ruefully at her. Sara wiped her eyes, took a deep breath, eyelash extensions thankfully still intact, and went to search for Julien.

She found him giving the chefs instructions.

"Julien? Excuse me. I am so sorry. What can I do to get my job back?"

Julien sighed, dismissed the chefs, and turned to her. He crossed his arms over his chest defensively, pressed his lips together, and arched his eyebrows with a look of both resignation and pity. Finally, he dropped his arms, let out a sigh, and rolled his eyes.

"I knew you would do this. Luckily for you, the French are very forgiving. If you apologize to the blonde gentleman from earlier, you can have your job back."

He smiled humorlessly.

"Well, that's easy. What's his name?" She beamed, relieved he wouldn't subject her to something like work without pay.

"Oh, let me see. It was an E something..." Julien twisted his mouth in thought. "Ah, yes. Ezekiel Cane. I believe he's staying at the Fairfield Inn. Debra will no doubt have his contact info; you can check with her. Good luck."

Sara's mouth fell open as Julien walked away. Ezekiel Cane? No way. That handsome gentleman was Ezekiel Cane? She had thought he looked vaguely familiar. She could never have imagined she would run into him, of all people, here in New York. He was the one person she could confidently say she had actually hated growing up. Great. This apology was going to be far more complicated than she thought.

The next morning, Sara caught a train from her apartment and then walked down to the Fairfield Inn, part of a high-rise building not far from Times Square. Standing in front of the double sets of sliding doors at the entrance, she felt a knot twist in her stomach, inwardly kicking herself for letting Ezekiel Cane see her as a waitress after all these years, when he obviously was better off staying in this nice hotel and rubbing elbows with the clientele she'd been serving.

"Hi. I'm here to see Mr. Ezekiel Cane?" she said as she approached the man at the reception desk.

"One minute." The man typed something into his computer, then placed a phone call. After speaking hurriedly, he hung up. "He's not in his room, Miss. Do you want me to take a message?"

"Um, no. Do you know where he might be?" Sara asked, hoping not to have to postpone this humiliating task any longer than necessary.

"You could check the breakfast bar or the outdoor dining area of our rooftop restaurant. That's a popular spot for our guests at this hour."

"Thank you!" Sara replied, not waiting to hear his "you're welcome" before walking towards the elevators to find the restaurant. She spotted him as soon as she walked out onto the rooftop deck with expansive views of the city. She hated that he'd grown up to be so handsome. Were transformations like that even possible? He was reading a large book, a Bible perhaps, as he leaned back, relaxing in his chair. As Sara watched, trying to gather her courage, a waitress approached him. She attempted to offer him more juice, even though Sara could see that his glass was practically full. She rolled her eyes. It was so clear the waitress was looking for reasons to visit his table. He said something, and the waitress blushed before leaving. Well, it was now or never. Time to face the past she had successfully run from for three years—until today.

CHAPTER 2

*E*zekiel looked up from the well-worn pages of his travel Bible again; it was hard not to stare at the cityscape spread before him, especially with the warm light of a late spring morning catching and reflecting off countless windows and multicolored architectural structures. He had been to New York before, but it struck him again why so many people were drawn to this city; however, it wasn't the architecture on his mind just now. Woven through his meditations on the Psalms, he kept having flashbacks to the events of the night before, at the charity gala he'd scored a ticket for after a couple of phone calls. And... her. Sara Ward, in person.

It had taken Ezekiel all of two minutes to spot her amongst the crowd. He was sure that his sudden increase in heart rate and the fluttering sensation in his chest was just excitement at seeing an old friend he hadn't been in contact with for years. Dressed to the hilt in some period costume, she definitely did look distractingly gorgeous, though. He'd decided to hang back for a while before speaking to her, instead just chatting casually with other guests in what appeared to be her zone of the room. After he'd seen her return to the kitchen several times for refreshments, he'd managed to work his way quite close to her. And then that jerk had attacked her. He thanked God again he'd been close enough to get in the way of his punch. *Then again*, Ezekiel chuckled to himself, *she was holding her own pretty well without my help! Was she always so tough, or has the city just rubbed off on her?*

Whatever the case, he was even more surprised that she didn't seem to recognize *him* when he came back to the kitchen to try and smooth things over with her boss. He'd seen enough to know it wasn't her fault, but he couldn't do much to help her after her tirade in front of Julien. He almost laughed aloud at the thought of her chewing him out the way she did. Man, she had spunk! And possibly some unresolved anger issues... well, he'd keep praying for her. And hopefully, talk to her more in the coming days. That is, if she'd let him...

"EZEkiel Cane."

Ezekiel knew who it was before he looked up.

"Sara Ward."

He flashed her a smile. She hadn't changed much at all. Well, except for her hair. The long, curly, dark chocolate locks that had developed coppery highlights every summer from the sunlight were now a dark shade of red, or more like burnt orange. But she was still a gorgeous woman with a unique set of emerald green eyes, perhaps made even more striking by her new hair color. She'd always been tall for her age as a kid and had grown into her fit, athletic body very nicely over the years. She could have been a model; he knew that for a fact through the grapevine, but for some odd reason, she'd always shied away from 'girly' type aspirations and preferred instead to play the tomboy. Albeit a lovely tomboy...

"Some things never change," she said, snapping him out of his reverie.

She nodded her head towards his Bible as she sat down opposite him at the outdoor table for two. He would usually have opposed anyone interrupting his morning quiet time, where he liked to read God's word in peace, but this time it seemed more like a divine appointment.

Sara looked around her at the upscale restaurant decor, industrial and spare with stainless steel tables and chairs, and long, low glass panels instead of walls, to better showcase the city skyline around them. "Did you know it was me last night?" she asked, her tone insinuating she already knew the answer as she focused back on him.

Ezekiel smiled again.

"Yes," he admitted, finding the situation rather amusing. If he hadn't been confident it was her already, her reaction to the situation was confirmation enough. Sara Ward had always had a fiery personality. "Some things never change," he teased, repeating her words to her.

She didn't look amused.

"Whatever, Cane. Look, I need you to call my boss and tell him I apologized to you."

Ezekiel feigned a frown. He tilted his head as though thinking it over. "I don't know. Wouldn't that require you actually apologizing?"

Sara glared at him. She shook her head. "You're just as annoying as ever."

Ezekiel was sure he could hear her teeth grinding if he listened closely enough.

"That's slander, Miss Ward," Ezekiel retorted, smiling at her. He had never tried to be annoying, though admittedly, he did like to tease her; hence, he could never see why she hated him so much.

Sara shook her head again in obvious frustration. "This was a mistake."

She stood up.

"Okay, wait," he said finally, his hands up in mock surrender. He didn't want to be difficult about it, and of course, he wanted her to get her job back. It was the right thing to do, and he sensed God had orchestrated this situation. He needed to make the most of it.

"I'll call your boss," he said, his tone more serious now. She sat down. "In fact, I spoke to him for a while last night after you left, so he is expecting to hear from me. But I need something from you, too." She gazed at him warily. "I need your help with a story I'm working on."

"A story?" She looked intrigued in spite of herself. "Let me guess, you work in Hollywood now and want to make a movie in New York?"

Ezekiel chuckled at the fact that she thought he could be the Hollywood type. Younger him would have never fit that profile.

"No. I'm a journalist. An investigative journalist like your dad..." He stopped talking, realizing what he had just said. Her expression turned thunderous. "Sara, I'm sorry, I didn't mean to mention..."

"Forget about it," she muttered tersely and looked away. The last thing he wanted to do was remind her of the past and scare her off. The fact was, they had practically grown up together. Their families had once been so close that they had gone to the same schools, the same church, and even had dinner together once a week. But as they'd reached high school, things had changed between Ezekiel and Sara, and for reasons he couldn't understand, she had grown to hate him, seeming to take every opportunity to make it clear in both words and actions during that turbulent time. He had tried at various times to talk with her about it, but it never went anywhere good. So much had happened since then, yet she still apparently held her grudge. Even now, he couldn't shake the desire to make things right with her, if he could only discover what he'd done wrong in the first place!

"What do you need my help with?" Sara changed the subject.

He frowned. "Sara..."

"The story?" Sara interrupted. He understood she did not want to talk about the past. He would leave that discussion for later.

"Right. Well, I was writing an article on the Wentworth Corporation, 'America's Partner in Growth?'" He recited the company's famous motto, which conjured up decades of commercials depicting successful American industries from oil to manufacturing and even technology, looking at her face for signs of recognition. "The company's CEO, Donald Wentworth, Jr., the second son of the founder Donald Wentworth Sr., just died recently. He is to be succeeded by his son—well, you know, Donald Wentworth III."

"And this is relevant... why?"

Ezekiel shot her an incredulous look.

"Because my article was supposed to be on whether the company that handles the Wentworth Corporation's health insurance was contributing to company deaths by funding unhelpful treatment protocols. That story had to be scrapped."

He looked around and then pulled his chair next to hers to sit side by side. He leaned closer. The scent of her soft floral perfume caught him by surprise, and he shook his head slightly to focus his thoughts back on the topic of his investigation.

"While I was researching, I discovered something else: one of my trusted sources claims that Mr. Wentworth's death was ruled a homicide by an autopsy report, but the records were sealed for some reason by the corporation itself, and the police investigation seemed to just disappear. At least, there has been no apparent ongoing effort to solve the murder, implying a cover-up of some magnitude."

Sara turned to him, unimpressed by the serious allegations he was making.

"This is still just a newspaper story to me. What is my part in all this?"

"Right." Ezekiel had forgotten that not everyone found every little detail of an investigation as intriguing as he did. He often found himself carried away by the stories he investigated. "Here's where you come in. The Wentworths host an annual charity gala, and I need to be involved in it to complete my investigation. I have a hunch it's somehow tied to the murder, odd as that sounds. However, it's a very private event, planned by an in-house team they pick from the best events companies. Word on the street is that Donald the third has a new direction for the company and that this event is crucial. He gives the outward appearance of just powering on, in spite of his father's recent untimely and mysterious demise, as if it were of no real consequence. But I know there is more to it, and I need to be there."

"So... you want me to help you go undercover as an events planner?" she asked incredulously, putting two and two together.

"Well, only one of us here works for the Marionette, one of the city's most exclusive events companies," he replied with a confident smile.

She stared at him for a moment. He could see the wheels turning behind those intense green eyes.

Suddenly she held up her hands in protest. "Wait, I'm not sure you understand, Cane. I'm just a server at the Marionette. I'm not an event planner. My friend, Debra, is. Why don't you ask her? I'm not even qualified to apply for that Wentworth job." She frowned at him and crossed her arms, sensing she may have deterred him. No way did she want to spend days or weeks on end working closely with Ezekiel Cane. True, she wanted a chance at event planning, but at the cost of enduring his presence forty plus hours a week? She didn't see it happening.

"Actually, I already knew that," Ezekiel conceded. He looked down, then gave her a bashful look. "You know, I'm not too bad at my job. So, after you left the kitchen last night, Julien and I had a great talk. I had the chance to share with him about my part in my uncle's investment business, and how I would be interested in becoming a primary investor in the Marionette. That is, if he wouldn't mind me shadowing some of his key staff for a time to see the company's operation up close and to ensure it's one that we feel confident investing in. He was pretty excited at the prospects. In fact, when I told him I was impressed with your work in particular, he told me that you had been the assistant for last night's party, and he had actually been considering you for a promotion–before he fired you in the heat of the moment. He seems a little... on the dramatic side. But there you have it: you can keep your job, *and* if you decide to work with me, you can try your hand at a serious promotion."

Sara couldn't believe it. Ezekiel had dropped into her life out of nowhere it seemed, and turned it upside down. Or was it right side up? She felt herself blush, and didn't know if she was embarrassed or just frustrated that this exasperating man had somehow magically managed to hand her the best offer she'd had in ... well, years, but at the same time caused her such torment just by his presence.

It was too much. She had to get out of there, to think clearly. "I can't believe this, Cane. You really are full of yourself, aren't you? I'm out of here." She stood up and walked toward the door leading inside. He should have known she would be difficult about it.

"Well, I tried," he said quietly, watching her walk farther and farther away.

I didn't ask you to try, he immediately sensed in response. He knew that voice.

"I..." Ezekiel caught himself before he began to argue with God. If God had told him to get her on the story, she must be essential for his success. He sighed, stood up, and chased after her. She had gone down the elevator and was already out the main door when he caught up to her. They entered the street.

"Sara." She ignored him. "Sara, please. Look, I know it's a lot to take in all at once, but I saw you last night, you were amazing. You have a way with people; they're drawn to you. And the party itself was really marvelous." He grinned while dodging people on the sidewalk, trying to stay alongside her as she almost race walked away from his hotel. "Remember the homecoming dance you helped plan back in high school? The disco one? You missed our ten-year reunion, but seriously, people were still talking about it fondly. I know you can do this, and you'll be the exact partner I need so I can uncover vital information for my story. Where else would you find an offer as exciting as that?"

"I don't know. But I won't find it by talking to you," she retorted, not sparing him a glance.

"Okay, wait. I'll pay you for your work on the story as well." He would have said anything at that point just to halt her brisk pace and engage her in conversation again, but he guessed he had said the wrong thing.

She stopped abruptly, turning to face him. She scoffed. "Okay, so Sara is poor; throw money at her." She folded her arms.

"No! That's not what I meant at all. I just meant that I get paid for my work, and it would only be right to pay you for your work."

He swallowed. He didn't want to upset her. It was glaringly apparent to him that her feelings about him hadn't changed over the years.

Sara rolled her eyes. "I think it's fantastic that the moment you, of all people, decide to waltz into my life is when I'm down on my luck," Sara said. She closed her eyes and sighed before opening them again. "And now, unfortunately, you're the best option I'm presented with for help. So, as much as it pains me to say it...." She looked up at him. He tried not to feel any hurt at the amount of pain and distaste in her features. "I'll do it. But once we're done, please, just disappear."

He desperately wanted to ask her what he had done to so deeply offend her. He needed to understand why she hated him, but he knew it would be premature, not to mention selfish, to bring that up. Of course, not everyone would like him; he had to live with that. It was part of being an investigative journalist. He knew it was his calling, and he had to answer that call. But Sara had always been special to him, and the memories of her and their families were bittersweet. If the most she could offer now was to help with the story, then he would have to accept that, but it wasn't what he desired in his heart. He preferred reconciliation, and he had been praying for that.

"It's a deal," he said, his mood dampened by hers. God would really have to help him now.

CHAPTER 3

$\mathcal{E}$zekiel had invited Sara to lunch to discuss the details of his plan. She entered the little café and spotted him seated alone. She was still wondering if the torture of working with him was worth her promotion at the Marionette.

"Hey." He smiled, his face lighting up as he did. That face again. What business did he have being that handsome? His broad jaw was covered by a well-trimmed stubble, his dark blue eyes striking. Sara looked away.

"Hi." She sat down. "I am meeting Debra soon. I have to convince her to submit us to the Wentworth Corporation as the representatives for the Marionette. She should have been the one to apply for that gig, and I would have considered myself lucky to be her assistant. Now I'm asking her to give up the lead position to me. I'm hoping she'll do it if she knows I can pay her back. And if she talks Julien into it, he'll listen to her; he always does. He loves her work, and totally trusts her. I suppose you have already worked out how you can attach yourself to my team after your talks with Julien? You'll be my unofficial slash official assistant ... or something? Anyway, if we're selected, we'll get called in for an interview, and if they like us, they'll hire us to plan their event."

"Thank you, Sara. Although we didn't need to get right into that." He gave a small sheepish smile.

"I don't think you and I have anything else to get into." She wasn't about to tell him anything about her life. He stared at her thoughtfully for a moment, and when she thought he was about to say something, he instead called for the waiter and ordered coffee.

Sara played with her hands awkwardly.

"So, why didn't you become a pastor?" she asked. Maybe if she got him talking, he wouldn't ask about her. Besides, she couldn't deny that a little part of her wasn't curious about him.

"God didn't ask me to. Or, at least, He hasn't yet."

Sara frowned. He was one of the lucky ones, she decided, to feel such a direct connection to the divine. She had never experienced God the way he did.

"What led you to become a waitress? We both know—"

"We both know nothing." She cut him off. The last thing she wanted was him commenting on her life choices.

He raised his hands in mock surrender.

"Okay. I'm sorry. Not my business."

"I'm sorry. I just–you're not someone I want to talk about my life choices with." She looked away.

"I understand. Completely. You don't like me."

She looked up at him. He almost looked like he cared, the way his lips twitched downwards. She was surprised to find there was a momentary pang of sadness on his handsome features, but it was gone too quickly for her to decipher what it meant.

"Let's talk about the story. How does it go?"

He seemed to jump at her change of subject. His eyes lit up as they always did when he was talking about a story. He seemed to come to life around his work. The truth was out there, and Ezekiel Cane would be the one to reveal it.

"Yes. So, we need to plan the event in order to gather solid evidence for the story."

She nodded and tried to listen as he explained his strategies as an undercover journalist. She wasn't sure she even heard half of it. She felt so tense around him; all she could focus on was her posture and not looking directly at him. Would she give something away of herself if she crossed her legs, if she met his gaze? Would he see her past, her present, flash through her eyes, and feel he knew her? She needed to keep the distance between them. Ezekiel cleared his throat.

"Were you... even listening to me?" he asked.

"Hm?" Sara just wanted to get their little meeting over with.

Ezekiel sighed. "Sara, can I ask you a favor?"

"Another one?" she snapped.

He recoiled and took a breath. "Look, I would appreciate it if we could be civil to each other. I won't have a problem with that, but I need you to try on your end too."

Sara rolled her eyes.

"Of course, you wouldn't have a problem with that. What did people call you in high school?" She thought for a moment. "Ah, yes. Sugarcane. And why? Because of how 'sweet' you were."

"Well, no one calls me that anymore. But please, do. I don't mind being sweet," he teased.

"Oh, and it's so sweet of you to blackmail me into helping you," she mocked.

"I told you before: I was helping you get your job back regardless," he remarked calmly. "You could have just gone back to waitressing and hoping for that promotion. Instead, you agreed to help me, and take the promotion early. Let's just focus on learning some fundamentals of being undercover. Okay?" he said. Sara could tell she was annoying him. She kind of liked the feeling.

"Fine. Sorry. Can you tell me again how this works?"

"No problem," Ezekiel grinned.

After their lunch, Sara's next task was to persuade Debra to help them make the whole plan possible. She stopped at her local café to buy Debra's favorite drink.

"Hey," Sara greeted Debra as she walked into their apartment. "I brought you coffee ... and a scone!"

"You what?" Debra stopped reading her book, peering up over her reading glasses from her place on the sofa. When she saw Sara carrying the coffee and brown pastry bag, Debra jumped up to take it from her friend. She inhaled the delicious aroma and sighed with pleasure before she began to sip the dark liquid. A peek inside the paper bag revealed her favorite maple scone, and she popped a corner of it into her mouth, savoring the texture. Then she paused dramatically and narrowed her eyes in suspicion.

"Wait," she eyed Sara. "Why did you bring me this? It's not anywhere near my birthday."

She held the coffee away from her as though it might be poisonous. Sara lifted her eyebrows. Debra was always suspicious.

"Because I love you, Deb. Gosh, way to make me feel like a horrible friend," Sara said, pouting and acting as if she was offended.

Debra lifted the corners of her mouth in a fake smile. "Good one. What's the real reason?"

Sara hated that Debra knew her so well. "I need a favor," she conceded.

"There it is. What can I do for you?" Debra asked, her tone light-hearted as she took another sip of her coffee.

"Ezekiel Cane, the man who took the punch for me at the party the other night? He agreed to get me my job back, but he asked me to help him with something." Sara puffed her cheeks out and blew out a rush of air. "I can't believe I'm doing this, now that I think about it, but here goes...."

Sara sat down at the kitchen island and started to tell Debra about her deal with Ezekiel.

Debra put down her coffee cup. "So let me get this straight: you want me to tell Julien that he should submit two people, neither of whom is an actual event planner, to the *Wentworth Corporation* on behalf of the Marionette for their big annual gig?" Debra clarified. Sara nodded sheepishly, suddenly realizing the risk to which they'd be subjecting Debra. She hadn't even thought of that before. She'd only thought Debra might be upset about losing out on the chance at the assignment herself. "I could lose my job for something like that! I mean, what if it doesn't work out, or you get caught?"

"See, but it will work out. You can help us and everything," Sara pleaded, trying to convince herself as well as Debra. "And he promised to pay me, so I can share that with you, since you'd basically be giving me your position for the time being. Come on, I don't want to do this anymore than you do, but I already agreed to it, and I can't pull it off without your help."

Debra hesitated for what felt like a good five minutes, seeming to stare through Sara, then nodded slowly.

"Fine."

"Really?! You are the best! Thank you! I seriously owe you."

"I'm only doing it because you brought me coffee," Debra

mumbled as Sara did a celebratory dance around the living room. Debra couldn't help laughing at her clumsy friend, all limbs, as she shimmied across the room.

25

CHAPTER 4

Joe was a friend of Ezekiel's from college. He was the only son of David Galligan, the owner of Galligan Oil, but you wouldn't know it from how laid back he was. Joe didn't like to showcase his family's wealth, almost apologetic in his humility, and kind to everyone, regardless of their station in life. At least, that had always been Ezekiel's impression of him over the years.

"Hey, man!" Ezekiel greeted Joe with a wide smile and a friendly punch to Joe's shoulder. It had been almost a year since they'd seen each other in person.

"You look great, Zeke. You're definitely keeping in shape," Joe laughed as they man-hugged and then sat opposite each other.

"Likewise. I have to thank you for agreeing to help again. I know it's always a risk for you every time you use your connections to help me," Ezekiel said sincerely. Joe was like one of those God-sent friends he could always trust with his stories.

"Hey, with how business is at the company, I might have nothing to lose," Joe said. Ezekiel didn't have time to ponder the words before Joe spoke again. "I've called a contact in the Wentworth HR and you'll for sure get the interview, but word is Belinda Wentworth is doing the interviews herself, so, at that point, I can't guarantee you get the job."

"I'll prepare as much as I can for that part. Thank you," Ezekiel said.

Joe nodded. They fell silent.

"So, this Sara Ward you asked me to also get an interview for, is this the same Sara Ward from..."

"Yep. Ironic, I know," Ezekiel cut him off.

"I thought you said she hated you. For the whole first year of college, half of everything you told me about your life had to do with her and how she didn't like you." Joe leaned forward.

"She didn't like—I mean, she doesn't like me," Ezekiel sighed. "Honestly, as kids, I could understand picking some random reason to hate someone, but I thought she would have let that go by now."

If he was being honest, it bothered him that she didn't like him, which affected him even more because he didn't know why.

"And you don't know why?" Joe said, echoing Ezekiel's thoughts.

Ezekiel shook his head thoughtfully. "I don't have a clue."

"Why don't you ask her?"

"No. No, I can't do that," Ezekiel shook his head emphatically. "Our whole childhood experience seems like a sore topic for her."

Joe sighed and sat back.

"Is she helping you with the story? I mean, is she a part of it, or does she just genuinely want to work for the Wentworth's?"

Ezekiel looked up at his friend.

"Why do you ask? You know I only discuss my stories on a need-to-know basis."

"Hey, I'm just trying to help you here," Joe shrugged.

Ezekiel realized that Joe had helped him too many times for him to be hiding information from Joe about his story. He was used to being guarded, but he didn't need to be around Joe.

"Yeah. She's helping me, although she is mainly doing it in hopes of a promotion at her own company."

Joe nodded. "I see."

They ordered their food and ate. The conversation turned away from the story, and soon they were catching up as they always did. It was good to hear what was going on in Joe's life and to know his friend was doing well. Only later did he remember he'd not asked Joe what he meant by his comment about his work at his dad's company.

A few days later, Ezekiel walked into a mini-conference room in the Marionette building. As he expected, they had gotten the call to come in for the interview. Debra insisted that they practice for the interview because it reflected well on her and the Marionette if the people they had submitted got such an exclusive job.

"Welcome to Client Management 101," Debra smiled and wiggled her eyebrows. Ezekiel smiled back. He had never met Debra; he only knew of her because she was Sara's friend and agreed to submit their names for the Wentworth interview. She seemed friendly enough though, unlike Sara.

"I don't think we've met," he said as he extended his hand.

"No, we haven't. But I've heard quite a bit about you," Debra replied with an amused grin.

"Oh. Only bad things, I'm sure."

"You would be correct," Sara said as she strode into the room.

Ezekiel decided to ignore her as he took Debra's hand and kissed it.

"Ezekiel Cane."

Debra blushed.

"Debra Wallace."

"Who has a boyfriend," Sara interjected pointedly as she took a seat at the conference table. Debra glared at her.

"That was totally unnecessary," Debra muttered sideways to her friend. Sara only smiled sweetly.

Ezekiel crossed to the table and sat beside Sara.

"Sara," he nodded professionally, deciding against the friendly handshake he'd offered Debra. It seemed important to move at her pace. If she only wanted them to speak when necessary, he would respect that. If she wanted them to be friends, he wouldn't mind that either. It was all up to her.

"Ezekiel," she replied without looking at him. Her flat tone did not surprise him. As she began paging through the folders laid out on the table, Debra took a seat opposite them.

"I've heard Mrs. Wentworth is conducting the interviews herself, and I'm sure she is no stranger to event planning, so you'll need to know your stuff too," Debra informed them, folding her arms. "Let's start with the essentials."

She dropped a massive binder on the table with a resounding thud. Ezekiel gulped. Oh boy, this was the part of his investigation he wasn't sure he liked: going undercover in an industry he knew next to nothing about always meant a steep learning curve.

"This will be a breeze for me," Sara said, throwing a cocky glance in Ezekiel's direction. He shook his head.

"Good, then you wouldn't mind answering some questions. What's the first thing you ask the client about the event?" Debra squinted, focusing on Sara.

"Event goals and objectives. What do they hope to achieve with this event?"

"Ok, smarty pants. Do you make the budget for high-profile clients, or do they give you one?"

Sara smirked.

"You make the budget, of course. I thought we were here to learn. I'm not learning."

She faked a yawn. Ezekiel watched the two friends with amusement. It was nice to see a side of Sara that wasn't angry, annoyed, or scowling.

"Oh. You want to push it, do you?" Debra leaned forward, the playful tone of her voice giving away how much she was enjoying this. "Branding! Does the event have its own brand, or does it match the client's?"

"It..." Sara started to reply confidently, then stopped. "Wait."

She paused; her face thoughtful. Ezekiel could guess that it depended on the client.

"Wouldn't it depend on the client?" he said quietly, more so thinking out loud than speaking to anyone. The two women turned to him with surprised looks on their faces. Ezekiel laughed.

"Oh, c'mon. I was guessing."

"You guessed right," Debra smirked, obviously impressed.

"You sure there isn't something you're not telling us, Sugarcane?" Sara teased, a surprising mix of playfulness and astonishment lighting up her features.

Ezekiel smiled, feeling a bit proud of himself.

"Maybe I'm a natural."

"Oh, please," Sara rolled her eyes and gave him a playful shove. It seemed being around Debra put her at ease. "Wait till we get into the nitty-gritty stuff."

"Like color schemes," Debra said, her face full of mock horror.

Ezekiel glanced between the two women silently for a moment.

"Bring it on," he said finally, with a challenging grin.

"Ohhhh. Ok, Sugarcane," Sara whooped. "Debra?"

Debra nodded.

"Color schemes."

She moved the first binder aside and thunked a second one down in front of them. The sheer size of it made Ezekiel think that maybe he had spoken a little too confidently.

Several hours later, they had made it through most of the binders, at least on a surface level, and it was getting dark outside.

"Hey guys, I gotta run. It's getting pretty late, but I expect you two to keep studying," Debra winked, packing her things into her bag.

"Thank you for all your help, Debra. We'll try not to let you down," Ezekiel smiled at her.

"Oh, I know you won't. Success is your only option. Goodnight, guys." She left the room.

"It's just you and me now," Ezekiel joked.

Sara didn't look up. "Didn't you hear her? Back to work."

He watched her for a moment. She was obviously more at ease around him now after a day in Debra's company. But her walls had started to rebuild themselves as soon as Debra left. Maybe it would be up to him to help break through them a bit.

"You know, I feel like taking a break." He jumped up abruptly.

She looked up at him, unamused. "Sit back down, Sugarcane."

"I think I've heard enough about monochromatic color schemes and vendor relations." He gave her a look that said, *You know I'm right*, raising one eyebrow.

He could see her mulling it over.

"Ok." She dropped her pen and sat back. He smiled victoriously, crossing to the window, and perched on the sill.

"New York looks incredible at night," he admitted, the view making him appreciate the creative ability God had given man.

"It's not too bad," she shrugged as she wandered over and plopped on the other end of the sill.

He watched her as she admired the view. As he did, he felt a warm glow rise inside his chest; she too appeared happy in the moment, surveying the city.

"You know, I remember when we were kids, Sunday evenings were the highlight of my week." He waited to see if she would react, but she stared steadily out the window.

"Hmm," she murmured as though she'd barely heard him.

"My parents were super relaxed when we were at your house or when you guys came over." He smiled at the memory. "The laughter, the conversation. I mean, we were kids, so how much of it did we really understand? But it just felt good, like a safe space. I don't know if you ever noticed, but I didn't get along with many kids at school. But at home, or in church, or with your family, I felt accepted for the most part. That felt good."

She finally turned to him, a distant look in her eyes, as though she was reliving the memories he had spoken.

"That's one way to remember it."

She gave a brief, tight smile, then looked away again.

He knew something must have happened between them, and he just wanted to find out what. He knew Sara didn't want to talk about it yet though, so he wouldn't press his luck tonight.

"Where did you go to college?" he asked, changing the subject. Maybe she would be more forthcoming if he eased her into it.

"Michigan." She turned to face him now. "Let me guess, you went somewhere close to home, like UCLA?"

"Stanford," he corrected.

Sara nodded. "See, I know that because you weren't looking to run away from Santa Monica, unlike me."

She was right. Ezekiel knew she had run as far away from California as possible.

"Which is why you chose to settle in New York."

"I'm not doing too well, but New York is a big city, and I felt like I wanted to blend in. I didn't want a nosy community or Sunday family dinners. I just wanted to be a girl in a city. It's silly, I guess." She looked down.

"No. It's not." He shook his head quickly. "You have your reasons."

She looked up at him. "I did some research on you," she confessed.

"Oh. Did you?" he asked with an amused grin.

"Yes. Mr. Ezekiel Cane, hotshot fast-rising journalist," she said in mocking grand tones. Ezekiel couldn't think of a reply. He didn't understand why she sounded so bitter about it.

"Do you only hate me, or is it the whole world?"

Sara couldn't help her jaw dropping in shock at his pointed question, but, truthfully, she wasn't sure of her answer. She turned away in silence once more and looked out over New York.

"Are you okay?" Ezekiel frowned. Sara had to admit that she hadn't expected his question. She stared at the dazzling lights of the city, blocking out her view of the stars.

"What does it matter?"

"We were probably friends at some point, Sara. I mean, we grew up together, all those dinners and..."

"Will you stop bringing up our damn childhood," she burst out finally, walking away from the window. "Why do you have such a rose-colored memory of it all anyway? I was miserable growing up, and you made it all worse when–" She stopped and turned back to face him, hating the look of pity on his face.

"Don't do that," she scoffed. "Don't pity me."

"I just want to understand." His tone was somber, serious. "I don't mean you any harm or hurt. I never have, so I don't understand why you get upset every time I'm around."

She eyed him wearily. It was late, and she was tired. She couldn't deal with this now.

"It is what it is, Cane. If it makes you feel any better, I feel upset or angry all the time. Sometimes at just who I am or how my life has gone so far." She looked him in the eyes. "If I didn't have to see you, it would just be one less problem."

Ezekiel opened his mouth to speak; the look in his eyes seemed to communicate genuine concern. It unnerved her.

"Sara, I..." He stopped as though he didn't know what to say. He probably didn't.

"Hey. We should get some sleep. Tomorrow is a big day." Sara walked back to the table and gathered her things. "We have to actually get the job if the investigation is going to work. I don't need to be an investigative journalist to know that," she joked, hoping to change the subject altogether. She headed for the door. "See you tomorrow, Sugarcane."

He still looked solemn, but he managed a smile.

"You too, Ward."

She left.

CHAPTER 5

zekiel walked into the waiting area of Mrs. Belinda Wentworth's office less than five minutes after Sara. She looked down as he took the seat beside her and hoped he wouldn't bring up their discussion from the previous evening. She had revealed way more than she had intended.

"Hey. Ready?" he asked quietly. She turned to him. He was smiling at her. Her breath caught as his blue eyes sparkled. She coughed and looked away. He had caught her off guard, she decided. She hadn't been expecting him to be so close.

"Fine, fine," she said hastily before his hand could reach her shoulder. She pulled away slightly, and he let his hand drop back into his lap.

He looked unsure, but he shrugged.

"I prayed a lot about this interview. I have a good feeling."

She didn't reply. Of course, Ezekiel Cane would pray about it. Sara was sure he prayed about everything.

"From the Marionette?" an attractive, dark-haired woman about their age called out.

"That's us," Sara answered, standing up quickly. Ezekiel followed after her as the woman ushered them into the office. It was a massive office, imposing, and clearly designed to convey the corporation's wealth. From the minimalist style of the decor to the choice of artwork hung about the room, it screamed affluence.

Belinda Wentworth was seated behind an enormous, no doubt one-of-a-kind desk. She looked every bit the ruthless business matriarch that the media made her out to be. Her silvery hair was cropped in a slanted bob, and she wore a classic navy designer suit with a white silk blouse. A string of pearls clung to her throat, and her manicured fingers were decked out in rings set with large stones of varying hues.

"Sit," she instructed, though it was more of a barked command.

She did not look up from the documents she was reading. They did as she asked, seating themselves opposite her. It felt like minutes passed before she finally looked up. She scrutinized them for a moment before starting.

"You two are from the Marionette. They're good, so I'm expecting you to measure up," she clipped, her face straight. She took a breath. "Okay. I assume anyone appearing before me today knows a great deal about planning an event, so I'm not interested in that." She sat up tall and leaned forward. Her gaze was intimidating. "Why should I trust you? This event is highly exclusive and will involve sensitive details our corporation wouldn't want in the wrong hands. Why would I trust you with that?"

Sara spared a quick glance at Ezekiel. He looked like she felt: almost panicked and unsure of what to say. They had spent all day yesterday studying color schemes and budgeting, and this was what she was asking instead? Belinda raised an eyebrow expectantly.

Sara sat up and smiled with a confidence she willed herself to display. An idea had sprung to her mind, almost out of nowhere. She ran with it.

"I know exactly what you mean, Mrs. Wentworth. Are you familiar with Truman's Toys?"

Mrs. Wentworth raised her eyebrows dubiously but replied, "Yes, I am aware of them. Why?"

Sara nodded and continued, "Well, I have a very unusual link to that company that I think may interest you. When I was little, a cousin of mine came to stay with us with his parents. He was skinny and painfully shy, and it looked like puberty wasn't treating him well. He also had this stuffed rabbit. A small, shabby little thing, really."

Mrs. Wentworth looked intrigued.

"I was walking by the 'man cave,' where the adults were gathered that evening, and I heard them talking. His parents were so embarrassed and scared for him. He had no friends, and he was getting bullied. They had tried therapy, changing him to another school, anything they could think of to help him, but in spite of their best efforts, he was just this shy twelve-year-old who still carried a stuffed animal everywhere, even to classes. They had come to their wit's end."

Out of the corner of her eye, she could see Ezekiel's confused expression but ignored it.

"Cutting this long story short, I listened to them discuss how they were going to steal the rabbit from him while he slept and throw it away, and they would just not mention it. I thought this was cruel, and despite not being supposed to have heard any of it, I barged in uninvited and made it known to them what I thought." She continued, trying to rush through the story. "They told me not to tell, and tried to explain that throwing away the rabbit secretly would help them to help him."

Belinda looked expectant; she was waiting for the point of the long story. Sara couldn't believe that she hadn't cut her off by now. "However, I managed to convince the family–and later my cousin–that this toy could be the key to welcoming his new adopted sister into the family. And I was right: when his adopted sister, Sophie, arrived at their home, he gave the rabbit to her and never looked back. He became a believer in the magic of toys. You may know him now as Truman of Truman's Toys."

"Why, yes, that is indeed a very interesting connection you have. Truman's Toys is a very successful company," Mrs. Wentworth said, intrigued by details she'd been unaware of regarding Sara's well-known cousin, as she leaned back in her seat.

"So Mrs. Wentworth, if what you need from us is secrecy to help the Wentworth Corporation, which will, in turn, help your clients and stakeholders, then we want to help you help them. I've understood the value of privacy and discretion, as well as creative problem-solving, from a young age. I believe these values will be an asset for you if you choose us to plan your event."

At first, the older woman said nothing, didn't even move. Then, a slow smirk grew on her face. She looked impressed, in spite of herself, as she sat back.

"I like you," she nodded. "What's your name?"

"Sara Ward," Sara stated with all the confidence she could muster.

"Sara Ward," Belinda repeated.

They finished the interview, and as they left the Wentworth Corporation, Sara couldn't believe what had just happened.

"Where did *that* come from?" Ezekiel asked her, sounding amazed.

"I don't know," she laughed excitedly. "That was so unreal! One minute I didn't know what to say, and then it was like my brain just started talking."

"That was great, Sara! It really was," Ezekiel said, his tone sincere. All those years I had no idea Truman was your cousin. That certainly was a well-kept secret!" Sara looked at him. They were walking through New York now, just the two of them. Sara didn't mind walking; it was a beautiful day, though rain clouds still lingered in the sunny sky after morning showers.

"Thanks," she smiled. "It was thrilling. What you do is thrilling." She had to admit; he was like a spy or a secret agent, getting to put on various personas for investigations. "Is that why you do it?"

He glanced at her.

"No," he replied. "I do it because I believe God led me into it, but the thrill is definitely one of the perks."

She only nodded. She may not view God the same way he did, but she sure wasn't going to discredit his beliefs.

"Why do you choose to work at the Marionette as a waitress?" he asked.

"Money," Sara answered simply.

"I know you have a degree in media and PR. Why don't you use that?" he countered. She turned to him with a look of surprise.

"How did you know that?"

He rubbed his neck. "I—You know. I keep in touch with your folks and...." he hesitated. "...I ask about you."

They stopped walking. She stared at him in disbelief.

"Why?"

"I guess I want to know that you're okay. You were a big part of my life growing up. Friends or not," he admitted. Sara felt a strange warmth in her chest. She didn't know what to say; she could only blink at him.

"Ezekiel, that's..." She stopped abruptly as it suddenly began to rain. "Oh no."

"Here, put this over your head." Ezekiel quickly took off his jacket and gave it to her. They hurriedly found a taxi, for which Sara was grateful. They sat quietly inside, the only sound the windshield wipers ticking back and forth. Sara glanced at Ezekiel. His hair was wet, tousled a bit, but he still looked so handsome. He turned, and his eyes met hers. She swallowed and looked away from him quickly.

Finally, the taxi pulled up to her apartment. The rain had let up to a drizzle. Ezekiel got out of the cab with her.

"I guess I'll call you if Debra hears from the Wentworth Corporation," she said, her voice trailing off awkwardly. It was probably the rain; she felt cold and out of sorts.

"Yeah, that'd be great. Uh... Thank you again for doing this," he stammered. She nodded and turned to walk away. "Sara?"

"Hm?" She turned back around.

"My jacket."

"Right." She realized she was wearing it over her shoulders. He reached out to help her take it off, his hand brushing her shoulder. She felt a rush of heat where his hand had touched her. She cleared her throat, keen to be rid of the unexpected feeling.

"Well, I'll see you," she said hastily and hurried into her building.

CHAPTER 6

It hadn't taken long after the interview for the Wentworth Corporation to call and say that the Marionette had gotten the job. Ezekiel thanked God for how smoothly everything was going so far.

"This is where you guys will be working. You have this as an office area, and there's a small connected conference room through that door."

A professionally attired, dark-haired young woman showed Ezekiel and Sara around their new office at the Wentworth building. She had called it 'small,' but the conference room was bigger than Sara's apartment.

"If you have any questions, my name is Carly, and I am your go-to girl. I am Mrs. Wentworth's assistant, and as this event is very important to her, it is likewise important to me," Carly informed them.

"Nice to meet you, Carly; I'm—"

"Ezekiel Cane, and she's Sara Ward. I know who you are. Any questions?" Carly asked. She had a *go-go-go* vibe to her. Ezekiel could tell she had to be an efficient person to work with Belinda Wentworth.

"None on my end," Ezekiel smiled. Sara shook her head. Carly clapped her hands together.

"Good. I'll leave you to it."

Then she left the room. Ezekiel turned to Sara.

"So, what do you want to do now?" he asked, casually leaning against what he guessed would be his desk. There was one on the other side of the room for Sara.

"Maybe actually plan the event? We've got a lot of work to do. Places to go, people to meet. We've only got two weeks. Get off your butt!" She put her hands on her hips. Ezekiel thought she looked rather cute when she was being bossy.

"And what exactly, might I ask, do you find so amusing?" She raised an eyebrow.

He hadn't realized he was smiling.

"Nothing. Nothing at all. Let's go, boss."

He stood up. Ezekiel had known he would have to do the actual event planning tasks, but he'd never realized how much work that actually was. Until now.

They spent the next week going from vendor to vendor for one thing or another–catering, decorations, lighting, sound, entertainment—the list seemed endless. Then they would compare prices. Sara was a natural at it, though. Ezekiel found himself hanging back and watching in amazement as she handled most of it. He was mainly there to carry shopping bags or drive her places.

"What do you think?" She turned to him abruptly in the fifth store they'd found themselves at that day, and it wasn't yet noon. "Is the price too steep for customized gift bags? It's only about a hundred guests. Maybe we go with the plain ones?"

Ezekiel hadn't been paying attention.

"Whatever you decide is fine with me. You're doing a great job," he assured her.

She frowned.

"But I want your input. A second opinion. What's the point of you coming if we don't do it together?"

"Um. Okay." He cleared his throat and looked at the plain bag sitting on a table and then the customized samples. "We could..." He hesitated, thinking about his answer. He wanted his response to be what she wanted. "We could work the customized bag into our budget and see if there might be something else we could trim just a bit."

She blinked at him for a second, then smiled.

"Yeah. You're right. That works great." She turned back to the lady who owned the store. "We..." She stopped and turned to him again, then smiled. "Thank you."

"You two are so lovely; I must say," the lady spoke up. She was an older woman, maybe in her late sixties, stylishly dressed but still giving the impression of being the grandmotherly type. They gave her confused looks. "Oh. Don't mind me; I love that you are both here together. It's just that the grooms rarely come in with their brides, and even when they do, they just busy themselves on their phones. Oh! And the way you look at her. Oh, my heart," the woman gushed, her hand over her ample chest in a dramatic gesture. Sara half expected her to swoon.

Ezekiel didn't know what to say to that. How had he been looking at Sara?

"You're mistaken," he said quickly.

Sara spoke up. "We work together. We're planning a corporate event."

The woman frowned. "Oh. Excuse me. I'm so sorry. You could have fooled me."

They both offered her awkward smiles, and Sara hastily continued discussing the bags. Ezekiel glanced at Sara. She seemed unaffected, but he felt unnerved by what the woman had said for some reason. How *did* he look at Sara? He hadn't noticed any particular change in his demeanor. Maybe it was just because they'd known each other so long; there must be a hint of nostalgia that the woman was picking up on. Yes, that was it, he decided, relieved.

They went to one more store before Sara declared she was tired and that they needed to get lunch. They chose a small cafe nearby and ordered the daily special without even perusing the menu.

"Well, you have to admit, some of this is fun," Sara said, referring to the work involved with planning an event. Sara couldn't believe he wasn't enjoying himself more.

"A little," he conceded. "But it's rather stressful." At the start of a small frown on her face, he rushed on, "You're good at it, though. Patient with the vendors," he said sincerely, and she looked down. "You're good with people."

She looked up at him, smiled briefly, and then turned to look out the window. She had her hair up in her usual sleek, classic bun, but a few wavy strands had fallen down the sides of her face. The way the light from the window was hitting her made her look dreamy, like a watercolor painting. Ezekiel felt his pulse quicken as he took in the sight of her. He cleared his throat and drank from his glass of water. He shouldn't be staring at her.

"When we were younger..." she started to speak, then paused. She turned to face him. "When we were younger, my family wasn't as great as we'd seem at those Sunday night dinners."

She leaned forward, resting her arm on the table. Ezekiel leaned forward too, paying attention.

"The issue was that my dad had wanted a son." She smiled again, but it was a sad smile. "Unfortunately, they had me, and my mother could never conceive again. He tried to hide it; he tried to do dad stuff with me, but he always ended up showing how disappointed he was with me."

She was staring forlornly at a faint spot on the table.

"I didn't get this at first, so I tried so hard to be the child he wanted, but, as you know, I could never be his son. As the years went on, it was clear he was happier providing for me than interacting with me, but to me, it felt like he was trying to pay me off and that I was an inconvenience. By my early teens, he would get upset and ask me to leave if I tried to spend time with him. Sometimes he didn't seem to want to see me or talk to me. One day I heard him tell my mother, 'I just can't connect with her.' Which, of course, hurt terribly."

The waiter brought them coffee at that moment, and they thanked him. Then Ezekiel turned back to Sara and waited for her to continue. She took a sip of her cappuccino, sighing before launching back into their conversation.

"At some point, I got angry. I started to rebel—to be the opposite of everything he wanted me to be. In the process, I hurt my mom too, but she always took his side, so I figured she deserved it too." She laughed a mirthless laugh. Ezekiel had had no idea. He had just thought she was a wild child, a rebel without a cause. He felt sorry for her, and instantly his view of Mr. Darren Ward was shifting. He guessed if he'd looked hard enough, he might have seen it for himself.

"My folks started getting close to your folks." Her eyes met his for a second before dropping again. "And my dad all but fell in love with you. It felt like he talked about you constantly. 'Did you hear about this or that accomplishment? What a fine young man!'" she mimicked her father bitterly.

Ezekiel felt his heart sink. Of course, it made perfect sense to him now why she would hate him. Her father had taken him under his wing and been a mentor to him from the get-go when Ezekiel had been just a kid. Darren Ward had been a significant influence in Ezekiel's life, even in his career. Yet, he had done so at his daughter's expense, and Sara held that against Ezekiel and obviously against her parents as well.

"Watching you grow close to a father who decided he couldn't be bothered with me hurt so much." She shut her eyes. "So, when I look at you," she said, opening her eyes and looking right at him, "It's hard not to see someone who got the father's love I never really knew myself."

Ezekiel didn't have any words. He could see the bitterness in her eyes even though her tone was quiet. They just looked into each other's eyes.

"I'm sorry." It was so inadequate, but there seemed to be no way to convey just how much he meant those words.

She looked away. "Sad to say, but many of my life choices have been driven by a need to upset him. As you can see, it hasn't led to a life of any great purpose. I haven't spoken to either of my parents in three years." Ezekiel's eyes widened in surprise and dismay.

The waiter came over and placed their food in front of them, though they'd apparently both lost their appetites, and the delectable entrees went largely untouched.

Ezekiel couldn't help but wonder if she had ever tried going to God with this hurt that she felt. He was the only one that Ezekiel knew could bring people back from the deepest pain.

"What about God?" Ezekiel finally asked.

She smiled knowingly, and in her expression, he could almost hear her saying, *I know all about that.*

"I've heard the whole nine yards. We grew up in church together, remember? So, you know I'm not an atheist." She began to push her food around with her fork.

"Why don't you talk to Him about this? Sara, it sounds like you've been really hurting for a long time. Don't you want it to end?"

"To end? Ha! That's rich." She shook her head. "What I think about

God is...." She hesitated, thinking as she poured some salt over her fries. "He has favorites. You're one of them. I'm not, and I don't think I want much to do with Him. I'm sure He knows I haven't been a good person if we're being honest."

Ezekiel frowned. He couldn't believe how wrong she was.

"Sara, it's not like that. God isn't like that."

"Hey." She raised a hand to stop him from speaking, her defensive mask falling back into place in an instant. "Can we not continue this discussion? Forget I even said anything, alright? Let's just eat."

She didn't look at him and focused on her food. His frown deepened, but he decided not to push it. He nodded and followed her lead by concentrating on his food instead, which could have been cardboard for all he tasted. He knew he couldn't let it go, though, especially now that he was fully aware of what had been causing her untoward contention. And he wouldn't. Maybe this was why God had brought him back into her life, to help her find Him.

The next day, Ezekiel wrapped up his prayer time and stayed there for a minute. He was so grieved over what Sara had told him the day before, but he knew God had a plan for her. He felt more at ease as he stared at her name in his prayer book. He'd written it in large capital letters. He sighed and put on his suit jacket. It was time to meet Carly for what he hoped would be an enlightening business dinner.

CHAPTER 7

*S*ara was pacing the living room.

"I shouldn't have told him all that stuff. I don't know... I just ... he just ... he's easy to talk to."

She groaned, then went to sit by Debra, taking the bowl of ice cream from her and scooping out a large bite.

"Honestly, I don't see why you're so worked up about it. So, you two are becoming friends. Why is that such a big deal?" Debra shrugged. She picked up the remote and began scrolling through Netflix. They were sitting on the floor of their apartment. Occasionally, when they could afford the time, they liked to have nights where they intentionally hung out instead of just living and working together.

Sara glared at her friend.

"No! We're not friends. I mean, I'm just spewing hate his way 24/7, and in return, he's nice to me." She sobered, thinking about the look in his eyes when she had told him why she hated him. "Sometimes, I almost think he cares."

"Sara, that's what friends do!" Debra shook her by the shoulders. "Being friends with him could bring you some much-needed closure. Or not. But you have nothing to lose. Why are you fighting it?"

Sara stared at Debra as her words sunk in. Maybe she was right, Sara began to realize. She remembered the compassionate look in his eyes when she had admitted how she felt. It was still so hard to let go of the hurt she'd carried for so many years, but perhaps it was time she became the bigger person and made an effort to forgive him.

"You know what? Maybe that's true. Would you mind if we take a rain check on the movie?"

Debra nodded. Sara put down the ice cream, grabbed her coat and shoes, and left the apartment; she would find Ezekiel and apologize. None of it was his fault. Maybe they could actually start over and even be … friends? As her train rattled along the tracks, she mulled over the idea of a friendship with Ezekiel Cane. She was surprised to find that it wasn't a repulsive thought; in fact, thinking back to the way he'd looked at her in the rain the other day and how she'd even had fun showing him all over the city in their travels amongst the various vendors, watching his smile as she made arrangements... yes, she was beginning to see this man in a new light.

She walked into his hotel with a sense of determination. For the first time in a long time, she felt like she was doing the right thing. She headed for the elevator; he had given her his room details in case of an emergency. As she approached the doors, she stopped, spotting Ezekiel walking into the building from the entrance on the other side of the room. He looked relaxed in a casual sweater and tailored jeans, his blonde hair swept roughly to the side, and he chuckled as he pushed open the heavy glass door.

She took a step in his direction but stopped when she saw Carly, dressed in jeans and a red flowing top, step in after him. She froze. Carly laughed and touched his shoulder playfully, and he smiled back at her. Suddenly, Sara felt exposed. She couldn't let them see her. Her breath caught in her chest, and she blushed hotly as she retreated back through the lobby, weaving around the glass-tiled columns to avoid being seen.

Once outside the sliding glass doors, Sara took several deep breaths, relishing the crisp night air filling her lungs and calming her startled nerves. Ezekiel was probably just friendly with everyone, including her. A flirt, she decided. It was his job to be friendly and get people to talk, to share details with him. He didn't actually want to be friends with her. He was just doing his job. She laughed at herself as she walked away from the building; she was stupid to have even gone there. He had a whole life, a great life compared to hers, and she had decided she wanted no place in it. She was losing focus. He was still the person who reminded her of her childhood pain, and here he was laughing and having a good time with some woman he just met at the Wentworth Corporation. She shook her head and headed home.

The next day, they had to brief Belinda Wentworth on the progress of their planning. When Sara arrived, Carly and Ezekiel were chatting. She rolled her eyes. In a workplace, it would be nice if he kept things professional.

"Hey," Ezekiel called when he saw her. "I was waiting for you."

"Were you?" Sara snapped before she could stop herself.

He frowned and walked over to her. "How are you doing this morning?"

She didn't look at him as she bent over to sort through some documents on her desk.

"Doesn't matter." She stood up straight and faced him. "I'm ready for the meeting. Let's go."

She saw his look of confusion but didn't give him a chance to speak before she walked away.

After the meeting, which was a resounding success, Ezekiel blocked Sara in the hallway before she could walk away.

"Move," she said, not looking at him.

"I know you're usually not fond of me, but today you're downright cold," he said, his tone accusatory. She looked at him.

"One of us actually has to plan this thing, and since you have an investigation to conduct, I guess that would be me. Let's not waste any more time 'working together.' You do what you're here to do, and I'll do what I'm here to do," she whispered so that only he would hear.

She tried to push past him, but he caught her arm. She sucked in a breath at the tingly sensation where he touched her skin. He shook his head.

"I'm confused. I thought we were...." He hesitated. "I thought we were at least being civil to each other. What changed?"

At her glare, he let go of her arm.

"I don't know what you mean, Sugarcane. We both have work to do. Let's not forget that I don't like you, and this is just a job." She walked away.

A few hours later, Sara was sitting in her office, going over the arrangement of the room for the party. She wondered why the Corporation had refused to provide them with the guest list.

"It would make my life a whole lot easier," she mumbled. Next, she picked up the line-up for the event. It was filled with blanks. The media team she had hired had also called her and asked her for the PowerPoints, yet Mrs. Wentworth's office had kept delaying.

"Sara." She looked up to see Carly had walked into the room. "Where's Ezekiel?" Carly asked.

Sara tried not to roll her eyes.

"I don't know. I haven't seen him since the meeting," she said, not looking away from the document she was reading.

"Okay. Belinda wants to see you," Carly said and started to leave the room.

"Sure thing, I'll call Ezekiel." Sara reached for her phone.

"No," Carly said, stopping her. "Just you."

"Oh. Okay." Sara blinked, trying not to be nervous. She knew that Ezekiel pulled minimal weight in the actual planning, but she didn't think Belinda Wentworth knew it.

She knocked on the large oak door of Belinda's office and then pushed it open when she heard a summons from within.

"You wanted to see me?" she asked, stepping into the office.

"Come in. Take a seat," Belinda smiled. If Sara hadn't been nervous before, she certainly was now. Why was Belinda Wentworth smiling at her like that? It looked more predatory than friendly. Sara sat down and folded her hands in her lap in an attempt to hide her nervousness.

"I think that I've told you that I like you. Haven't I?" Belinda sat up and leaned forward. Sara only nodded. "I've been impressed with all that you've been doing," the older woman added.

"It's really been a team effort..." Sara began lamely.

"Don't try to be humble, sweetheart. Being a woman in business, I can tell you that it wasn't humility that got me to where I am now," Belinda reprimanded. Sara kept quiet. "Well, I guess I should get to the point, shouldn't I? I want you to stay on as a part of my company. My son is the new CEO, and he's instigating a number of excellent changes. As a mother and a major stakeholder, I want to see him succeed. I think he could do with someone on his team he can trust." She leaned in closer. "Someone *I* trust. Like you."

Sara blinked at her. "I...I don't—"

"I would be offering you an executive position, of course, with a very attractive salary and generous benefits. I see a whole lot of me in you. Knowing the important role I played as an executive helping my husband build this empire, I realize that's just what my son's tenure needs."

Sara couldn't tell if she was being pranked or if someone was playing some cruel joke on her. She was tempted to glance around for a hidden camera.

"You don't even know me," she blurted out, thinking out loud.

Belinda laughed.

"I know enough. Please consider my offer. You don't have to say anything right away."

Sara looked down and nodded. Should she actually consider this? It would be such a great step forward, but it would be crazy. They were trying to expose the company for wrongdoings after all. She stood up and walked towards the door in a bit of a daze.

"And Sara?" Sara turned around. "There's a party tomorrow night. You should come. I'll introduce you to Donald and some other key people from the company. I'm sure you two will hit it off." Belinda smiled. Again, Sara could only nod. "Carly will give you the details and find you something to wear. You can go," Belinda dismissed her, and she left the office.

Sara couldn't sleep that night. She lay awake, staring up at the ceiling. She didn't want to feel like she owed any loyalty to Ezekiel, but the truth was he had been nothing but sweet and kind to her. He had even been fun to be around sometimes. At least when he didn't remind her of what she hadn't had as a child growing up. In exasperation, she asked aloud, "What do I do? Please help me! I'm so tired."

She turned over again, pulling her covers up to her neck. She closed her eyes, and before her in her mind's eye, were two nail-pierced hands reaching towards her, lit by a blue fire. As she reached out to take those hands, the warmth from the fire consumed her, and an incredible warmth saturated every cell in her body. Love as she had never known. *Beloved, I have come to speak with you.*

Sara felt tears flow down her face as she communed with God, her body fully at rest for the first time in years.

CHAPTER 8

*E*zekiel didn't have time to ponder what had just happened. He thought he had been making some progress with Sara but guessed that in her mind, he would always be the person who had stolen her father's affection. Ezekiel sighed and made his way to the little hole-in-the-wall bagel shop several blocks from the Wentworth Corporation, where he and Carly had agreed last night would be an innocuous enough rendezvous point so as to not draw any attention to themselves. Just to be safe, he chose the most circuitous route he could think of to get there, but still, he found himself nervously glancing around for any suspicious-looking persons. He had to chuckle at himself in spite of his jitteriness–he realized he was specifically assuming any criminal types following him would be big, beefy, muscle-bound goons. Apparently, he'd watched too many mystery movies.

As he approached the bagel shop, he was thanking the Lord that Carly's conscience had finally driven her to seek him out. From the things she had told him, the Wentworths all seemed to love their business, and their family life revolved around it, so it was a true mystery as to who and why the senior Wentworth had not only been murdered, but that no one in the family seemed bent on bringing the perpetrator to justice. However, Carly had also mentioned during last night's conversation that Donald Junior had been close to his father, but they seemed to have had a falling out not long before the older Mr. Wentworth's death. He wasn't sure just what evidence she had, but he hoped it would be enough to reveal who ordered the autopsy records sealed, which may, in turn, lead to the 'why.'

"There you are," he greeted Carly as they approached the shop from opposite directions. She looked as nervous as he felt. It was sobering to realize she was putting her job, if not her very life, at risk to do the right thing by helping to expose evil. Once inside, they ordered a couple of bagels with lox 'schmear' and chose the tiny table furthest from the front window of the shop. As they were waiting for their order in silence, Carly reached into her large purse, which looked more like a small carry-on bag to Ezekiel, and withdrew a business-sized envelope with his name on it.

Glancing around one more time to make sure no one was paying attention to them; he slipped a single sheet of paper out of the envelope and skimmed it quickly. Eyes wide and face blanched, he muttered, "Bingo." The document was a copy of the order to the coroner's office, just as he had suspected. He shook his head sadly as he saw Donald Junior's signature at the bottom of the page. He had hoped the top-secret document relating to Donald Wentworth II's death would help him establish that something was amiss, but it nonetheless brought him sorrow to see evidence in black and white as to the depths this family had fallen, and for what? Greed? Jealousy? Power? Unfortunately, his job now was to prove motive, but if he could get a confession, it would wrap the story up nicely. That is, if one could use the term 'nicely' in relation to a murder investigation.

* * *

Joe had received an invitation to an exclusive party given by a wealthy family in New York, which the Wentworths would be attending. Ezekiel was grateful when Joe invited him, as he figured it would be advantageous for him to go. He was hoping to find one or two people who might be willing to talk to him about the Wentworths. Surely someone in their tightly knit inner circle might slip and divulge something that could help lead to motive in this investigation, especially after they'd had a few drinks under their belt or sash, whichever the case may be.

"Thanks for inviting me, Joe. I really appreciate it. I wonder if there's anyone here, I could talk to about the story discreetly," Ezekiel said, looking around the room. It was full of men in thousand-dollar suits and women in elegant cocktail dresses, jewelry sparkling in the light of the numerous elaborate chandeliers adorning the ceiling.

"I wouldn't dismiss it. People do tend to talk a lot more when they're drunk," Joe said, confirming what Ezekiel had presumed about the guest's potential 'loose tongues.' "And don't thank me. I need this."

Ezekiel was confused about Joe's meaning, but he didn't get a chance to ask because someone else came in and caught Joe's attention.

Ezekiel had begun to casually meander around the room, trying to blend in and appear disinterested as he listened for any useful tidbits swirling in the conversations around him; he stopped when he caught sight of Sara. What was she doing here? She looked stunning in a shimmery gold midi dress that seemed to flow as she moved. He was about to walk up to her but stopped when he saw Donald Wentworth III touch the small of her back, and their heads bent together as if in intimate conversation. She smiled and laughed. Ezekiel didn't know what was happening, but he knew that Donald III was dangerous and that Sara shouldn't be moving with his crowd.

He strode up to them.

"Sara! I didn't know you would be here." He wanted to shove Donald's hand away from her.

"You don't know everything that I do," she replied with a bland face, though her green eyes were flashing a warning. "Excuse us."

She smiled and walked away with Donald in tow. Ezekiel stood there in shock. Was she out of her mind? Had she forgotten that they were investigating these people for murder? Ezekiel couldn't help the anger rising within him as he watched them. Belinda Wentworth had joined them, dressed like the queen she obviously thought herself to be, with no shortage of royal blue silk and diamonds.

If this was what Sara wanted, he could not stop her. He made his way through the crowd, down the elevator, and out into the street; he couldn't face polite conversation with strangers right now, murder investigation or not. He needed some air.

When Ezekiel reached his hotel room, he opened the door and then slammed it behind him, rattling the pictures on the wall. He leaned back against the door, attempting to slow his breathing, and loosened his tie. He couldn't even understand why he was so upset, nor why he'd blown his chance to gather more information, but he knew what to do about it and Who to go to.

"Lord, I know you want me to share Your love and keep praying for her, but she's so difficult! She's spending time with the very people we're trying to investigate," Ezekiel prayed, his voice thick with emotion. "I know You know all and You see all, but she could jeopardize the story, not to mention her life! What if she pushes me away completely? Then how will I help her?" He shut his eyes and fell to his knees. "Lord, I don't know why I can't escape this urge to help her, but I trust You. It's just difficult to love someone who hates you," he admitted quietly. He realized he was currently in a position Jesus must have found Himself in dozens of times.

My beloved, all is not always as it seems.

As he heard the words in his spirit, a sense of calm slowly washed over him. He released a breath. That was all God said to him that night, and he was content with it. He would choose to trust God, because he knew that God's ways and thoughts were far greater than his own, as the scriptures said.

* * *

JOE CAME to Ezekiel's hotel room the next day.

"Hey. What happened? I had no idea when you left last night."

"I'm sorry about that." Ezekiel rubbed his neck and walked into the kitchen area of his room. "Coffee?" he asked Joe.

"No, no. I'm good, thanks."

Ezekiel made a cup for himself and leaned against the counter, sipping it.

"Did you get anything for your story last night?" Joe seemed a bit on edge.

"Uh. No, I left early. I'm sorry about that."

"Why did you leave early?" Joe took a seat at one of the barstools in front of the counter.

"I know, but I don't know," Ezekiel tried to explain. "It's Sara, right. She's walking around with Donald Wentworth, who has questionable ethics at best, and whether he had anything to do with his father's death? I don't know. I just think that she needs to be more careful. I can't help but imagine that this is the reason she's been so cold to me."

"Okay, I understand you are concerned about the company she is keeping, but why do you care if she's cold to you? From what I understand, she's always been cold to you," Joe said.

Ezekiel sighed.

"I don't know, okay? It's just that it's been different since we've been working together. Suddenly, I'm getting to know this woman I had supposedly known my whole life but apparently never known. Not really. And I liked it. I liked her energy, her laughter. I liked being on that side of her."

"Well, as long as you don't fall in love with her," Joe said pointedly. "Because I don't need to remind you that she hates you. I think she's doing a good job of reminding you herself."

Ezekiel shook his head and scoffed, "I'm not in love with her. I just enjoyed being her friend, that's all."

Ezekiel felt Joe's eyes on him. It was apparent Joe didn't believe him.

"You know what? Let's get back on track here. The story." Ezekiel sat beside Joe. "I found evidence that the cover-up came from Donald. All I need is for him to give some sort of motive in maybe his speech or something like that at this event, and I'll have all I need."

"Sounds like you've almost wrapped up the story." Joe nodded.

"Why would he do it, though?" Ezekiel wondered out loud. From what Carly had told him, he and his father had been close, until that last falling out, but still... things didn't really add up.

Joe looked down.

"America isn't what it used to be. People, companies. They're forced to change and evolve or get swept away," Joe said solemnly. The tone of his friend's voice caused Ezekiel to look up.

"Is everything okay?" Ezekiel asked. "I mean with you?"

Joe's eyes snapped up quickly, and he plastered on a huge smile.

"Sure, life is fine. Never better! Anyway, I should get going. Busy day at the office today." Joe stood up, and Ezekiel escorted him to the door. *I ought to pray more for Joe, too*, he thought.

Ezekiel got ready for the day and headed to the venue they had booked for the event. It was already four in the afternoon and he knew that most of the work would be done already, but he decided that it was better late than never. Tomorrow was the main event and it would hopefully lead to the end of his investigation, or at least Sara's involvement in it.

He forced his mind away from that. He didn't like that many of his thoughts these days involved Sara. She was a grown adult, and she could handle herself. He had to leave her in God's hands.

He walked into the main hall and spotted her. She was standing in the middle of the room, which was beautifully decorated with elaborately decked out tables seating eight each, covered with the finest in china, cutlery, and crystal. Each place setting had the elegant custom bag they'd chosen, filled with delectable custom-made candies. The centerpieces on each table were nothing short of amazing, one of Sara's stunning finds in a tiny, tucked away florist shop she knew of, that no doubt would soon be enjoying a booming business once the party goers learned of it. It was one of the things Ezekiel admired about her: she was determined to find and help unique, small businesses in her pursuit of delivering an excellent result. She seemed to derive more pleasure from that than planning the actual event, a compassionate side of her he'd not seen before, but was truly moved by. As he observed her, she was going over last-minute details with the set-up team. She had her hair in a thick ponytail down her back, but some strands had come loose. She looked like she had been working hard, but she seemed radiant, in spite of her casual appearance, with the passion evident in her features as she gave instructions.

Ezekiel walked over to her. She turned around. He had startled her, he could tell.

"This all looks wonderful, Sara. You really are a natural at this."

She smiled, her cheeks turning a light pink.

"I don't know. It's not that great." She looked around at the room almost nervously, then down. Ezekiel couldn't help but smile. Then, she looked up at him, her face serious, her eyes intense. "Ezekiel, I should apologize..." she started to say.

"No," he stopped her, stepping close to her. "You don't need to." He could feel himself getting heady again, being so close to her, all his senses firing at once. "I should have trusted that you can handle yourself. You're a very strong and capable woman, and I know you'll always do what's right."

She took in a shaky breath. She bit her lip and instinctively

Ezekiel's eyes dropped to her lips. He looked back up at her eyes, and saw a look of turmoil. It was like she was fighting within herself. He frowned. Why did he find himself leaning closer? His heart was beating more rapidly as their lips came closer together.

She closed her eyes. He closed his. It felt like his heart would stop when their lips finally met; he realized everything in him wanted this moment to happen.

"Mr. Cane." Sara jumped back as Belinda Wentworth entered the room. Ezekiel had never been in a situation with worse timing in his life.

"Mrs. Wentworth," he said, his tone betraying his annoyance.

"It's nice of you to join Miss Ward finally. You could pull your weight more," she said, then turned to Sara.

"The room looks delightful. I love it." She smiled; a gesture Sara returned. Ezekiel kept looking at Sara, but she wouldn't look at him. Belinda walked to the other side of the room to inspect it, and Ezekiel took the opportunity. "Sara, I didn't mean to–"

"Let's not talk about it, Cane. I have work to do, and like she said, you should pull your weight more."

Sara's tone was brusque as she walked away. Ezekiel looked at her blankly. It was like she had turned a hundred and eighty degrees when Belinda came in. He shook his head and turned away. He should have realized that maybe they had both just been caught up in the moment.

The rest of the day, she avoided him like the plague and stuck to Belinda Wentworth's side until he left. He decided to forget what had happened, no doubt a result of an obvious momentary lapse of judgment.

CHAPTER 9

It had been a long day and Sara was exhausted. She just wanted to get home and shower. She most definitely felt relieved that the event was tomorrow; Sara was thankful she could get it over with and finally get some rest. She was also glad that her time on the story was ending. Sara didn't want to think about what had happened today–or had *almost* happened.

"Sweetie, let me give you a ride," Belinda offered as Sara walked out of the building.

"No, I'm fine, thanks; I can walk," Sara said politely.

"No. I insist," Belinda said, her face straight. Sara understood that it wasn't a request.

She slid into the back seat of the luxury car next to Belinda. She hadn't heard of the brand of car and didn't recognize the logo on the front of it.

"Donald enjoyed meeting you the other night. He had a lovely time," Belinda said as the car slid away from the curb and melted into traffic. Sara kept a smile on her face. Belinda Wentworth was an intimidating woman. When Sara didn't say anything, Belinda moved on from the subject.

The older woman pulled out a flash drive and handed it to her. Sara slowly took it, confused.

"It's the guest list and the multimedia for the event. I'm giving them to you because I trust you," Belinda said, her tone very serious.

Sara looked down at the flash drive and then back up at Belinda. She knew what that meant. It meant that whatever was on there was incriminating. She tried to stay composed and not feel unnerved.

"Thank you for trusting me."

"I've more than trusted you, Sara Ward. I've made you a wonderful offer too. I've invited you into mine and my son's lives. It's a rare privilege."

The look on Belinda's face made Sara want to crawl into herself. She swallowed.

"I understand that you have some reservations. I'm not blind. I could see what was happening between you and Mr. Cane."

Sara's eyes shot to Belinda's. Belinda wasn't supposed to see that.

"I assure you. It's nothing. It was just in the moment," she said. Belinda only smiled.

"I want to show you something. I had someone look into Mr. Cane."

Sara's eyes widened in alarm. Oh no, Belinda probably knew that he wasn't an event planner. Suddenly, she was painfully aware that she had gotten into the car with Belinda, and no one knew where she was at that moment.

"There's no need to be tense, Sara. We trust each other, you and me." Belinda touched her shoulder. "That's why I'm giving you a gift."

Sara watched as she pulled out a document. It couldn't have been less than four pages long and then a second one.

"These are his call records. The first record details a call to the Marionette before he came to New York. He didn't bump into you by accident; he meant to find you. He asked about you."

Sara took the documents from her in disbelief.

"That's not true. It was a coincidence..." She stopped short as she read what was on the page.

She felt like the air around her was growing thin. Why had Ezekiel never mentioned this?

Mr. Cane. Yes, Asking for a Miss Ward. Can I know if she's assigned to any events within the first week of September? The call transcript read. She'll be working at a party that week. Would you like the details? Sara stopped reading. Ezekiel should have mentioned this.

"That's not all, dear," Belinda interrupted her thoughts. "Read the second one." As Sara started to read, her heart dropped. She didn't know why it hurt this much, but she knew this was what betrayal felt like. "I'm only trying to help you," Belinda said, but Sara barely heard it. She was angry, her blood was boiling, her heart was breaking, and all she could see now was Ezekiel Cane in her mind's eye.

They pulled over outside Sara's apartment. Sara got out of the car and headed into her building without a word. She was trying so hard to manage her emotions. She was feeling so many simultaneously and didn't notice him standing at her door until he'd said her name.

"Sara, we need to talk."

Sara looked up into Ezekiel Cane's blue eyes. They were so clear, and spoke of honesty, though she realized he didn't have a shred of that in him. Sara hated that he looked so handsome. She hated that he was even here.

He took a step toward her and she took one back. She looked up at him and saw his surprise at the look on her face.

"What's wrong?"

"You won't like anything I have to say to you, so I suggest you leave," she said through gritted teeth.

"Sara, if this is about us almost kissing, we're adults..."

"It's not about the stupid kiss!" she yelled. He looked taken aback. "I thought that I hated you before, but I think I hate you more now for letting me believe that maybe, just maybe, I had been wrong to hate you all these years. You made me feel like I could trust you!"

"You can trust me. Sara, that's all I've been trying to say to you." He stepped closer and touched her arm gently. She shook him off and stepped backward.

"No. I can't," Sara said, her voice breaking. She threw the documents at him. "You were more his son than I'll ever be his daughter. I should have expected this."

She watched him read the documents and stayed quiet. They were snippets from calls between Ezekiel and her parents. He had been telling them everything about her since he had come to New York. She had fought so hard for years to distance herself from them, shut them out, keep them in the dark, and even though now she knew that she had to forgive them, as God had instructed her when He spoke to her, it didn't make the betrayal hurt any less.

"Sara, I can explain."

"Save it." She grabbed the documents from him, walked into her apartment, and slammed the door. She released a breath, all her strength leaving her; she didn't know how to deal with this. She slipped into bed and repeated, "Lord, help me." Somehow, she knew He would.

The next day arrived and Sara attempted to pull herself together. She looked at herself in the mirror as she put one final pin in her hair. An elegant woman looked back at her. Early that morning, Sara had looked at the flash drive Belinda had given her. It had horrified her, especially Donald's speech and the other information on it. All she needed was a smile that she could fake and to do one thing after the other, and, somehow, she would get through the day.

The guest list wasn't any less terrifying, making Sara cautious as she walked into the hall. She recognized the guests by their names because she had done Google searches on most of them. Novak Viktor, a Russian arms dealer with powerful connections to the Kremlin. Santana Lopez, wife of the ex-Mexican President who was jailed for corruption. She still had many ties to prominent politicians in Latin America. Sara watched them all converse. Crooks, corrupt leaders, and a good handful of them internationally wanted criminals.

Sara tried to remain calm as Donald got ready to take the stage. She looked up, and her eyes caught Ezekiel's from across the room. The overhead light cast a surreal glow over him. He looked terrific, his hair perfectly styled, his suit expertly tailored. She wanted to look away, but she found she couldn't. It was that feeling when two people spot each other from across a room, and felt like they were the only ones there. Her breath caught, a hollow feeling in her stomach. She didn't want to feel this way for him. There was so much between them that she wasn't sure they could surmount.

Two bodyguards approached him and spoke to him. Sara's eyes widened and she blanched. She knew what was happening. His cover was blown. He glanced at her again as they escorted him from the room, but she looked away this time, desperate to maintain her composure. She turned around, only to bump into a dark-haired woman.

"I'm so sorry," Sara said, looking up to see that it was Carly. "Carly.

Hi," Sara said in surprise. She noted the man with whom Carly's arm was linked.

"Oh. Sara, this is my husband, Jonathan." Carly smiled at Sara's confused look. Sara shook her head.

"Right. You're married." Sara shook Jonathan's hand.

Carly smiled and looked around. "Is Ezekiel here?"

"Actually, you just missed him. Is there a message I can take to him?" Sara asked cautiously.

Carly leaned closer to her.

"Tell him I said good luck. And that no matter how tonight goes, I'm still willing to go on record about the things we discussed for his story." Sara's eyes widened. Of course! Carly had been helping with the story, she realized belatedly.

"Well, I'll be sure to pass on your message."

"Ladies and gentlemen. Thank you for coming tonight. To the rebirthing of a company." Everyone's attention turned to the stage, where Donald was now speaking. That was Sara's cue. She took a deep breath for courage and slipped out of the room into a side corridor. She knew this had to work. She stopped when she heard voices and flattened herself against the wall.

"Lord. Do your thing. Protect us and make this mission successful, or whatever you plan to do," she whispered.

Ezekiel sat in a chair in the middle of a dimly lit room, just like he'd seen in so many movies, but he'd never imagined real criminals actually did this. The guards left the room after securing his hands to the chair with zip ties. He knew what this meant, bizarre as it all seemed: his cover had been blown.

"Lord, thank You that You are the God Who makes a way where there is none. Please help me now."

"Of course, you would be praying." Joe walked into the room.

Ezekiel looked up slowly in shock. "Joe. What are you doing here?" he asked. His mind raced, scanning through his memories of all their recent interactions. What had he missed?

Joe laughed.

"That's a rich question. You know, Cane, I have always known that you would get in over your head sooner or later," Joe sniffed.

"What are you talking about, Joe?" Ezekiel asked. He refused to believe what was becoming crystal clear: Joe had somehow betrayed him.

"I'm talking about the damn Wentworths, Ezekiel. You just had to mess with the Wentworths. I didn't want to do this, but you left me no choice. The country isn't what it used to be. I tried to warn you. We were going under, and Dad sold in a moment of desperation."

"Your father sold Galligan Oil!? Why wasn't it in the press?" Ezekiel asked. He was still having a hard time comprehending that Joe had actually betrayed him. This plot was becoming more predictable by the minute but he never in a million years thought he'd be in the middle of a nightmare like this, investigative journalist or not.

"Because it was an underhanded type of deal. Wentworth Senior worked it all out, but it left my father no better than a slave to Donald Wentworth. He would have ruined our whole family."

"So, when I went to the Galligans for help to kill my husband, they were much obliged," Belinda Wentworth said as she walked into the room. "I've known about your plans from the beginning, Mr. Cane, and I have waited so eagerly for this moment."

"Why would you kill your husband? You were happy." Ezekiel could see the Galligans' motives, but not Belinda's.

"We *were*," she said, walking closer to him. "But he'd lost his mind. He couldn't see that things had changed, and the business needed to change with the times. I, however, could see the writing on the wall, so to speak. All our political connections had begun to disregard us, literally avoid us, if you can believe that. We were losing our clout in Washington and other key power centers, so it was only a matter of time before our empire would follow suit."

Ezekiel was still confused.

"So, what? You conspired with your son to kill his father?"

"Oh my, no. Donald Junior had no idea. He loved his father too much. But neither would ever put himself aside to protect the treasure that we had built." Her eyes glazed over as she spoke. "I knew it would be easier to whisper in my son's ear, little by little. Like getting him to agree to this event, where he will unveil our plans to create alliances with the guests so that we can expand our sphere of influence beyond US shores. We should have made this move years ago, but it's better late than never. Our enterprise must expand its horizons now."

"By working with criminals."

"What difference does it make? They're just useful idiots anyway, though they don't realize it. The company success is what matters and if I succeed, they may survive, of course, providing our business is mutually beneficial." She turned to Ezekiel now and smiled, her eyes strangely vacant. "But it was never my plan to play second fiddle to my son. I don't have the heart to murder my own child, but I'm not above framing him for his father's murder and organizing tonight's gathering of criminals with an intent to commit treason."

Ezekiel stared at her in shock. She was mad, at best, possessed at worst, and he strongly suspected the latter.

"Oh, don't look at me like that. The Wentworth corporation will thrive under my rule, and I'll have him out in no time, or at least moved to a comfortable prison." She smiled. "That's where you come in, Cane."

"Oh, I have a part to play in this?" he asked. A lot was wrong with her if she thought he would help with her scheme.

"Yes. That's why you're still alive, Ezekiel. So that you can finish your article." She smiled deviously. Ezekiel looked between her and Joe.

"Except, you'll write what you initially thought, that my son is behind everything, with no involvement from me whatsoever. You'll do this, or I'll take Miss Ward down with me if you expose me. I'm sure you are intelligent enough that I don't need to provide details of just what that means."

Ezekiel's eyes snapped to hers when she mentioned Sara.

"You wouldn't dare..."

"Dare what? Hm? Did you really think I'd just magically taken an interest in her? *Trusted* her? Why? Because of an awkward childhood story?" She laughed. "You must think me stupid." Her tone had turned ominous.

"You know, I had a feeling that you didn't like my story and all that friendliness was a load of garbage." Everyone turned to the door in surprise as Sara stepped into the room.

Belinda's eyes widened. "What are you doing here? You're not supposed to be here."

"No, actually, I am. See, I wouldn't expect you to understand, because I didn't for the longest time, but the strangest thing happened to me. One night I was tossing and turning, considering your weirdly generous offer, and... God came to me. And as plain as the nose on your evil face, He told me you would try to use me and just to follow His lead instead."

Sara smirked in Ezekiel's direction. Ezekiel was in awe that God had spoken to Sara and brought the answer to his prayers. God never ceased to amaze him.

"Well, *God* should have told you not to come here because it is such a waste that you have to die now, instead of when I'd originally planned. You could have been most useful to me in my plans for Wentworth." Belinda faked a frown.

"Not so fast," Sara warned. At the same time, they heard a commotion from the main room.

Belinda looked at Joe. "What is going on?"

"The police," Joe answered after a quick glance into the hallway, with an anxious look at Sara's calm face.

"I've been wired this whole night, and they have heard everything you've said," Sara stated confidently, a relieved smile flickering across her face.

What a woman, Ezekiel couldn't help but think. If he hadn't been tied up, he would have hugged her until she was breathless. He would thank her and tell her how beautiful and strong she was. Since he was still tied up, he gave silent shouts of praise to the Lord for this miraculous deliverance.

The police reached them in mere seconds, having been stationed at various locations around the building, waiting for the signal. Teams of armed officers had begun to break up the party in the main room, with two particularly burly cops unceremoniously escorting Belinda out in handcuffs, along with a few other choice characters who had been in attendance at the event. Joe seemed to have disappeared before the police came into the room. In the flurry of activity that took place during the raid, Ezekiel had no time to wonder if Joe had been captured elsewhere in the building, but a sense of deep sadness over Joe's betrayal gripped his gut, the only damper on this satisfying end to the entire adventure. He made a mental note to re-double his prayers for Joe and perhaps pay him a visit in jail.

The remaining partygoers, who were innocent but fearful of any negative publicity, made a hasty exit, and the dazed and confused staff were left holding half-empty trays of hors d'oeuvres and drinks. Ezekiel had finally been untied and set free, questioned by the detectives who had come in just after the arrests, and was standing outside the venue talking to an officer when he saw Sara walk out of the building. She looked divine in her long-sleeved emerald velvet dress, her hair expertly pinned up in a smooth chignon, remarkably still in place in spite of all the excitement of the last half hour. It was as if the entire escapade had not fazed her at all. Ezekiel felt his chest tighten as she strode toward him. The weight of what she'd accomplished began to sink in, and on top of it all, she was radiant: the color in her cheeks enhanced the green of her eyes, and he was suddenly overcome. But she could have been killed in there, all because he'd asked her to be involved in this crazy investigation. Would she ever forgive him now?

"Sara I..."

Without a word, she cut him off, rising on her toes and kissing him. Impulsively he wrapped his arms around her and kissed her back. He felt warmth seep through his body. His mind muddled completely, his words forgotten as he took in her scent and her taste and the feeling of holding her. When she stepped back, it took him a minute to steady himself.

"Why?" he asked. "I thought you still hated me."

"And you're going to hold that over my head?" she joked, laughing.

He laughed too. "What changed?"

"I read the full transcript of the phone calls," she admitted sheepishly. "Something I should have done right away." Ezekiel looked away. He rubbed the back of his neck.

"I hope that you understand that I didn't do it to hurt you or betray you. I did it to give a dying man some peace. I know that it wasn't my place, but I was with my dad a lot leading up to his death, and I... just wanted to encourage your dad somehow."

Sara's eyes shot up to meet his.

"Your dad–your dad died?" she asked, her voice breaking as she did. "Ezekiel, I had no idea."

She hugged him. He held her tight before letting go.

"That's why I kept telling your dad about you. He's dying, Sara, and his one regret is how he treated you all those years. He can't stop talking about it."

He placed a hand on her cheek.

She smiled. "I know. I understand now. And I know God is going to help me restore that relationship."

She kissed him again. Ezekiel felt truly at peace. He had thought she was abandoning him for the Wentworths, but she had had a plan all along. Correction: GOD had had a plan. When God had told him that things were not always as they seemed, it made sense now.

"Ezekiel Cane," she said, grinning up at him. "I don't think I hate you anymore."

A wide smile spread slowly across his face.

"Well, I guess that's a good place to start over, isn't it?"

She chuckled.

"Look out!" someone shouted behind them.

It felt like slow motion to Ezekiel as they turned around just in time to see a gun pointed in their direction. They didn't even have time to move before the explosion of a gunshot ripped through the air.

LOVE NEVER LOST

BOOK TWO

CHAPTER 1

"Mr. Cane, your story is indeed groundbreaking and a shocking indication of the bigger issue of corruption in American corporations. Please, tell us about your process of going undercover. Our viewers will want all the details of such a harrowing endeavor!"

Ezekiel cleared his throat, his face grave as he addressed the interviewer, an attractive, professionally dressed young woman a few years his junior.

"It can be dangerous," he acknowledged solemnly. "And there's a lot that goes into it. It all really depends on the environment. The Wentworth story was less perilous at first but rapidly escalated." The woman nodded intently as he spoke. "Usually, the outcome wouldn't have been a fully recorded confession. That is indeed rare. In most cases, an investigative journalist would uncover damning evidence, and the police would do the rest, but I had exceptional help with this particular story."

"So, you acknowledge that your work is potentially fraught with danger?" she asked. In hindsight, Ezekiel knew he should have seen the leading question for what it was. It's why he preferred long-form print journalism: plenty of time to craft the story, present the evidence, and tackle the opposing views with sound reasoning. None of this TV sleight-of-hand drama.

Yet he had known the Wentworth piece would attract major media attention. He'd not only exposed major corruption at the highest level, but a murder as well, and in the process, toppled the Wentworth empire.

"I believe I mentioned that, yes. There is always that possibility," he nodded cautiously.

"Right. So, I have it from a credible source that you blackmailed a fellow civilian into helping you with this hazardous investigation, endangering their life, and that they were seriously injured–perhaps even almost killed–in the process. Did you, Mr. Ezekiel Cane, recklessly jeopardize another civilian's life for a story?" Her expression was almost menacing.

Ezekiel could only blink at her. His pulse was pounding in his ears, and he forced a ragged breath as sweat began to bead around his temples. Suddenly the harsh lights in the studio seemed to intensify, blurring his vision. He held up one hand to block the nearest light, and tugged at his shirt collar. The show host looked at him expectantly, but the only words that came to Ezekiel's mind were a panicked prayer for help.

He knew he was technically innocent. True, his uncle had invested in the event planning company the Marionette, and had given Sara Ward a promotion as the lead event planner for this event, but she had decided to work with him on the story of her own accord. Then again, that didn't relieve the guilt he still felt over the traumatic injury she'd suffered—a gunshot had grazed the back of her head, resulting in a severe concussion. And now Ezekiel had walked right into this TV woman's trap, and he couldn't defend himself against the assault of painful memories flooding over him. He coughed, almost choking, trying to compose himself again.

"I... I...." He looked into the camera and then back at the host. "Excuse me."

He pulled the lapel microphone off his shirt and nearly ran off camera, bile rising in his throat.

The video cut to Miranda Twain, acclaimed host of the wildly successful Wide-Open show.

"That was the now notorious Ezekiel Cane, up and coming investigative journalist, avoiding questions about what many are calling his *questionable methods* in obtaining evidence for his explosive story that brought down the Wentworth empire." She shook her head. "When we come back, I'll have guests with me to discuss: investigative journalism, is it still journalism or has it become vigilantism? Stay with me. I'm Miranda Twain, this is the Wide-Open Show, and we'll bust this issue wide open."

Brant Wilford turned off the TV and turned to Ezekiel, his expression grim.

"You could have said *something*."

"What could I possibly have said that would have done any good? It's basically all true." Ezekiel sighed.

"You said you didn't blackmail her."

"I didn't! You know me, Brant. I don't do those deals. But I–" he stopped short. Ezekiel was disgusted with himself. For weeks, he had wrestled with guilt over what had happened to Sara, and despite crying out to God repeatedly, couldn't shake the weight of what she'd suffered bearing down on his conscience.

Brant sighed and ran a hand down his face. He leaned back in his chair.

"Ezekiel, you understand that we love you here at the Daily Times, and we want to support you through thick and thin, but if you don't speak publicly on the matter, people will continue shredding you, dragging your name through the mud–and the Daily Times by extension–as the face for everything wrong with journalism."

"What would you have me do, Brant?" Ezekiel asked, exasperated. He despised whining, and bristled at the sound of his own voice, but he had no one else to talk to for advice. Brant was the Chief Editor at the Santa Monica Daily Times and had a seat on the board; overall he was a kind man but clearly nearing the end of his patience over this issue.

"I don't know," he sighed, his face lined with worry. "Take another interview. Pacify the situation somehow. Work a little harder on overcoming this stumbling block. Anything to get past this."

"You mean lie? You know I won't lie." Ezekiel's tone was firm. There had to be a way to protect Sara from further harm and keep his name in the clear, without stooping to that level.

"Great. We love that about you at the Daily Times, but you need to find a way to fix this, or corporate will be forced to take action."

Ezekiel's gaze met Brant's. They were good friends, and without a trace of arrogance, Ezekiel knew Brant considered him one of the best journalists the Daily Times had. Ezekiel knew Brant was on his side; but he may not get the rest of the board to agree with him. The board could ask that Brant fire Ezekiel, even if Brant didn't want that for the Times. Ezekiel knew well that Brant wouldn't do that lightly, but if it meant salvaging the Times and several dozen jobs he'd have no choice. "Look, Brant, you've always backed my work, and I'm not about to throw away the partnership we have. I just–this cuts deeper than any story I've ever done. I couldn't protect her in New York. I can't risk her being hurt further by revealing any more than they already know."

"You're a great journalist Ezekiel, but at some point, you are going to have to learn how to manage all the press stuff for your work, even if it feels like you're standing in front of a firing squad." Brant's tone was low, almost pleading. "Why don't you get her to come and tell the media the truth?" he suggested.

Instantly, Ezekiel was taken back to that night. His chest tightened and he felt the heat rise up his neck at the memory of her lips against his, her scent ... and the bliss that, for one moment, everything was perfect–and then it was not. Joe Galligan, Ezekiel's once-trusted friend, had somehow managed to evade the police round-up inside the Wentworth gala, but then was spotted trying to escape the building. In a fit of rage and panic, Joe attempted to shoot his way out. He only managed two shots before being taken down, and one of them grazed the back of Sara's head. Ezekiel shut his eyes against the stabbing memory: her confused frown, and the way she'd just crumpled. He had caught her; held her in his arms, her blood soaking through his sleeve. He kept his eyes shut tight for a moment, a barrier against the guilt and the dull ache in his heart.

"I'm sorry. That won't be possible. But I'll make this right. I will," Ezekiel said with renewed conviction and left Brant's office.

* * *

Ezekiel pulled up to the Ward residence fifteen minutes later than he had said he would. He had spent most of the journey there asking God for the strength to face what he was about to do. He stepped out of his car and walked up the front steps to the door. He was about to knock on the large solid oak door when it swung open. Mildred Ward stood there frowning at him.

"I was waiting for you."

"I'm terribly sorry. I was...."

She smiled and raised a hand to stop him, her mood suddenly shifting at his apology.

"You don't need to explain. You have a whole life of your own. Really, it's nice of you to come."

He smiled back at her. Mildred Ward reminded him of her daughter, except her hair was shorter, wispier and streaked with gray, and she had a slightly smaller frame than Sara's tall athletic build. Ezekiel had last seen her at her husband Darren Ward's funeral several weeks earlier. Darren, who had been like a second father to him. Grief had clearly descended on Mildred; the skin on her face sagging as if she had aged years in a matter of weeks.

"I've wanted to come by sooner. I wish we'd had more of a chance to talk at Darren's funeral. I've just been so busy wrapping things up in New York."

"It is good you are here now. And there will be plenty of time to talk about Darren, moving forward. Let's get going."

Mildred shut the door and walked to her car. Ezekiel followed.

"I brought flowers," he said, stating the obvious, as he clambered into the passenger seat of Mildred's car. He raised the colorful bouquet for her to see.

"How nice of you, Ezekiel." She offered him a wilted smile. "I wish I had been a better mother to her. Being alone in the house since her father passed seems to have left me with nothing but memories of a broken family. One that I could have at least tried to repair, but I never wanted to upset him, so I let him be a terrible father to her."

Ezekiel reached out and gently squeezed her shoulder as she drove.

"That's in the past. I'm sure you would change it if you could, but you can't. If you can, look to God for healing and comfort. I know He will make a way to bring beauty out of ashes in this situation. I think He's already doing so." Ezekiel knew this well of encouragement had to be coming from God, as he certainly had been struggling to find peace over the past few weeks himself. He breathed a prayer of thanks for the comfort he was suddenly able to share in that moment.

She smiled at him, a genuine one this time, full of emotion.

"I'm so proud of you, Ezekiel. And I want you to know that I don't blame you for the incident."

Ezekiel knew that her words should have made him feel better, but the all-too-familiar weight of guilt only seemed to press harder on his conscience. He managed a small smile and focused on the road in front of them.

CHAPTER 2

"What day of the week is it?"

"Tuesday."

"What time of day is it?"

"Morning."

"Twelve multiplied by four is?"

"48."

"Wow. That's great. That's all questions correctly answered, three days in a row now. I just need you to answer one more question for me. What is your name?"

"Sara Marie Ward," Sara sighed patiently, staring at the ceiling. She waited as the doctor wrote on the clipboard she was holding. What the doctor didn't ask, but Sara knew proved her cognitive abilities, was precisely how many dots were on the ceiling tiles. She had spent far too much time staring at them in the past several weeks, and silently mused that she was now qualified to answer that question, if it had only been included in her daily exam.

"This is excellent, Sara. Everything looks great. I'll go through the results of your labs and physicals, and hopefully, all will be good news."

The doctor smiled at her. Sara sat up.

"Thank you."

She nodded, hopped off the examination table, and put on her slippers. It had been almost five weeks since she'd been in the hospital. She did these tests every day, and even though the doctors hadn't explicitly said it, she knew that if her mental, physical, and lab assessments were in order, she would get to go home. She really wanted today to be that day.

"Hey there. Doc says I can take you to your room. Come on," Nurse Patty chirped, walking into the exam room.

"How do you think I did?" Sara asked, allowing Patty to support her by holding her arm. She didn't actually need the support, not anymore. Her balance and motor skills had improved dramatically over the weeks of rehab. More than once, she'd been told that a fraction of an inch closer to her skull may have killed her. Instead, her long hair covered the healing scar at the back of her scalp, and she almost felt normal as she talked and walked down the hallway. Now, if she could just remember how she had gotten into this state...

"You that eager to leave me, Sara?" Patty joked as they reached her room. Sara giggled.

"If I could take you with me, Patty, I would."

Patty smiled and led Sara to her bed. Sara thanked her as she made herself comfortable before plucking her Bible from the little bedside cabinet. Gratefulness swelled within her at the sight of the many cards and notes decorating the shelf and even the wall nearby (thanks to Patty's help). "Well, Miss Sunshine," Patty raised an eyebrow at her as she spoke, "I can't say I wouldn't be interested in meeting a few of these praying folks and asking them to have a word with God for me, too." She gestured at the card collection. "God must pay attention to them, because your recovery has been remarkable for sure."

Patty helped prop her pillows so that she could sit up and read. Sara opened the Bible to the book of Joshua. Early in her time at the hospital, her friend and roommate from New York, Debra, had brought some of her belongings from their apartment. Among them was a new Bible, which Sara didn't recognize at first. But as Debra placed it beside her, she felt a warm sense of welcome she couldn't explain. Where did that come from? Then, inside the cover, was her own handwriting. Dates from just weeks before, and next to them Bible passages that she'd copied from its pages. Sara searched her mind, but the memories of what had happened in New York that led to her encountering God for the first time in—well, ever—seemed hidden, as if behind a curtain. She just couldn't recall them. But the healing was there. She couldn't deny it. Her body was whole, and her heart was no longer fractured by bitterness at the wounds of her father's neglect.

Sara had spent much time during the past few weeks since the excruciating headaches subsided, reading the Bible and praying, and it had been the most edifying experience she had ever had in her life. Patty informed her on a regular basis that it was totally fine if she was feeling anxious or overwhelmed or weepy—that they were all absolutely normal reactions to a brain injury. Sara could only shake her head in wonder. "I just feel calm. Like, calmer than I remember feeling in years—certainly since before I moved to New York!"

"God got anything good to say to me today?" Patty asked, like she did every day.

"He wants you to know that He loves you," Sara replied with a smile, like she also did every day. She turned to the Book and focused on the words she was reading. Even though she wasn't deeply studying it, she could feel the Word change her every day, little by little, keeping her sane, helping her to hear God. The words came to life as she read, almost as if they were highlighted with a heavenly pen. Daily, a verse or sometimes several, would seem to leap off the page, and she knew it was God's way of getting her attention. It never failed to give her goosebumps and a sense that God was right there, working everything out for her good.

Sara was engrossed in her reading when she heard a knock on the door. She looked up as her mother walked in.

"Mom," she smiled, though it still felt slightly awkward. Losing her father had brought her and her mother closer together than they had ever been, and God had given her the strength to forgive both her parents from the heart. But it was strange not having the layers of hurt separating them as before, and Sara often found herself surprised by little things she'd never noticed about her mom.

"I do love it that you smile at me these days," Mildred smiled back. "I was sure you never would again."

"The wonders that God does," Sara quipped as she watched her mother come and sit beside her. "I wish I'd had the chance with dad before he...."

"I know. It's okay." Her mother squeezed her hand. "There's no point in holding onto those regrets."

Sara shook her head, blinking to stem the tears that had suddenly filled her eyes. *Easier said than done*, she thought. She had been in the hospital when her father died and not well enough to attend the funeral. Debra had sat by her side when the funeral was live-streamed, to support her, holding Sara as she sobbed over what might have been, what she'd missed out on all the years that she'd spent running away. Her mother had promised they would have a memorial ceremony when she was out of the hospital, especially for Sara, and they would scatter his ashes.

Mildred moved away, pulling a tissue out of the box from the nearby dresser. She moved back to Sara, blotted her tears, and leaned in to kiss her on the forehead.

"It'll be alright," Mildred whispered. She moved back to the dresser and picked up Sara's chart.

"I'm hoping they'll let me go home soon, maybe even today."

"I hope so too," Mildred smiled. It was obvious she wasn't sure what she was reading in the chart. Sara was wondering whether the doctors themselves could read their own handwriting, when her mother turned to face her. "Sara, sweetheart, there's someone here to see...." but her voice trailed off as Sara's eyes fastened on the man who'd just walked in behind Mildred.

"Hello, Sara," the man said softly. His eyes searched her face.

"Ezekiel Cane?" Sara asked in utter surprise. She hadn't seen him in years, and the last time they'd seen each other, she had hated him. Well, she had seen him on the news a bit lately, which was weird, but other than that, she had no idea what he was up to. "What are you doing here?"

"I...I...." He stopped, glancing at Mildred. He looked a little nervous, and Sara couldn't think why.

Of course, she realized suddenly. He was probably nervous because of their past—the hate she had sent his way for so many years.

"Ezekiel?" she said, her stomach clenching. Although God had healed much of her heart regarding her father, seeing Ezekiel made her aware that there was still more work to do.

He smiled a fond smile. Sara frowned and looked between her mother and Ezekiel.

"Sara, I should have come earlier, but there was a lot to wrap up in New York with the police and the news. I'm so sorry about your dad, Sara."

"Thank you, Ezekiel," she said, still puzzled. "I've seen you on the news quite a bit recently."

"I'm afraid so," he walked closer to her.

"I'm sorry, but I don't understand why you're here."

"You wouldn't. You've lost maybe three months' worth of memories?" he said gruffly, his brow creased.

Sara blinked at him, trying to connect the dots of what he was saying.

"This isn't our first meeting in years," she deduced. Ezekiel nodded. Her mind was searching, trying to pull back that curtain that blocked her memory. "Somewhere in the past three months, we met again?" He nodded again.

"I see," Sara said, frowning, and she only wished she really could.

"Sara, I never meant for you to get hurt or any of it."

"How would *you* hurt me?" Sara asked, confused by what he was saying. He looked down. He had been in New York, he was apologizing for her getting hurt, and they'd met sometime in the last three months. What did it all mean? "Did you have something to do with putting me in the hospital?" She straightened suddenly.

"I did. But it's not like that," he said quickly. "It was an accident."

Sara blinked at him again. Her head was beginning to hurt.

"What ... What do you mean? ... Ughh...." She groaned and pressed a palm to the back and side of her head.

"Are you okay?" He rushed to her side and rested a hand on her arm, but she pulled her arm away.

"Stop. I–Oww...." She groaned again as the pain increased, radiating into her face.

"Sara, dear, you need to stop trying to remember. The doctor warned against this." Mildred came and took Ezekiel's place beside her, rubbing her arm. "Just breathe. Let it go. Breathe in, 2, 3, 4 and out 2, 3, 4."

Sara focused on her mother's voice as she continued to encourage her to relax and breathe, and let it soothe her. She let go of what she was trying to remember and opened her eyes. Ezekiel's jaw was clenched when she looked up, and he avoided her eyes.

"I'm sorry. I should go," he said, his voice small.

"Wait. I need to know what happened." She stopped him before he could leave. She wasn't going to let him just drop this on her and walk away.

He turned to her. "You should watch the news," he shrugged apologetically.

He walked out of the room just as Nurse Patty walked in.

"I have wonderful news!" She beamed, oblivious to the air of sobriety. "You get to go home!"

* * *

SARA HAD THOUGHT it was great news when she first heard it, but after being home for nearly a week, it felt like a prison. What's worse, she wasn't actually *home*. Instead, she was staying with her mother for a little while before heading back to New York, just to give herself a chance to get fully back on her feet before re-entering the 'rat race' that was New York. And truthfully, more to give her mother a little more time with her so they could continue to rebuild their broken relationship. Her mother, at least, was thrilled with the temporary arrangement.

Sara, however, was bored, and for the past two days, all she could think about was Ezekiel Cane's bombshell. He had told her to watch the news. What did that even mean? How was she linked to the scandal those reporters kept talking about? She was so grateful that she only had short-term memory loss. She could remember clearly all her life events, painful as many of them were, up until the past few months. She knew work at the Marionette had been intense, but she'd been working toward a promotion. Other than that, everything seemed shadowed, hidden. Whatever event had brought on her memory loss, the injury that caused it, anything that might have led up to it–was a mystery. At her frequent inquiries, everyone was vague, quickly changing the subject. *As if I don't know that's exactly what they're doing,* she rolled her eyes in exasperation.

Over the past several weeks, though, she had experienced fleeting images here and there that made no sense to her. Her doctors were optimistic that in time she would regain even the past few months' of memory, though they were reluctant to give her any kind of expectation as to when that might occur. They were not even sure whether her injury itself was the cause, or if it was just her mind's way of protecting her from the trauma she had experienced. Sara was sure she wanted her memory back–or was she? Maybe it was better in the long run that she couldn't remember what had happened? Sara didn't know the answer, and agonizing over it certainly wasn't helping.

In frustration, she clicked her tongue and crouched down by the oven. Sara's shoulders slumped and she rolled her eyes, seeing that her cake hadn't risen after almost thirty minutes. It looked like an over-sized, overdone pancake... again.

"God, please send me something to do. I can't sit here and bake for the rest of my life," she whispered a prayer, "especially when no one wants to eat these dismal failures."

As though on cue, her phone rang. She picked it up from the counter and smiled as she saw Debra's name pop up on the screen.

"Well, hello you," Debra's voice smiled through the phone at her.

"I miss you! I miss New York!" So what if she sounded desperate? She couldn't go on like this much longer.

"Really? What exactly do you miss? The rude people or the rude weather?" Debra quipped. Sara laughed.

"I miss *doing* something–anything. Maybe even working."

"The Marionette?"

Sara thought for a moment. Did she miss the Marionette? She shook her head even though Debra couldn't see her. "No. Not that. There's more I could be doing than waitressing. I'm convinced of that now."

"Like what?"

Sara glanced at the oven once again before grabbing a bottle of coconut water from the fridge and walking into the living room.

"Maybe use my degree? I'm still praying about it, but I think it seems to be the direction God is leading me." She sat down on the couch.

"I remember you were pretty passionate about your training, so that could certainly be a great move for you."

Sara nodded slowly as she mulled over the idea. After graduation, instead of finding a job in public relations, the work she'd actually studied for–and that her parents had paid for–she had taken almost any other job she could find. She mostly hated those jobs, and it showed. She'd lost every single one, until the Marionette. But she had definitely succeeded in disappointing her parents; she closed her eyes and shuddered at the realization of how that had actually made her glad at the time. But now... everything was so different.

"So, I need to find work in PR."

"I guess I could keep my eyes open for any openings here in New York," Debra offered, then Sara could hear papers rustling. "Now tell me about this Ezekiel issue."

Sara let out a massive sigh. "They are hounding him because he supposedly almost got someone killed while he was working on his story in New York, right? Well... I can't stop thinking–was that me? Was he trying to tell me that *I'm the one* he... blackmailed? I just can't remember anything, though!"

Debra snorted. "That was not at all how it happened."

"But it makes sense. Why else would I have helped *him*? I hated him, Debra. Like, I don't think I even told you how much I hated the guy."

"Well, people have been known to change. Even you wouldn't believe how much," Debra said, the hooded tone to her voice betraying her. She obviously knew more than she was willing to share.

"What do you mean?"

"It's not my story to tell. Besides, I have to go. I hope you figure it out." Debra sent kisses through the phone before hanging up.

Sara shut her eyes.

"I'm so confused. Please lead me," she prayed aloud. The smell of smoke wafted into the living room, and Sara opened her eyes abruptly, realizing her cake was still in the oven.

"No, no, no!"

She rushed into the kitchen and pulled open the oven to find a blackened mess. Turning off the oven and dumping the ruined cake into the sink, she sighed and slumped onto a kitchen chair. Clearly, baking was *not* her next career move. Was it odd that she wanted to cry, she wondered? Her emotions were a seesaw. She knew the doctors had warned her about this, but the reality of what she was experiencing was exhausting.

Sometimes, new life can arise from ashes.

Really God? Sara shut her eyes. The smoke detector went off belatedly just then, and the sprinklers her mother had been convinced to install by her fire chief uncle sprayed water over her. *Just peachy,* she groaned, racing to shut off the alarm system and getting soaked in the process. At least the counters and floor would be clean... once she finished mopping them all up, of course. She was thankful her mom had taken the afternoon to run errands and wouldn't be home until dinnertime. Maybe Sara could eliminate the soggy mess before then. Including the cake.

"Of course," she replied humbly to that still, small Voice. "I am pretty sure You *can* bring new life. I already feel new in a lot of ways. It's just..." Sara exhaled as she surveyed the dripping kitchen. "Help me trust You."

Embrace it. Go with it, beloved. All things work together for the ones who love Me. You have been called according to My purpose for you.

Sara was about to ask what that meant when her phone rang again. She looked down at the unknown number.

"Hello?" she answered.

"Sara Ward. I'm Brant Wilford, and I believe that we can help each other."

CHAPTER 3

The last thing Ezekiel wanted to do on a Monday morning was get dragged into another argument with Brant, but he hadn't even reached his desk when Casey, the office administrator, informed him that Brant wanted to see him.

"I know it looks like I haven't done anything, but waiting it out might be the best strategy–" Ezekiel stopped short when he saw Sara Ward seated in Brant's office. He turned to Brant with a menacing look. "What is she doing here?"

"Hello, Ezekiel. It's good to see you again after you dropped that bombshell on me in the hospital and went AWOL," Sara replied sunnily before Brant could speak.

"Sara, I'm sorry about that. It's just–seeing you in the hospital like that, I thought you needed space and...." he faltered.

"You thought wrong," she stated flatly.

He shook his head. "I'm sorry; what are you doing in Brant's office?"

"He called me with a proposition."

Ezekiel couldn't believe his ears.

"A proposition? You have got to be kidding me." He ran a hand through his hair. "The situation is messy as it is; you can't bring her into it. She's suffering from a brain injury."

"Um, hello? I'm right here, and he didn't drag me here. I accepted his proposition."

"You don't even know what happened to you," Ezekiel turned to her.

"And whose fault is that?" she retorted.

Ezekiel blinked at her, then sighed.

"Listen, I have been warned not to pressure you into trying to remember things. But I can tell you in all honesty: I didn't blackmail you, okay? Those are all media lies. We met in New York, things happened, and you needed my help. I asked for something in return, and you decided to help me. I wish now... " he trailed off and gazed out the office window.

"What?" Sara pressed him. Her heart was pounding in her chest, and she was trying to ignore the pressure at the back of her head as her mind once again struggled against the shadows.

Ezekiel turned to see her searching his expression for clues, then shrugged and looked down. "I wish you could remember it all yourself. But you *can* trust me on this: you were there because you chose to be," he said evenly.

"But then I got shot in the head?" Sara's gaze shook him. Ezekiel inhaled sharply and looked away again. He could take the whole world accusing him, even on live TV if he had to, but he hated seeing what felt like blame in her eyes. He turned and crouched beside her chair, looking up into her eyes.

"Sara, if I could have stepped between you and that bullet, I would do it, a hundred times over." He shook his head, clenching his fists. "I just didn't see it coming. It should've been me." He hung his head. There was so much more churning inside him, but what else could he say? What if she never remembered? All he could do was wait.

Sara bit her lip. "There's more to it, isn't there?" she asked, her tone sober, her eyes understanding.

Ezekiel nodded.

"Let me help you." She leaned over in her seat and put her face close to his. Ezekiel was suddenly transported by her scent. She smelled clean and sweet. It was intoxicating. He had to stand up quickly, and her eyes followed him.

"Help me? How? Why?"

"It might sound weird, but I think God wants me to. I have this feeling, like–peace inside–about helping you. The media is slaughtering you. You need to speak out and control the story," she said calmly.

"She's right. I want her to be your publicist," Brant said, drawing Ezekiel's attention to him.

Ezekiel wasn't sure he'd heard right.

"You want *her* to be my publicist?" he repeated stupidly.

"Absolutely. This way, you get the professional help you need, and she gets to control what comes out about this whole situation–and what doesn't. It's a win-win."

Ezekiel looked between the two of them.

"Isn't it too soon for you to be working again? Why not work with another publicist?" he looked to Brant again warily.

"I wouldn't be comfortable with that," Sara piped up. "If I got into this whole mess with you, I think I should be the one to try and get us out of it. Besides, my doctors said it's fine for me to work, just not too many hours a week to start off. I want to do this," she emphasized, her eyes pleading with him. "Please."

She stood and closed the distance between them, laying her hand on his arm. Ezekiel knew that her emerald green eyes would be his undoing, and he found himself nodding as he looked into them.

"Well... what do you want me to do, Boss?" he sighed, his hands raised in surrender.

"Everything I say," she grinned triumphantly. "First, you can buy me breakfast. I think you have a lot to tell me."

* * *

AN HOUR LATER, Ezekiel sat across from Sara at the Breadbox Cafe a few blocks from his office, watching her eat a piece of sprouted whole wheat toast. He generally preferred to be the one asking questions, but this time it actually felt good to be talking. For the first time since leaving New York, he was able to sift through all the events that had taken place during the entire Wentworth investigation, with Sara listening patiently as he did so. He knew it was risky, given her potentially fragile mental state, but she'd convinced him it was worth it for both of them. He hoped she was right.

So far, she seemed to be assimilating the knowledge without any signs of anxiety, but finally, Sara reached out and put her hand on

Ezekiel's arm to pause him. "Wait–slow down. I need to understand. I still can't remember anything–it's all a total shadow. But I have to know–tell me honestly–how *did* you convince me to even work with you? I'm not accusing you of anything. It's just–I know how much I hated you before... well, before God. And I just cannot see how I would have gone along with anything you said?" she looked at him searchingly, her palms in the air.

"Well," Ezekiel chuckled, "it wasn't easy!" The memory of chasing her down on a New York City sidewalk sprung to mind. "But I was able to work a promotion for you into my offer, and I also promised that you would be paid for your time on my job. You still almost turned me down, but by some miracle, decided to go along with the plan." He placed both hands on the table in front of him and looked her straight in the eye. "I don't have anything to hide, Sara. I made it clear to you at the time that your job at the Marionette was secure, whether you decided to work with me or not. And I was thrilled that you took me up on my offer–even if you did make life ... challenging ... for a while there," he finished, his eyes hinting at a smile.

Sara's mind churned. While the past few months were still lost to her memory, she had a clear recollection of her life prior to that, and the memories of their teen years were as vivid as ever. She had unquestionably hated Ezekiel, as he represented all the rejection she'd felt from her father. But now, with the layers of bitterness and pain being peeled away by God's love over the past few months... Suddenly it slammed into her afresh that not once could she ever recall Ezekiel being anything less than kind and patient toward her, in spite of the vitriol she had spewed at him all those years. Her cheeks colored at the unpleasant memories of her horrible attitude toward him. In a moment of clarity, she knew. He was telling the truth.

When Sara didn't respond, Ezekiel continued. "So, basically, you almost single-handedly pulled the whole gala together in a matter of weeks, then went behind my back, got the police involved, and saved the day. ...and then Joe, obviously enraged, ended up shooting you, for which he is now in jail facing attempted murder and assault charges. He insists he didn't mean to hit anyone. Yeah, right," Ezekiel shook his head, rolling his eyes.

Sara sat in silence a moment longer, then she placed her toast down and focused her gaze on his. "I still don't remember," she acknowledged, "but... I believe you, Ezekiel. I can't think of any reason not to trust you. And like I said before, I believe God's leading me to help you now, and I definitely trust Him. But... that's not all that happened. Is it?"

He smiled, lifting his eyebrows. "You're intuitive."

"What else happened?"

Ezekiel continued to gaze at her, and the gentle smile on his face gave way to a longing look. He swallowed, praying he was doing the right thing in telling her.

"*We* did," he finally said, not taking his eyes off hers.

She drew her head back in confusion at first, her eyes narrowed at him suspiciously.

"Wait–what? *We happened*?" she repeated incredulously.

"Yes, we. You and me. We..." he faltered, unable to hide the edge of pain in his voice. It didn't seem fair; how many times would he have to start all over again with her? Her face softened as she searched his quizzically, then she shook her head once, and then again, as though trying to rattle the memories into view.

"But how could we... You mean that I...." she struggled to put her thoughts together, grasping for any shred of a memory, but unable to reach any.

"You didn't hate me anymore," he said simply. "Or at least, that was what you said. I never expected it, but we grew close." He tried to smile, but the look of pity on her face made it difficult. He drew in a ragged breath and let it out sharply.

"Ezekiel, I'm so sorry..." she whispered. "To lose, I mean– to not ..." she stammered, grasping for the right words and trying to remember, more frustrated than ever that she couldn't. *Of all the things to forget!* she wailed inwardly. "I can't imagine what that's like for you. I mean, me, not remembering... us."

"It's not something you can help."

She reached out and took his hand, squeezing it.

"I'm so sorry. I mean, actually, it's kind of amazing that I forgave you up to that extent. I guess that's really evidence that God *has* been changing me after all this time. But, I...." She looked down at their hands, then slowly drew hers back.

"Sara."

She looked up at him.

"It's okay. Really. Don't feel bad. Even though it's a weird sort of heartbreak to encounter, I honestly don't expect anything from you. You have been through enough, and I know you just need to take each day as it comes. Maybe... we could just try being friends, though? If you'd like?" Ezekiel offered tentatively.

She watched him for a long moment before nodding slowly.

"I think I can manage that," she replied. "I have to say; it is almost like waking up from a coma to realize you have become more than friends with someone you once hated."

Ezekiel chuckled in spite of his sadness. "I'm sure it is."

The waitress came to refill their coffee.

"Thank you," Sara said and waited for her to leave. "I'm sorry. For how I spoke to you earlier. I don't blame you. It's just hard sometimes, not being able to remember all this for myself. But I believe you."

"You don't need to apologize. I should be thanking you for choosing to help me."

"I told you, I'm pretty sure God wants me to," she said matter-of-factly.

Ezekiel frowned.

"I wish we'd had more time to talk about things before you–well, before you lost your memory. I never got to hear how it was that you came to reconnect with God in all this. It's the greatest thing that's come out of this whole mess, really, and ... well, it's what I was praying for," he admitted.

"Thank you," Sara said simply. She blushed again to think of how awful she'd been to him in the past, and there he was praying for her all along.

"But I guess that must all be part of the period you can't remember?" he asked.

"Yes! It's odd, isn't it? I woke up in the hospital just feeling His presence. It was as if he was carrying me through the fog into the light. I knew that it was God, and I've felt so full of peace since then, getting to know Him more." She was surprised by how easy it was to talk to him about it all, and she was grateful for it.

Ezekiel wanted to reach out and push a strand of hair behind her ear, but aside from fearing it would seem too intimate, he didn't want to distract her from what she was sharing. Her face was practically glowing as she spoke, and his breath caught at the intensity in her eyes.

"You had it right all along. With God. I wish I'd known growing up," she said sadly.

"You know now," he smiled.

"Yeah. I do," she smiled back. "It changes everything. Well, *He* changes everything..." her voice trailed off as she took a sip of her coffee and stared out the window.

For those few moments, Ezekiel could forget all the anguish of the past several weeks as gratitude swelled within him. Sara's physical recovery was awesome, sure, but seeing the transformation that God had obviously done on the inside of her stunned him. *Wow, God,* he prayed silently. Whatever happened, he felt sure of God's love for them both. Joining Sara in her gaze out the window, he continued to offer up silent praises.

* * *

TWO DAYS LATER, Ezekiel opened his apartment door to find Sara standing there, a smirk on her face and a large bag over her shoulder.

"Ward? What are you doing here at this hour?" It was six am, and Ezekiel was still groggy from being woken up by her knocking.

She rolled her eyes. "It almost sounds like you're not happy to see me. Excuse me." She pushed past him and into his apartment. He shrugged, shut the door, and followed her back in. She stopped in the middle of his living room, hands on her hips, just looking around. "Hm."

"What do you mean 'hm'?" he asked, rubbing his eyes as he moved to the kitchen to make some coffee. She didn't appear to be leaving soon, so he might as well get coffee.

"It's just very...." She hesitated as she thought. "...modern. I always thought of you as sort of a western, dark wood type of guy."

Ezekiel shot her a grumpy look behind her back and reached for his jar of coffee grounds.

"Coffee?" he asked, *not that you need any, Miss Perky at 6am,* he added inwardly.

She turned to face him and walked over to wait by the breakfast bar.

"Yes, please," she smiled. "Milk, no sugar."

He nodded and turned on the coffee machine.

She sat on one of the black metal barstools, and he stood across the counter from her as the coffee began to brew, the aroma wafting between them.

"So. What brings you to my humble abode at six in the morning?" he asked, stifling a yawn.

"Is it that early? I guess I'm a morning person now. I wanted to know if you had plans for the day," she answered rather innocently.

"Oh. Uh... I would have to double check my phone, but nothing urgent I can think of." He ran a hand through his hair, attempting to smooth it down a bit, having just gotten out of bed. Sara had certainly risen to the occasion and exceeded his expectations during their undercover job on the Wentworth story, but this was a whole new level of motivation. "Why?" he questioned.

"Because I booked you an interview."

Ezekiel's eyes widened in panic; he was immediately awake. "What? I can't do an interview today! What would I even say?" He threw his hands up and then pressed them against his forehead, blowing out a forceful breath.

"Relax, it's not today. It's tomorrow, and that's why I'm here: to coach you through it." She beamed. She was clearly pleased with her work, and Ezekiel couldn't help admiring her, especially as she sat there at his kitchen counter looking far too gorgeous for so early in the morning.

Ezekiel shook his head in resignation and huffed a sigh. "Fine. I didn't have any plans anyway. You know I'm trying to just lay low."

"Good. Because we have a lot to cover," she said, her tone stern.

He handed her a cup of coffee, and she smiled in appreciation before taking a sip. She brought out a binder from her bag and placed it on the counter. Ezekiel had a wave of déjà vu at the sight of it. All they were missing was Debra, and it would be just like their under-cover training session back in New York. To his great relief, this binder was a fraction of the size of Debra's binders. Suddenly he grinned broadly at her when it hit him: this time was especially different because now, they were officially friends. He took a sip of his coffee.

"Why are you looking at me like that?" she asked, and paused from flipping through the binder. Ezekiel started to answer that he was just remembering their training with Debra, when it occurred to him that she didn't actually share the memory. He shook the disappointing thought away.

"Uh—nothing. I was just...." Ezekiel paused, realizing that talking about something she couldn't remember might upset her.

She frowned, her expression growing somber. "You were remembering something."

He nodded.

"I was there, but I've forgotten."

He nodded again. He hated this.

Sara smiled, but it didn't reach her eyes. "That's okay. I'm sure this is difficult for you, knowing I don't have all the memories you have." She snorted. "Of course, don't get me wrong; it's also pretty hard losing three months of your life." Ezekiel looked down at the counter. Despite her facetious tone, the sadness in her eyes was revealing, and it pained him to see it. "Especially when something really important happened, and you can see how it hurts someone else."

Ezekiel's eyes flew back to hers, and he could see she was suddenly close to tears.

"Hey, please—don't feel bad. I'm fine, honest. In fact, I'm ready to set out on this adventure of friendship. I mean, we're even more than friends now," he said in a lighter tone, attempting to brighten her mood.

"We are?" she blinked at him, confused.

"We're publicist and client now. I'd say that's a big deal."

She laughed, and Ezekiel grinned. He liked that he could make her laugh.

"So, hotshot publicist. What do you have in store for me today?"

He came around the counter and sat on the stool next to hers.

"Well, the interview is with a local news station; I thought we'd start here in Santa Monica and see how it goes." He nodded along as she spoke. "The strategy is this: we keep all the conversation focused on how important your article was and how much better the world is now that the Wentworth corporation has been exposed."

"So, make them feel grateful for the story and hope they forget the methods?" he asked, and she smiled.

"Exactly."

"But they're still going to ask about it. They're interested in what gets views," he sighed.

"I know how the media works, thank you," she retorted. Ezekiel tried not to roll his eyes. "I will teach you how to truthfully dodge those questions or turn them around to focus on what *you* want to talk about."

"Okay. Let's do it." he said, a small sense of cautious optimism welling up in him.

"We're going to simulate interview scenarios, so I suggest you get ready for the day, and then we'll start. Last I looked, most interviews do not take place while wearing pajamas. Zoom calls maybe, but not interviews. I'll cook us something to eat while you do that."

"You've got a point there, and I definitely won't argue with a woman who offers to cook me breakfast." He saluted her and headed off to take a shower and get dressed. He didn't want to be in his pajamas all day anyway. When he came back to the kitchen, his eyes widened in surprise.

"Did you order in?" he asked, taking in the arrangement on his dining table.

She scowled at him. "I'll try not to be offended by that. Come on. We'll eat while we work." She beckoned him over and placed a jug of orange juice on the table.

"I didn't know you could cook a full breakfast with what was in my fridge. Actually," he corrected, "I didn't know *you* could cook, period." She gave him an impish grin.

He was surprised, pleasantly surprised. Living alone, he didn't eat many home-cooked meals, except when his mother stopped by with some leftovers. He went over and pulled out his chair. He tried not to think of how right it felt as she sat down for breakfast next to him.

"It's something I picked up living in New York. A hobby. Okay, a necessity. Things are expensive over there, and, as you may know, I wasn't extra buoyant." They both laughed. "Do you still pray before you eat?" she asked, and offered her hand to him. Ezekiel looked at it for a second before he took it, enjoying the warmth of her touch. He looked up at her, and she was staring at their linked hands; then her gaze came up to meet his abruptly. She smiled at him. Ezekiel wanted to believe that she could feel something, that whatever had sparked between them weeks ago might be strong enough to pull the memories back to her, but he wouldn't push her.

"Do you want me to pray?" she asked.

He shook his head. "I'll do it."

He forced himself to close his eyes. If he stared at her any longer, the urge to tell her how beautiful she looked might just overpower his will; some of her long hair had escaped her signature loose bun, and her cheeks were flushed from standing over the stove. "Lord, thank You for provision, thank You for Sara, and for me. We ask that You bless this meal and the hands that prepared it. We are grateful for being able to eat. Lord, provide for those who can't and help us find ways to help them. And Father, give us courage and words to say to bring truth to light during these interviews, much as I'd rather not do them.Thank you, Lord. In Jesus' name. Amen."

"Amen," Sara said too.

As they ate, they went through a few possible scenarios. Sara talked him through answers and taught him some tactics that he could use to steer the conversation. Ezekiel knew she was brilliant, but this was a whole new level of insight into her. The discovery should have made him happy, but it only made his heart ache for what could have been if she hadn't been hurt, if her memory hadn't been lost, if he'd somehow managed to protect her.

"Hey, did I lose you? Please say you aren't already getting stage fright after all this practice," Sara pleaded with him, noticing the faraway look in his eyes.

Ezekiel snapped back to the present. "No, no," he reassured her. "Sorry, promise–I'll stay focused. You... are really great at this stuff. I'm thankful Brant called you in. I needed this–needed you, to help me. Thanks," he recovered. *Stop rambling, dope*, he told himself. He was truly grateful for her; he just had to let go of what might have been, and appreciate that they could be friends.

CHAPTER 4

$\mathcal{E}$zekiel was already prepped to go on camera, and they were counting down to start the broadcast by the time Sara arrived. He spotted her behind the camera and smiled. She gave him a thumbs up.

"You've got this," she mouthed, giggling to herself at the sight of him with stage makeup on.

The red light went on, and the host looked into the camera.

"Welcome back this morning. With me for the next few minutes is one of the most talked-about journalists in America at the moment, Mr. Ezekiel Cane." The lady smiled into the camera. "Mr. Cane." She turned to Ezekiel. "Tell us, why have you decided to begin taking interviews again? The last one proved awkward, and you've been silent since then."

Ezekiel cleared his throat. "Well, the subject matter was and is still very delicate, so I wanted to ensure I was saying the right words, not rushing into saying anything I didn't mean or that could be misinterpreted."

"Are you saying you wanted to prepare what to say? Doesn't that seem a bit disingenuous?" she asked, her face straight.

Ezekiel's face dropped.

"No, ah, that's not what I meant. I would like to focus on a grander issue, the corrupt nature of American corporations."

"So, you're saying that the reckless endangerment of human life in the name of journalism is less important than corruption?" she asked. Her face was deadpan, and Sara almost didn't believe what she was hearing. Ezekiel chuckled nervously.

"No, you misunderstand me. I'm saying that the article has done a world of good, and–"

"And so, we should ignore the tragedy that could have happened in the process of obtaining information to create the article?" She cut him off.

Sara had to resist the urge to shout foul play. The interviewer was badgering him.

"You seem to be putting words in my mouth that I'm not saying," Ezekiel said, his tone edgy, red infusing his cheeks, in spite of the makeup.

"Well, you don't seem to be saying very much about the issue of concern, and it is my job to find out the truth and report it."

The woman smiled, but Sara scoffed at her obvious insincerity. This wasn't an interview; it was an ambush. Ezekiel looked more than annoyed.

"I believe that is the job of both our professions," he said through gritted teeth.

The producer made a "wrap it up" signal with his hands from behind the camera. The interviewer and Ezekiel seemed to have a bit of a staredown before she finally broke eye contact and looked into the camera.

"I'm afraid that is all the time we have for the interview this morning. We take you to our colleague on the streets for our live coverage of the community marathon for charity. I'm Cassidy Fields for the Good Morning Show. Grab your coffee and join us for more up to the minute news and commentary after a word from our sponsors."

Ezekiel all but tore the mic from his shirt before storming down the platform and off into the hallway.

"You'll be hearing from me," Sara tossed at the producer before running after Ezekiel. *Ugh, come on, God—what am I supposed to say to pick him up now?* she prayed silently as she followed him out to the parking lot. She reached him just as he was yanking open his car door. "Ezekiel, wait!" she called out.

He stopped with his hand on the open door. He turned around.

Sara stepped back as she watched a vein pulsing in his neck, his jaw clenched.

"That was a disaster. She had no intention of hearing anything but a confession of wrongdoing. Like an interrogation!" Ezekiel huffed.

"I'm sorry, Ezekiel, I had no idea that would happen. I obviously need to do a better job screening which interviews we do, but all interviews won't go as expected. We need to practice more," she admitted. She knew as his publicist, all the blame for this landed squarely on her, and she really did feel sorry.

"There's no way you could have known," he acknowledged with a shake of his head. He began to pace. She swallowed and sighed. "This is useless," he groaned.

"No one seems to want to listen to anything about the article..." she started.

"If we don't address the blackmail issue," he said grimly, his gaze fixing on hers as he stopped pacing.

She nodded, realizing the futility of the situation. "I'm the only other person who should know how it all happened, and I can't help because I've lost my memory." Without realizing it, she'd lifted her hands to her head, her face strained, trying to soothe the pressure that had started to build as she struggled against her own mind.

His face softened. "Sara, please don't look like that."

"Like what?"

"Like you're the cause of all my problems. I think I did a pretty good job causing this myself."

She tried to smile, but she knew it didn't reassure him. "We can't give up. I'm going to help you to untangle this mess."

"Right, " he said dryly, one eyebrow arched, a skeptical look on his face.

She swatted his arm. "Now is not the time to doubt my skills. We can think of something else. I just need to do exactly that. Think," she decided, finality in her tone as she began to walk away. "And pray. Pray more importantly."

She heard him sigh before climbing into his car.

* * *

THE NEXT DAY, Sara found herself heaving a disgusted sigh as she watched yet another cake refuse to rise in the oven.

"I know baking isn't supposed to be this hard. Something has to be missing; maybe the baking soda has gone bad or something?" she mused as she walked away from it and over to her computer that was perched on the counter.

She took a sip of her iced tea, staring at the interview invitations in her email. All for Ezekiel.

"Lord, please guide me. I know you nudged me in this direction," she murmured, scrolling through the emails. The doorbell rang. A welcome distraction, Sara decided, as she pulled open the door and frowned at the man standing there.

"Hello. Can I help you?"

"Miss Sara Ward?" he asked.

Sara wasn't sure she recognized him. In retrospect, she should have checked to see who it was before she opened the door, safe neighborhood or not.

"Yes, and you are?"

"Simon Mode, a reporter for Norton Media. I have it on a credible source that you were, in fact, the one involved in the Ezekiel Cane incident, although you are now working as his publicist. Would you please confirm that information?"

Sara only now noticed the cameraman standing behind him.

"Don't you have better things to do?" she demanded. "More important stories to report?" She slammed the door and leaned back against it.

Oh. No. Her name was out there. Her heart drummed in her chest as she forced herself to take several deep breaths. She guessed it wasn't actually very hard for these people to find all these details out, but it did mean things would change. A lot. Sara had to put that thought on hold as the odor of burning cake reached her nose, and she dashed back to the kitchen before she could cause another flood.

CHAPTER 5

"What nerve. Showing up at your door," Brant said, seething from his chair.

Ezekiel sat on Brant's office sofa and watched Sara pace. "Okay, so they know it's you. But I doubt they know the whole story. No one outside your family even knows about your memory loss, right?"

"True, and this complicates things," Sara sighed.

"I am sorry your name is out there, but it had to come out sooner or later," Ezekiel sounded resigned. It likely would have been a matter of public record.

"You obviously are not following Miranda Twain's narrative of the whole situation on the Wide-Open Show," Brant rebuked as he turned on the television.

"Well, I smell something fishy. For all we know, he's still blackmailing her, and this time, to be his publicist," Miranda was saying, as the recording played where Brant had paused it.

She was about to say more, but Sara snatched the remote and turned it off. Ezekiel ran a hand through his hair. "She's not even a real journalist."

"Yet people seem to believe her, credible or not," Brant said, "You have history with Miranda Twain, Ezekiel, don't you? Couldn't you talk to her?"

Ezekiel shot him a weary look. "I don't think that's a good idea."

Sara looked at Ezekiel quizzically and then paused. "So. I've made a decision." Sara stood up and placed her hands on her hips. Ezekiel admired the determined look on her face, although admittedly, it made him nervous about whatever plan she had up her sleeve. "There are some aggressive PR strategies we learned in college. Like stealing a narrative."

Ezekiel and Brant exchanged wary glances.

"And this would involve?"

"In unique situations, where the other party in a scandal is cooperative, the two parties can do press together. Press that shapes the narrative."

"You want us to do press together?" Ezekiel cocked his head in disbelief. "A few hours ago, you didn't want your name out there. I don't get it."

"Well, I don't personally want the limelight, but I was hired to help you, and professionally, I think this is the best option we have. Or would you rather keep stumbling along by yourself while Miranda Twain keeps making you out to look like a liar," Sara shot back, her tone bordering on snarky.

Ezekiel shook his head and stood up, stepping in front of her.

"You forget one crucial detail. You lost your memory! And unless you want to lie, having you at interviews will not do any good."

She narrowed her eyes at him. "You underestimate me. That's where the narrative comes in." She stepped away. "We're going to paint ourselves as exactly what we are."

"Publicist and client?"

"Enemies turned lovers."

Ezekiel almost choked on his saliva. He coughed. "What?"

"Well, come on. We aren't anymore, and we'll let them know that, but we can tell them about the parts before I lost my memory. We let them know that maybe," she said, stepping towards him, "maybe we are on that path again, just starting as friends after the accident."

Ezekiel blinked. He tried not to be enthralled by her eyes or by the softness of her tone. For a split second, his hopes had soared at the words 'enemies turned lovers,' but her next words brought him crashing back down again. "Something in there feels like lying..."

"I won't be dishonest." He turned to walk away, but she stepped around him.

"Ezekiel. If you could, trust me; I know what I am doing. Please, leave it to me,"Sara said."To recap, there's no dishonesty. We *were* enemies once–that is, I considered you *my* enemy–but then, we found feelings for each other. I lost all recollection of that. And now...." She paused, looking into his eyes, "Could you please trust me? After all, that is what Brant is paying me for."

When Ezekiel got home, he knew he needed to pray. They were receiving interview requests from across the country, and he needed to know what God had to say on the matter. For Sara, it would be easy to just fall into step doing her job with publicity, but he was the one nursing a broken heart, and now, doing interviews together, it would be even more difficult to guard his heart and emotions, striving to keep them reined in on that 'friendship' level.

Ezekiel sat on the floor in his living room, his head in his hands as he prayed. "Lord, I need You to guide me on this. I need You to lead me. I don't know why she lost her memory, though I'm beyond grateful it wasn't anything more than that. I know that Your ways are not our ways, but I need Your strength and Your help."

He waited, focusing on God, until eventually, he fell asleep stretched out on the floor, with the words *"this is the way; walk in it,"* echoing softly in his spirit. He knew that he had to trust God, and He would walk with him through it all. Though this may be one of the times it was not so easy to do.

* * *

A FEW DAYS LATER, he found himself on a plane seated next to Sara. She hadn't said a word to him since they'd first checked in. "Have I done something?" he finally asked her.

"No," she said simply, perusing the drinks menu.

He drew his eyebrows together. "You haven't spoken to me since we arrived," he said matter-of-factly.

"I didn't know I was obligated to." She didn't take her eyes off the menu.

"Of course, you are not obligated to, but ignoring me? How is that helpful?"

"All this time together can be quite intense; sometimes I like some quiet," Sara dropped the menu on her lap.

Ezekiel cocked his head to the side and raised his eyebrows in utter confusion. "Quiet when we are together?"

She looked affronted. "Sometimes... I just get overwhelmed by all this, and need a bit of space. I am sorry if it comes across as rude, that is not my intention." She offered him a smile as she rested her head against the seat back.

Ezekiel sighed. "I'm sorry that the schedule is so intense. I knew it would be a lot for you to dive right back into after everything you've been through. Maybe... if we could organize some fun activities, things might seem a bit more... relaxed?"

"Fun sounds good."

Ezekiel put his head in his hand as he spoke, "I sometimes forget that you have had a serious concussion and could struggle with fatigue. Please," he implored, looking up at her again, "can you let me know if you need to take a break?"

"I can look after myself, Ezekiel," Sara shook her head and reassured him. "You are not my keeper. You're overthinking things. If I need help, I'll let you know."

"As long as you're sure?"

"We're stuck together for the next few weeks while we travel and do interviews; let's just see how it goes. If anything needs to change for me, I'll let you know. I promise." She smiled, her eyes twinkling.

That was what worried Ezekiel; his good name was the most important thing to him and he wanted that to be restored, but not at the expense of Sara's health. He wanted them both to come out of this as colleagues and friends, happy and healthy this time. Still, she was right: there was no point worrying. It meant he wasn't trusting God to work in this situation. He forced a smile.

"What looks good?" He nodded towards the drinks menu.

Her smile widened.

"Most of it is alcohol, but we can order ice cream too." She raised her brows.

"In the morning?"

She frowned. "What? Don't you eat ice cream in the morning? Didn't you just say we need to have more fun? You need to learn to loosen up. Yikes, no wonder I used to make fun of you in school."

"I need to loosen up? Are you sure there's not something *I* should be teaching *you*?" he quipped, and she glared at him with a twinkle in her eye.

"I'll order it, and then we can talk PR strategy."

"Mm. Great, the fun stuff, I can hardly wait," he mocked, but he was smiling. Sara laughed and ordered three mini-cups of ice cream, one in each of the available flavors, chocolate, vanilla, and raspberry sherbert, all the while ignoring his protests at her decadence.

CHAPTER 6

"Y ou've both known each other since you were young, but Ms.Ward didn't particularly like you, is that what you're saying?" the interviewer asked Ezekiel. Sara watched him nod and then answer in the affirmative. Since she had lost her memory, they had decided that Ezekiel would do the talking, and she would provide mostly silent moral support. The interviewer looked at Sara, who only smiled. The interviewer narrowed her eyes at Sara almost imperceptibly, then turned back to Ezekiel. "If that's true, why would she be a part of your undercover work on the Wentworth Corporation? What could have persuaded her to be involved? Doesn't your past relationship make blackmail more likely as the motivation?"

Ezekiel glared at her and clenched his jaw. Sara knew he hated how these interviews revolved around the blackmail story and not the actual work he had done.

"It doesn't," he managed, and glanced in Sara's direction. She fixed his gaze with a warning glance, then quickly turned to face the woman again with a calm expression. *Man, she is cool under pressure,* he marveled, and tried to draw from her composure. He clasped his hands together in his lap and breathed out. "What I meant to say was, we are both adults now, and we chose to put our childhood issues behind us."

He smiled. Sara had to keep herself from facepalming. It was the most obviously forced smile she had ever seen. The interviewer looked apprehensive. "You know what? I think we've heard enough–" she began.

"It tells you a lot about the power of a faithful friend," Sara interjected suddenly. She needed the interview to end on a positive note, and Ezekiel wasn't being very helpful. Both of them turned to her in surprise. "It shows that when a person perseveres in kindness, change in relationships is possible, in spite of the odds."

She turned to Ezekiel.

"Ezekiel didn't need to change, though." She shook her head and smiled fondly. "He's always been kind and considerate, even as a kid, and he's always tried to do his best. He was so sweet the other kids used to call him 'Sugarcane.' People, including me, just didn't see the value in his friendship. I'm glad that I do now, though. And I have always known him as honest and trustworthy. That's why I chose to work with him in New York and why I still trust him now."

"That kind of loyalty is both rare and valuable," the interviewer commented thoughtfully, and Sara realized they were still on camera. She nodded, and the woman continued. "You have apparently decided to leave your career in New York and continue working with Mr. Cane, despite the fact that you almost lost your life working with him before. Tell me honestly, Ms. Ward, what do you think of Mr. Cane's Wentworth article?"

"I think it's masterful, and it reminds us of the importance of honest journalism, the kind that speaks the truth regardless of the potential consequences," Sara said.

The interviewer nodded along as Sara spoke. She wasn't even sure how she managed to sound so eloquent in the moment, but it just seemed to flow. A few minutes later, the interview was over, and they were ushered back to the green room by a producer's assistant.

"You were incredible." Ezekiel came up beside Sara at the snack table.

"I wouldn't say incredible," she replied, reaching for a cupcake and trying to stifle her smile.

"Really? She was eating out of your hand. The bit about the 'power of a faithful friend,'" Ezekiel whistled and poured himself a cup of coffee.

"You know, if you stopped being annoyed at them for asking questions about the blackmail issue, you could just answer it and move on to talking about the article," she pointed out.

"But the article is what is important."

"Yes, but the media tells the story that sells. And our beautiful friendship and possible blackmail is that story."

Ezekiel looked at her thoughtfully for a moment, then sipped his coffee.

"Thank you for saying what you said."

"All of it was entirely true. You are kind, and I feel regret every day we are together for treating you so badly growing up."

"Well..." he gave her a sly grin, "You could make it up to me if you feel *that* terrible..."

She narrowed her eyes at the mischievous glint in his.

"What exactly did you have in mind, Cane?"

"You see, I've never been to Michigan before, and since this is your alma mater home state... Come on, I want to take you somewhere."

He pulled her along, and she managed to snatch one more cupcake before letting him drag her off.

Sara didn't know what she was expecting, but a dollar souvenir store wasn't it. She folded her arms across her chest as she stepped in the door, wrinkling her nose and raising one eyebrow at Ezekiel.

"What? Just say it." Ezekiel turned to her.

"Why a souvenir store?" She looked around, "and a dollar one at that?"

"Because, my dad used to look for dollar souvenir stores whenever we traveled. It was fun. It's been a while since I've consistently been traveling, and since we'll be doing that for interviews, I thought we could continue my dad's tradition."

Sara smiled. She found it incredibly sweet that he'd had such a tradition with his father, quirky as it was. She had never had any with her father. But she guessed Ezekiel could have, as her father had loved him like a son. It was odd to think that he had probably known her own father much better than she had. She shook her head. *Not now, Sara,* she chided herself. *You can't change the past, just be a friend now.* "Okay, what types of souvenirs are we thinking?" she said aloud.

"Since I dragged you here against your will, I'll let you pick," he answered.

"That's gracious of you, kind sir. Fine. I'll pick." Sara meandered through the store, Ezekiel trailing after her. "Everything in here looks hideous."

"Everything in here also costs a dollar or less," he reminded her, and she laughed. Though in glancing around, he had to admit that either things had gotten much flimsier and cheaper over the years, or his memory of his childhood experiences was just a bit rosy-colored by the fondness of it.

"You know," Sara suddenly reflected, "if anyone had told me I would be friends with you one day, I would have laughed them out of the room."

Ezekiel couldn't help chuckling himself. "Yeah... I do remember you making it pretty clear on more than one occasion that I wasn't exactly your BFF material."

She threw her head back and laughed out loud at his understatement. "I know! But, you were so... *perfect*... and I found myself following a different path back then. Anything to get back at my dad..." she shook her head at the memories, less painful now, but not without sadness. "But now, looking back, I wish I'd paid more attention to you. Sorry," she shrugged, thankful again for how she was starting to see things differently now.

All the things she had told herself she hated about him: his integrity, loyalty, and good nature, were the things that now made her want to be friends with him even more. She guessed that, deep down, she had always known that it wasn't anything about Ezekiel himself that she hated. It was because her father had loved an outsider over his own daughter.

"I think that we don't always know ourselves very well. We try to decide who we are, based on circumstances and situations, but our lives, destinies, and who we become is also shaped by God. And lovingly so. I had no idea we would end up working together, but I believe our time together has been... well, a result of trusting God, right?"

Sara turned to him, impressed. She leaned on a shelf and eyed him thoughtfully. "That's true. So, in essence, our friendship, if God willed it, was an inevitability?" She wasn't sure how that conclusion sat with her, but she wondered what he would say.

Ezekiel tilted his head and smiled, "I wouldn't say inevitable... I mean, we had to agree with God, to actually follow those promptings, right?"

"Isn't that like some sort of test?" She picked up a random stuffed animal and began to squeeze and release it. He leaned on the shelf in front of him and focused his gaze on her. For a moment, he didn't say anything, only looked at her as he pondered. When Sara figured he would change the subject, he said, "No, I don't think it's a test. We do have free will. It's a little like GPS. If we go in a wrong direction that won't help us, either ignorantly or willfully, we can be re-routed if we're willing to listen and obey. To me, it's not so much about the actual events that happen but our character development through it all."

Sara raised her eyebrows, waiting for him to continue.

"I know that God can bring good out of all things no matter what happens. God is why we can fathom happiness, goodness, fun, and love. He ultimately shapes our lives and destinies in ways that work out for our good, regardless of anything momentary. For instance, the One who created us to experience enjoyment would surely give us many choices for where we'd find that enjoyment. A little like a playground. With His blessing, we can play on the swings or the merry-go-round; it's up to us. Even if we stepped outside His best will, say onto the road, and then got hit by a truck, that obviously would not be the will of a good God. But He can bring healing to us and use that experience for our good or the good of others.

God may have led us back together when we first met at that event, but we then made the free choice to work together for our mutual benefit. A bit like we are now. It's still our choice. And because we both desire, I assume, to do His will and bring Him glory, He is orchestrating circumstances to accomplish that through us."

Sara was awed for a moment. She hadn't thought of it that way and stared at him. There was so much wisdom behind his eyes; it was as if she was only seeing this depth to him for the first time. Suddenly, she was aware of how handsome he was. Handsome and wise, and she was lost in her thoughts.

"Do you like that one?" he asked.

"Hm?" she muttered.

"The stuffed bird. Do you like it?" he asked.

She looked down at the stuffed animal in her hands. It had to be the ugliest bird she had ever laid eyes on.

"What even is it?" she scoffed.

"I believe it's the state bird. Or an attempt at being the state bird."

Sara laughed, then tilted her head and looked at the trinket critically. "I think I'll take it. As a philosophical reminder."

"Of what?" he asked as they walked to the counter.

"I'm not sure," she replied definitively, and he laughed too.

The sales clerk looked at the bird and then at Sara.

"You're sure this is what you want?" Apparently, even *she* thought it was ugly.

"Yes," Sara said defensively, then turned to Ezekiel. "Maybe we can make a new tradition of it. We can buy the ugliest rendition of the state bird we can find for every state we visit. What do you think?"

Ezekiel didn't answer. His gaze was fixed on something else, his expression no longer full of laughter but clouded with... what? Sara turned and followed his gaze to a small TV mounted above the counter. It was the Wide-Open Show.

"Turn it up, please," Ezekiel directed, and the clerk obliged.

"*.... publicity stunt. His publicist just happens to be the girl he black-mailed, and we're to believe in some sob story about her memory loss and their friendship? Oh, please.*" Miranda Twain laughed from the screen. "*What should happen is that he should be locked up for his questionable....*"

Sara hadn't even realized she had grabbed the remote, let alone turned off the TV. Ezekiel turned to her. His expression was hard to read.

"Ignore that woman, she's...."

"Not a journalist. Journalists seek the truth," Ezekiel finished for her. Sara could see the muscles in his jaw clench. She took their purchase from the clerk.

"Let's go." She extended her hand to Ezekiel, which he took, and she led him out of the store.

* * *

A FEW HOURS LATER, Sara had her phone propped up on her hotel room desk with Debra on video chat, while she avoided sorting through her emails.

"You should have seen his face. I don't know why he cares so much about Miranda Twain."

Debra was cooking at the other end. "Have you asked him? Maybe they've had some run-in, you know, in the past. And Miranda Twain is like the journalist of journalists. At least, that's what she'll tell you she is."

Sara pursed her lips in thought. "Still. She's being extraordinarily cruel to him; it's almost like she's personally offended by him. She hasn't invited him for another interview either, to actually get the truth, so how can she claim to know anything?"

"You could reach out to her," Debra suggested.

Sara laughed. "Sure, and risk Ezekiel firing me and maybe killing me, too?"

"Then let it go."

Sara sighed. "I guess you're right. I just don't like to see him so upset. It's not like him, but somehow she just really gets to him."

"And you don't like when he's upset because...."

"He's my client, and my friend," Sara replied, "obviously. And in case you're wondering, that's all we are.".

"Are you sure you're not being unnecessarily opposed to the idea of the two of you getting back together?"

"I'm sure I know my own feelings," Sara snapped a little more harshly than needed for one who couldn't even remember the past three months, let alone her 'feelings' about it. "Look, it's not like that," she continued, more subdued now. "He's a great guy, I am glad we are friends now–not enemies, but that's it. And... I guess I admire his understanding and love for God, which is yet another thing I missed out on while growing up."

"The first being a friendship with Ezekiel?"

"Yeah, well, that and a relationship with God, with my parents..." Sara trailed off, then sighed. "Anyway, I should go and get dinner, and then get back to my emails. Your cooking in the background is making me even more hungry."

"Well then, I hope to see you whenever you guys roll through New York. Give Ezekiel my best."

"Of course! Maybe we could do a double date?" Sara suggested "It's about time; we need to get to know Mike. Make sure he is a man worthy of you," Sara grinned at her.

"Um, about that..." Debra frowned. "Things with Mike hadn't been going so well, so we agreed to call it quits."

"And you didn't tell me?" Sara whined. "I should have been there for you, Debra!"

"No, it's fine," Debra assured her. "You've had a lot going on. Really, it is. Looking forward to seeing you both soon, though. I'll fill you in on all the details later, don't stress." Debra blew her kiss, which Sara returned and tapped off the call.

Sara threw some sweatpants and a jacket over her nightie and left her room, searching for food. She found it quicker to go down and order from the kitchen than to call room service, and this hotel didn't seem to mind.

CHAPTER 7

*E*zekiel was sitting in the armchair in his hotel room. He felt more at peace as he read his Bible. He knew he shouldn't have let Miranda Twain get under his skin, but with their history, he was not surprised. But he didn't want to think about that now–or her. It was certainly not easy to ignore her, though, as she continued to make herself, and her opinion of him, prominent on the airwaves.

He flipped the page. He had found himself intrigued and drawn to the life of Moses, his closeness to God in a time when God just wasn't that close with anyone. He could only imagine what that must have been like, to experience the face-to-face encounters that Moses had had with the Creator of the Universe.

"Lord, I want more of you, and please guide me," he prayed. He was beginning to feel like he wasn't where God wanted him, not really, not anymore. But the way his career was shifting–all the publicity, the personal attention, rather than a focus on the issues–it was wearing him thin. It had never been his goal to be famous; just finding the truth and getting it out to people, that's what mattered. He hadn't put much thought or prayer into it yet, but now was a good time. "I know that as I trust You, You will direct my steps. Teach me to be a man after Your heart, Lord."

His thoughts were interrupted by a knock on his door. He placed his Bible on the desk and went to open it.

"Sara," he said, surprised. She beamed at him. She had a tray of covered plates in her hands.

"I was downstairs getting dinner, and I thought maybe you hadn't had dinner either."

Ezekiel frowned. "You brought me dinner?"

Her smile dropped, and she faltered, "Oh, uh, I'm sorry. You've probably already eaten. I should take this...."

"No! No," he hurried, "I was just caught off guard. What a treat, thanks. Come in."

He took the tray from her and stepped back to let her in before shutting the door with his foot. She stood awkwardly in the middle of the room as he watched her. She crossed her arms and glanced around, then uncrossed them and put her hands on her hips.

"Where do you want to set that up?" she asked, nodding towards the tray.

Ezekiel looked around. It wasn't a large room.

"Let's eat on the floor," he decided. "It'll be comfortable on the carpet."

She nodded and helped him lay out the food on a blanket he pulled from the nearby closet. Sara had brought some appetizers as well as a chicken curry and fried rice dish.

"Good choice," he commented as they began to eat. He watched her for a moment as they ate silently. She seemed to be thinking about something. "Penny for your thoughts?"

She looked at him, held his gaze briefly, and then focused on her food again.

"There're a few of them. Probably worth more than a penny," she teased.

"I'd pay," he said with all seriousness, before he could stop himself.

She looked up at him then, and Ezekiel couldn't decipher the look in her eyes before she looked back down at her food.

"Well," she said quietly. "I'm thinking about two things: God..."

Ezekiel nodded.

"...and you." She looked up again, this time as if looking for his reaction. Ezekiel waited.

"And...?" Ezekiel said.

"For one thing, I don't understand why Miranda Twain aggravates you so much. And, I don't know why God asked me to help you.

Frankly, I don't know why you're in my life. I mean, don't get me wrong; it's been great seeing you in a new light and all, knowing you're actually a good guy and not a horrible person deserving my wrath... but, I don't know... sometimes I wonder why I am not just moving on now?"

Ezekiel was glad she was thinking of him, but he wasn't sure he liked her questions.

"Why does God do what He does? That's a question I don't think anyone can answer. For a while, when we first met again, I thought that God wanted me to lead you to Him."

Sara nodded, still unable to remember that meeting. "And did you?"

"No. I deviated from that job and fell in love with you," he smirked.

She didn't seem to find it as funny as he did; she looked more thoughtful than amused.

"But I prayed for you. Encouraged you, and God seemed to handle the rest. Perhaps bringing me back into your life has helped you to confront your past a bit more and bring some healing?"

She stopped eating and looked up at the ceiling for a long moment, as though searching for something there. "It's odd not remembering my own salvation story and finding that God has healed much of my heart, helping me to forgive my Dad. Maybe God helped you to bring things to the surface?" she wondered aloud as she looked back at him. "It's also odd not remembering falling in love with someone," she chuckled then, a small quiet one, but still a chuckle. She took a sip of water.

Ezekiel nodded slowly. It was calm and quiet, as the dim orange lights cast a cozy glow around the tiny room. "I know it's got to be hard for you," he said softly.

"No, I think it's harder for you," she replied, gazing intently at the pattern on the wallpaper. They had been sitting side by side, but she turned to face him. "I'm sorry, Ezekiel. I truly am."

"You have nothing to be sorry for."

Sara nodded. "You're a good person. Thank you for looking after my father when his only child cut him off."

He hadn't expected that. "Don't say it like he didn't give you a reason to. I never knew back then what you'd gone through."

She looked down. "Now that he's gone, I can't help but think that it shouldn't have mattered. I was too harsh."

He caught her chin and tilted her face up so she was looking at him.

"Sara, in the end, he knew that you loved him and wanted to make things right."

"Because of you. Because you told him."

Ezekiel nodded. "Yes. But Sara, you can't carry guilt over it forever. You let yourself suffer for so long in an attempt to avoid him and the pain he caused you, and now that he's gone, you want to live in guilt and regret still?" Ezekiel smiled a rueful smile.

"Wouldn't I deserve it?"

"Of course."

She frowned at him as he continued.

"We're all guilty, we all have regrets, we all deserve punishment, and even death. But thankfully for those of us who have chosen to follow Christ, He's in the process of renewing our hearts and minds. And even though we sometimes suffer the consequences of our sin and wrong choices in the past, He is incredibly able to take what the enemy of our souls meant for evil, and turn it into something good. The trial is over, Jesus took your place in payment for that sin. So don't let that enemy continue to try to rob you of what Jesus has done for you by wallowing in guilt and regret. Even your earthly father wouldn't want that."

He held her gaze, then she smiled back at his serious look.

"I believe you," she scarcely whispered, but Ezekiel heard it.

He couldn't tear his gaze from hers. There was such an intensity in her green eyes as she processed his words. They'd both stopped eating.

"Do you feel like you have a lot to figure out?" he finally asked.

She nodded. "Quite a bit, actually. I want to start living again. Not under the shadow of what my father did or who I was. I was living as a victim."

"I hope being my publicist has helped," he tried for a joke.

"No, but being your friend has," she leveled at him with a glowing smile.

"Touche," he smiled back. Ezekiel hadn't expected that, but it warmed his heart. He was grateful to help her in any capacity, whether as a friend, or more, though he hadn't allowed himself to think too much of that possibility.

"I just want you to be happy and whole, Sara," he said.

"I'm fine. And we're fine. We're doing well as friends, don't you think?" she asked, as she placed a hand on his shoulder and squeezed.

Ezekiel tried to ignore the warmth of her touch and the scent of clean flowers that seemed to emanate from her. "Right." He swallowed. "I mean, yeah..." He watched her eyes, surprised she hadn't withdrawn her hand yet. Her lips were still parted as though she were about to speak, and he noticed her breath seemed to catch. He waited, unable to stir from the moment.

Slowly her hand brushed along his shoulder to the nape of his neck; her eyes focused on it. Ezekiel held his breath. He couldn't tell who was leaning closer as her hand came to rest on his face.

"Ezekiel," she whispered tentatively. Ezekiel almost didn't hear it. Maybe it was the warm orange glow on her skin or the sparkle in her eyes, or maybe the heat of her hand on his skin, but he didn't have time to ponder it as he kissed her.

She seemed to fall into it. His hand went around her waist, and she leaned into him. Ezekiel's senses flooded with the nearness of her again, his mind dizzy in her scent, her taste.

Abruptly, she pulled away. She gasped as she jumped up and stepped away, her eyes wide and her arms wrapped around herself. "I...."

It took Ezekiel a moment, but he also stood up, ran a hand through his hair and blew the air out of his lungs. "I'm sorry. I shouldn't have done that."

"No. I'm sorry. I... I shouldn't have...." Sara stopped and stared at him in confusion. "Maybe this friendship thing was a mistake."

"No. It's not. I...."

"Ezekiel, that can't happen again," Sara said quietly, now with her head in her hands.

He stayed silent for a moment. "Why are you fighting this?"

"Fighting...?" She swallowed and scoffed. "I'm not fighting anything." She looked around the room as though for support. "What just happened was–was just in the moment. The lights are low, we were sitting close together, and your cologne is–" She seemed to catch herself.

Ezekiel shook his head. "I don't get it. Why did you come to my room? Why bring me dinner?"

"Because we're friends. That's what friends do," Sara insisted.

"Yes. But I don't think friends go around kissing each other."

She glared at him, but didn't reply.

"I'm sorry. It's just... you don't remember *us*, but I do. Maybe it's easy for you, to just enjoy spending all this time together... but you need to understand, Sara, it's not the same for me. I really want the best for you, whatever that is, but this...." he sat back down with a grunt on the armchair where he'd been before. Her features softened, and she shut her eyes and then opened them as if re-calibrating.

"Look, I've been selfish," Sara apologized. "I don't want to mess with you. I just want to move on, not get stuck in the past. Maybe it's just better if we see each other as colleagues, okay?"

"Sara--" he stood up.

"Goodnight," she said with finality and left his room.

Ezekiel wanted to toss something across the room, but he knew better. Colleagues? Was that really all she wanted? Fine. If she didn't want their friendship anymore, he would leave her be. *No problem,* he told himself, but he wasn't sure who he was fooling.

CHAPTER 8

Sara hadn't slept well. Flashes from the past had disturbed her dreams. A window from the past had opened, a memory of a passionate kiss tugging at her. It irked her that the kiss had unsettled her so much when she wanted to be calm, confident, and professional. She was trying to be easygoing about the whole thing, but now she felt battered by it, as if tossed about on a wild ocean in a tiny rowboat.

Sara checked the time on her phone. She was waiting in the hotel lobby for Ezekiel so that they could leave for the airport. She saw him come out of the elevator and sighed.

"Well, it's about time," she said as she picked up her bag.

"I'm sorry," he said simply, his curt tone catching her off guard.

"Okay," was all she could say as she walked with him out of the hotel to where their taxi was waiting. He watched as the taxi driver loaded their luggage into the trunk, and then Ezekiel held the door for her. As she entered, her shoulder brushed against his chest, and she faltered at the nearness of him, almost losing her balance. *Get it together, Sara*, she admonished herself.

He frowned at her as she caught herself. She attempted a casual smile and cleared her throat.

"I'm sorry. I was just um... I think I tripped."

He nodded, shut the door behind her, and then climbed into the car from the opposite side, sitting next to her. She hated that she was so aware of him suddenly. Why couldn't things just be easy, like before...? The car felt a bit too small for them. When had they started using compact cars for taxis anyway?

"To the domestic terminal, please," Ezekiel called up to the driver. The driver nodded and pulled the car into the flow of traffic.

"I hope that last night...." she whispered, hoping the cab driver wouldn't hear.

"Last night was fine. I understood you perfectly. I'm fine. I can be your client, and you can be my publicist." Ezekiel kept his eyes on the road ahead of them.

Though whispering as well, his demeanor was calm and casual, but Sara didn't feel the same. Something was different. "You're a bit cold."

"What makes you say that? We've barely been together five minutes today. I'm just respecting your wishes."

She frowned at him. "Great, then. Thank you."

She crossed her arms and looked out the window. The rest of the ride was quiet. When they arrived at the airport, they moved through security without a word between them, and were soon standing in line to board their flight.

She pulled out her phone, but it fell to the floor. She didn't notice Ezekiel reach for it, so when she bent, he did too, his hand covering hers as she touched the phone. She snapped upright so quickly that she hit him in the nose on her way up.

"I'm so sorry!" She grabbed his shoulder as he stood up with his hand clutching his nose. "Ezekiel, are you okay?"

She didn't know why she had reacted so sharply to his hand on hers. Electricity had flowed through her body as he touched her. She rummaged through her purse and pulled out some tissues to hand to him.

"I know we're only work colleagues now, but I didn't think you would beat me up." He smirked.

She glared at him.

"Don't joke about it. I'm genuinely worried I hurt you."

"Worried about me?"

"Yes," Sara said.

"I'm sorry. I'm fine. Look." He moved his hand. "I'm not even bleeding."

She looked a bit closer. He was a little red at the site of impact, but he wasn't bleeding, so she stepped back.

"I'm sorry I hit you."

He touched her arm lightly, and her breath caught. *Ugh,* she thought, disgusted at herself and the color she could feel rising in her face.

"It's alright. It was a mistake," he said casually with a wave of his hand.

She blinked at him, then reminded herself to close her mouth before she started drooling. Why *did* he have to be so attractive?

She managed an awkward nod and a smile, then thanked God when their flight was called to board. *It was that stupid kiss,* she told herself. The way he'd held her, his lips against hers. It had unnerved her, and now... other memories were resurfacing. The doctors had told her she may have some emotional swings as she continued to recover, and especially as her missing memories began to return. That was probably a big part of it; she was vulnerable and moody because of the brain injury.

When these weeks of interviews were over, she needed to make a clean break from her past, she resolved. No more thoughts of her father's rejection, or how she used to hate Ezekiel. He had forgiven her, God had forgiven her. She was free to move on with her life, her only focus on pleasing God. She nodded as she looked out the small oval window at the ground dropping away beneath the airplane, satisfied with her decision. After all, that was why she knew nothing could happen with Ezekiel. He was too wrapped up in her past.

* * *

THE FOLLOWING two weeks were what Sara could only describe as a whirlwind. They had traveled so much that Sara was sure she had enough airline loyalty points to fund a honeymoon, though what made her think of a honeymoon was a mystery. They were up and down the country, from coast to coast, interviewing with different shows. The media seemed to be eating it all up. Well, except for Miranda Twain. Ezekiel had finally mentioned to Sara that they had been colleagues once in the past, but when Sara had tried to press him for more details, he had clammed up.

When they mentioned Sara's memory loss at the live taping of one show, the audience was awed. Sara did most of the talking, primarily singing high praises of Ezekiel, and then Ezekiel would talk about the article.

"What a wonderful turn of events, like something out of a novel," Chuck Henderson said, a popular nighttime show host.

"Oh, exactly. I find it hard to believe myself at times, having forgotten ever living through it. But it's been wonderful to experience my reconnection with Ezekiel all over again." Sara beamed, still hesitant to share that her memory was returning. That could wait for later, she reasoned.

She smiled at Ezekiel. He forced a smile back, but she ignored it. He was still relentless in maintaining a professional distance.

"Oh, please!" Chuck gushed, leaning back in his seat and looking at his audience, "I think I'm going to have a fit at how moving that is. What a kind thing to say. Tell us about the undercover work, Mr. Cane." Chuck said, turning back to Ezekiel.

Ezekiel seemed to light up as he shared about the investigation and the article. The two weeks had followed in that vein. Sara would talk about the material that would capture the audience's hearts, and then he would get to talk about the article.

Despite their professional agreement, Ezekiel had wanted to continue with the plan of souvenir hunting in each new city.

"This isn't exactly part of my role as your PR manager," Sara had pointed out when he invited her along at first. "I can just find something else to do while you shop; I know it's important for you to keep your tradition, though."

Ezekiel had considered her words briefly, then seemed unmoved and replied, "No, it's fine. We should be seen in public on this tour, right? And this is a pretty safe outing as colleagues. Unless you'd prefer to do your own thing?"

"No, I'm fine. Let's go," she'd managed nonchalantly. So they had.

At first they had sought out the most basic tourist shop there was and planned to buy the cheapest, most ghastly souvenir they could find.

"What about this one?"

Ezekiel reached past Sara to grab a glass figurine from the shelf beside her. Sara didn't realize she had turned her head slightly, following his woodsy scent. He pulled his arm back, and she almost followed.

"Are you okay? You look a bit dizzy."

She looked up at him and nodded, feeling her skin flush under his gaze. It had to be those blue eyes. She cleared her throat.

"I think that works. Let's pay."

She walked away from him.

"Hey, Sara?"

"Hmmm?"

"I have an idea."

"Oh?" Sara said.

"Follow me," Ezekiel said. Taking the figurine from her hand and setting it on a nearby shelf, he walked out into the sunshine and down the street, then turned around and ran backwards. "Come on, Sara, this will be fun."

Sara ran to catch up with him, and they walked into a nearby mall, then straight into the massive Truman's Toys.

"This is cute," Sara said, as she picked up a small teddy bear with a flowery dress and a fur coat. "Better than an ugly state bird." She pressed it against her face before picking up another bear, this time dressed in shorts and a striped shirt, and handed it to Ezekiel.

"Maybe we start a new tradition. You know this is my cousin's business?" Sara asked. "It would be great to support him. Even if it is in a small way."

"Yes, I did know," Ezekiel said, "Remember how...." He stopped abruptly. "I think I'd rather have a remote controlled drone," Ezekiel said, and put the teddy bear back on the shelf.

Sara frowned. She knew he was keeping something from her, from the gentle way he looked at her.

"Well, you can get the drone. It's your choice," she said, and took her bear to the counter to pay for it. She stood back and watched him as he made his purchase, her stomach twisting.

The more time she spent with Ezekiel, the more unsettled Sara felt. And it was a problem, because they were always together. With several more weeks to go.

CHAPTER 9

*E*zekiel took another sip of his soda, sitting across from Brant at the hotel restaurant. "So we are back to just colleagues again."

"And how is that working out for you, Ezekiel?"

"I still feel quite raw about it all to be honest," he said, eating a fry from his plate.

"Soon this interview series will be over, and life will be back to normal, you'll see," Brant waved his drink at Ezekiel.

Ezekiel looked at him and sighed. "Whatever 'normal' is."

"New opportunities will show up for you, Ezekiel. And for Sara as well. In the meantime, you have to accept that she does not want a relationship with you and let her go."

Ezekiel nodded. "Yes, I know. It's not what I want though," He sighed again. "You said you had something to tell me?"

"I do. It's something great, actually." Brant sat up straighter.

"Well, don't keep me in suspense."

"You've been nominated for a Pulitzer for your work on the Wentworth case."

Ezekiel froze. For a moment, he thought he hadn't heard right.

"How can that be possible?"

Brant tilted his head.

"What do you mean? You've worked for this. You deserve it."

"I–I–" Ezekiel closed his eyes for a moment. "Thank you, Lord," he said softly. And he was thankful, but a part of him felt oddly cold, not bursting with joy or fulfillment. A part of him almost didn't care.

"I know I should be ecstatic, but something feels weird," Ezekiel shrugged.

"There's a lot going on right now, that's why," Brant said.

"Ezekiel."

Ezekiel shot out of his chair as Sara appeared behind him. He looked at Brant, and Brant shifted in his seat. How long had she been there? Had she heard Ezekiel say that he didn't want to let her go?

"I was, um... I thought we could practice. We have an interview soon. It's okay if you would rather eat. Also, the Wide-Open Show has invited us to an interview," Sara said simply, and then turned and walked away.

"Sara, wait."

She stopped as they reached the hotel lobby.

"I've been nominated for a Pulitzer, by the way."

"That's great news," she said in a flat tone.

Ezekiel frowned. This was more than he could take. It almost felt like they'd gone back in time to their early days in New York. Her coolness chilled him.

"I'm sorry," Sara said. "I don't know why I said it like that. I'm happy for you. I really am."

"Thank you. The truth is, I don't know if I'm as happy as I should be," he confessed.

"What does that mean?"

"I don't know exactly. It's just, I've felt lately like I'm not doing what God wants me to be doing, like maybe journalism has been a season of my life, but now... maybe He's leading me to a new path."

He knew this was the last thing he should be saying to her, but he couldn't help himself. He shouldn't be troubling her with his problems, treating her as before when they were friends, opening up his heart to once again be trampled upon. She didn't scoff or turn away, though. She stepped closer to him.

"What *is* in your heart, Ezekiel? You know that Bible verse, "delight in the Lord, and He'll give you the desire of your heart," or something like that? Maybe this was the right thing for a time, but maybe He's nudging you to do something else now, something that inspires you more."

"Do you think you know what He wants you to do?" He didn't know why he was asking her that.

She tilted her head in contemplation for a moment.

"No. Not entirely. But I'm doing some of what I know. Helping you. And believing God will direct my next steps, not that it seems clear at the moment."

"This would be the second time He's had you help me. Thank you. I just don't feel what I am doing is particularly worthwhile."

"Ezekiel, you are so hard on yourself. Enjoy this win for a moment," she smiled, and he did too. "A Pulitzer is a 'well-done' from people who know your field very well. And even though you feel a bit iffy about your future, you should enjoy what you've achieved. You went above and beyond for that article. You can thank God for this success."

"No, I thank you, too," he said softly. "It was you, and God."

"That's not how I remember it."

"You don't remember it at all," he reminded her, with a crooked grin. She gave him a withering glare, but her face soon cracked into a smile.

"Well, actually..." she began.

"Yes?" Ezekiel stared at her. "Is your memory returning?"

She nodded. "Bits and pieces are returning. Also, I read some of your other work."

"That's fantastic! It means that you are healing. And, wow... you made an effort to read more of my work? Thank you. That means a lot to me." Warmth filled his chest.

"It's all part of the service providing excellent PR," she smiled at him wryly. "Honestly, though, it's a wonder you didn't get nominated for a Pulitzer sooner."

He stared at her, suddenly feeling a sense of pride in his career or, more so, that the woman he so admired, who seemed to know him better now than almost anyone else, saw the value in his work.

"I've had an amazing publicist. But, are you okay?" his eyes searched her face.

"You didn't need a publicist. Your work would have stood out for itself. And yes, I am fine." Sara turned her head away.

Ezekiel didn't laugh, and he didn't smile. He was worried about her and felt the failure of their friendship was his fault. He shouldn't have kissed her. He wondered exactly what she was beginning to remember.

"Sara, I'm sorry for everything. For kissing you, it was a mistake...."

"You apologize a lot," she said, cutting him off and stepping back as if he'd slapped her. He blinked at her. "Let's just go. We have an interview," she reminded him and turned to walk away.

He nodded and followed after her. Whatever pleasant moment they'd been having had passed.

* * *

THE INTERVIEW WAS GOING WELL as usual, and the interviewer was getting ready to wrap up.

"It has been great having you two on, really."

"Thank you," they both replied.

"Just before we go, though, what made you agree to start doing interviews with Ezekiel, Sara? I mean, you're a publicist, and usually, publicists work behind the scenes."

"I thought it was best. People knew who I was anyway, and there was no point letting a lie live on."

"Fair enough," the woman nodded. "To be honest, when the Daily Times reached out a few weeks back asking if we were interested in an exclusive on Mr. Cane's alleged blackmail victim, we declined, but we certainly regret it now, having met you."

Ezekiel froze and then slowly turned to Sara. She had frozen too, but her smile was still in place, so she looked unhinged.

"Come again?" she managed.

"I said we regret it. This has been a fantastic interview," the woman smiled at them, unaware of the tension brewing.

Sara nodded slightly and then turned with a thunderous look to Ezekiel.

"*You* put my name in the media?" Sara said through clenched teeth.

Ezekiel shook his head. "Why would I do that?"

"So, you mean to tell me that you had no idea that the paper you work for put my name in the media to save you?!" She stood up. Ezekiel stood up too.

136

"Maybe we should discuss this off-camera. I'm sure there's a reasonable explanation," he said, as calmly as he could manage. He was just as flustered by the news as she was, even more so by her assumption that he was to blame.

"I'm not discussing anything," she spat out, pulling off her microphone and walking off the set. Ezekiel huffed, and then turned to see the interviewer looking at him in disbelief.

"I had no idea she didn't know," she offered. She seemed genuinely sorry.

"Yeah. Thank you," was all Ezekiel could manage to say, before walking off camera in search of Brant. He found Brant in the parking lot and rushed towards him.

"I didn't know," Brant insisted.

"Like heck you didn't!"

"Okay, wait. Calm down." Brant raised his hands in defense. "I knew they were considering it. I just didn't know that corporate would go ahead with it."

"Is that even legal?" Ezekiel pressed him.

"Technically, they can do that, because her name could have easily been found elsewhere."

Ezekiel shut his eyes and ran a hand through his hair.

"What do I do now?"

"What do you mean?" Brant asked.

"You saw what just happened, didn't you? She thinks I was involved."

"You have to try to talk to her. You're an honest man, and she'll believe you," Brant suggested. "She has no reason not to."

"Yeah. Right." He began to walk away but paused and turned around. "Brant?"

"Yes?"

"Tell corporate I quit." Ezekiel hadn't been prepared to quit on the spot, but once it came to him, he knew it was right. His mind whirred with thoughts about what he could do next. Perhaps he could catch up with his uncle, who had invested in the Marionette, the event planning company that had started the whole process. He could take some time off, maybe volunteer at his father's charity. He so needed to move on, but first he needed to sort things out with Sara.

"Ezekiel, you're being rash; you–"

Ezekiel gave Brant a withering look, shutting him up.

"I'll let them know." Brant nodded, resigned.

"Good," he said before leaving. He had had a glimmer of hope when Sara had said she had some memory returning, but now his hopes were dashed. Now he knew they wouldn't part as friends, but he didn't think he could stand it if they parted as enemies.

CHAPTER 10

Sara was packing her bags when Debra's call came through. She almost didn't want to pick it up because she wasn't sure whose side Debra would be on, but she picked it up anyway.

"Hey, I'm busy, and I already know what you're going to say, so... you can just get straight to the point."

"Okay," Debra shrugged. She knew Sara didn't mean to be edgy; it was just her way when she was stressed. "Why did you burst out at him like that? On live TV, no less."

"I guess I'm a bad publicist. Sue me."

Debra wasn't fazed a bit. "You know I'm not talking about being a publicist," her voice had taken on a motherly tone.

"I was upset! How could he do that? And who knows, what if I misjudged him all this time? Maybe he's not as good as we all think."

"We both know you don't believe that. Ezekiel had nothing to do with it, and if he did, he had a good reason."

Sara scoffed as she threw some more clothes into her bag. "A good reason to put my name out like that without asking me?"

"Does it sound like something he would do, though?" Debra sounded reasonable. Sara sighed and slumped on her bed.

"I just... I can't...." Sara looked out the hotel window as her words faded into thoughts.

"You can't... what?" Debra pressed her gently.

"I can't fall in love with him!" Her hand shot up and covered her mouth in shock. Had she just said that out loud?

"Why not?" Debra didn't seem shocked.

"Because I need to move on! I'm not that kid anymore, trying to get back at my dad, nursing all the old wounds. He embodies so much of my past. I don't want to go backward!"

"But you're not moving on, Sara. Don't you get it? You're just giving it more power over you. You overcame it and fell in love with him before; you can do it again," Debra reasoned with her, and, deep down, Sara knew she was right.

"It doesn't matter, though," she shook away the thoughts. "He's over me now, and I don't want to pull him back into it. I told him that I didn't want to be anything more than friends, that I didn't even want to be friends, and I walked out on him."

"Sara, you can't know if you don't try."

"I'm not entirely sure I want to."

"Hey, I'm really sorry, I have to go. There's this new lunch hour thing we do at the Marionette. I can't miss it."

"It's noon?"

"It is."

"Okay, thanks; talk to you later," Sara rushed to turn on the television as Debra hung up the phone. The Wide-Open Show was already on. She was supposed to be there, and Ezekiel must have tried to reach her about it, but she had ignored his calls.

"Mr. Ezekiel Cane, it's good to meet again." Miranda Twain smiled widely at him, but her smile contrasted the general mood on the set. Even Sara could tell how tense Ezekiel was from the set of his jaw and the glint in his eye.

"You too, Miranda. Thank you for having me back." Somehow, Ezekiel felt disingenuous saying that, because at the moment, he felt anything but thankful.

"We felt it only fair to allow you to return and explain your previous visit with us, short-lived as it was," Miranda continued, looking very much like a panther evaluating her prey and how best to go in for the kill.

Sara could feel her heart in her throat. This interview was the most important one of all; it would finally give Ezekiel a chance to explain–

and hopefully redeem–himself. Sara sent up a silent prayer as she sat back and watched.

"Miss Ward isn't with you today," Miranda cocked a dark eyebrow at him.

"Astute as always, Miranda. Suffice it to say she had her reasons, and I had mine."

"It seems that you had a bit of a falling out?" she prompted.

Ezekiel just stared at her, waiting.

"Over you... lying to her?" Twain started on the offensive, but Ezekiel remained surprisingly calm.

"No. I never have, and I never will. I don't believe in lying. You would know that, of course, because you and I used to work together. No, the truth is, I prayed, and I believe God led me to seek Sara's help on the Wentworth story."

"And did *God* lead you to blackmail her?" Miranda persisted ruthlessly, unrelenting.

"No. There was some history between our families, but that's in the past anyway," he sighed. "When I first saw her again after all those years, there was an incident that sort of threw us together."

"By 'incident,' you mean I insulted a customer and got you punched in the face. Gracious of you not to tell America about my spunky side," Sara said to the TV, hands on her hips.

"An incident?" Miranda looked slightly confused, which was somewhat surprising. Ezekiel would have thought she'd done her homework more thoroughly before this crucial interview. However, she was apparently wondering why a seemingly unimportant 'incident' had any relevance to the story.

"Be patient, Miranda," Ezekiel chided before continuing. "Anyway, she lost her job over something that wasn't entirely her fault, and her boss gave her a sort of challenge."

"Yes. *Challenge*. I was so naïve. I would apologize to you a thousand times over now. Thank You, God, for changing me." Sara wasn't sure why she was talking to the empty room. But Ezekiel had never told the story out loud. She had only done her best to give the significant points in interviews, but it was nice to hear Ezekiel share the story.

"The challenge involved me. I simply wanted to be honest. Sara would do as her boss said, and I would let him know. And then, I added that I could use her help. My uncle was investing in the Marionette, the event planning company that was instrumental in the investigation. The event planning helped us to get close to the Wentworths. The company profits also helped to fund the investigation. There was an opportunity for a promotion for Sara, if she wanted it. Even so, she was reluctant. Sara Ward is very stubborn." He smiled, and oddly enough, Sara did too, even though she wasn't sure if it was a compliment.

"And did you hold her job over her?" Miranda drilled again. *Man, she's dogged,* Sara fumed.

"No, not at all. I told Sara I would get her job back for her regardless, but Sara was interested in the new role as the lead event organizer. And, I assured her I would be paying her for her help, since I was getting paid to follow the story," Ezekiel explained.

Miranda nodded, her lips pressed together. "Right. So, what happened?"

"Sara accepted the challenge; we went undercover, spent a lot of time together, and her then-defensive nature, stubbornness, and occasional crazy behavior gave way to an entertaining and caring young woman." Ezekiel couldn't stifle the grin that spread across his face at the memories of their time together, when he'd first fallen for her.

"I wasn't *that* stubborn...or crazy!" Sara muttered, rolling her eyes, but grinning all the same.

Miranda raised a brow, obviously waiting for the point.

"I fell in love with her. I'm not sure at what point, but I did. And for a moment, I thought I was losing her."

Sara nodded at the memory, surprised that she was now remembering so much.

"Oh yeah," Sara mused. "That woman... Belinda! Yes! The call transcripts!" she exclaimed as the images flooded her mind, finally. "I found out you talked to my dad behind my back, and then God...."

"But it turns out she was a more brilliant investigator than I was." He smiled, then his face went grim. "And then she got shot by Joe Galligan, who had managed to escape the initial police round up, and I can only assume he was after me and took revenge. Unfortunately, Sara was the one who was hurt."

Suddenly, Sara grabbed the back of her head, a sharp pain piercing her thoughts. She groaned as she fell over onto the floor. The trauma of the shooting came back like a wave. The panic in her heart, the pain, the blood, and Ezekiel's frightened face looking over her as she tried to breathe, tried to hold on to consciousness. Then everything went dark.

She moaned and sat up, forcing herself to breathe more slowly to steady herself. She could no longer hear the TV; her heart was beating too loudly in her ears. Suddenly everything stilled as she remembered the kiss, the shock, and his wonderful smile—the bliss before the pain.

Sara clutched her chest as loud sobs overtook her body. She had fallen in love with him! How could she have forgotten? How could she have forgotten what it felt like to let love relieve pain and hurt? To let love wash away the past?

If Christ could start afresh with her, surely... Sara could start afresh with Ezekiel, no matter their history? She stopped sobbing, sat up, and wiped her tears away. She knew what she had to do.

"And now?" Miranda Twain was asking, drawing Sara's attention back to the television. Miranda was at the edge of her seat, waiting eagerly for Ezekiel to speak. He sighed, looking straight into the camera.

"And now I guess there is no us." His solemn tone pierced Sara's heart.

Miranda was unusually quiet for a moment. She looked genuinely sorry.

"Well, I owe you an apology, if what you're saying is true," she finally stated. It was the sincerest Sara had ever seen Miranda Twain.

Ezekiel only nodded.

"Let's talk about the article."

Sara had heard enough; she stood up and left her room. She needed to talk to him and ask him one question, one thing: whether he loved her, or not? If he said that he didn't, she determined, then that would be it. But she had to know.

When God had led her to help Ezekiel, perhaps it was more than just with a story or some interviews. She could barely sit still in the cab ride to the Wide-Open studio. It seemed to take hours, but she knew it was only a short drive. Sara was sure that the interview would just be wrapping up by the time she got there. She admitted to herself now that she had fallen in love with him again, even before remembering the first time. If God were in this, surely memory loss wouldn't be enough to stop it?

She paid the cab driver in a hurry, leaving her change with him as she dashed from the cab and into the studio. She almost ran, anticipation fueling her. Maybe Debra was right, and this *was* how God wanted her to move forward?

"The Wide-Open Show, please," she asked, flashing a press pass at a woman walking by.

"Oh, just down this hallway," the woman gestured.

She nodded and said a quick thank you, turning around to start down the hallway when she saw Ezekiel come around the corner at the other end of the long hallway. Her heart caught in her throat at the sight of him, and she stopped short. She watched as Miranda rounded the corner, too. They obviously hadn't seen Sara yet.

Sara frowned as she watched them talk. There was something not professional about their conversation, something almost intimate. Sara blinked, willing her mind not to jump to any conclusions. Then, Miranda leaned up and placed a kiss on Ezekiel's cheek before hugging him. Sara's face flushed as she watched Ezekiel hold Miranda tightly; suddenly she felt as if she was intruding. It looked too intimate for her to be there, the whole thing. Now it all made sense, why Miranda Twain seemed to have such a powerful effect on him. *I've been so blind,* she scolded herself inwardly. *He's probably been in love with her all along. I just got in the way,* she shuddered at the thought. She had to get out of there. She stepped back behind the corner to be out of sight as they broke apart. She was willing herself to move, but her steps kept faltering until a confused-looking Ezekiel was suddenly standing in front of her alone.

"Sara? What are you doing here? I thought you'd decided to leave?"

The question she had wanted to ask suddenly seemed to stand between them in her mind. She should just ask it, just say it. Tell him she remembered everything, and ask if he was still in love with her. He leaned towards her as he stepped closer.

"What are you doing here?" he repeated, softer this time.

She shut her eyes. Now. Ask it now.

She opened her mouth. Ezekiel touched her arm.

"What is it?" his eyes searched hers.

"Ezekiel–"

LOVE CALLED TO SERVE

BOOK THREE

CHAPTER 1

Sara sighed and focused her attention on the conference room through the all-glass walls, watching the people inside. For three months now, she had been an associate at Mode, an elite New York PR firm, and she still wasn't allowed into client meetings.

Sara knew this was only because she was an associate on Eleanor Fetch's team. If she'd been assigned to a different manager, maybe she would have actual responsibilities, not just those of a glorified personal assistant. But Eleanor, one of the top execs in the company and a multi-award-winning PR manager, commanded all the limelight for herself. She was good, and she knew it. Eleanor stepped out of the conference room as if on cue, smiling as she waved the client's team goodbye.

Sara shot up.

"Eleanor, I have the print samples you asked for." She tried to keep pace with Eleanor as the slightly older woman strode through the communal office. "The ones you wanted to show CallTown Media?" Sara extended the rolled-up prints, not mentioning that she'd stayed up all night working on them.

"That's great." Eleanor kept on walking, then pulled out her phone and focused on it. "Did you schedule my 10 o'clock?"

Sara juggled the prints as she simultaneously avoided tripping while trying to check her own phone for Eleanor's schedule. "10 o'clock...10 o'clock. Yes. It's scheduled. You should see it on your calendar. The meeting with Peppy Cola," Sara confirmed.

Eleanor stopped abruptly, and Sara stumbled, narrowly avoiding a collision with her. Finally, Eleanor looked at her. "That's good. I'll need you to call ahead and take their coffee orders. Have everything laid out in the conference room before 10 and then clear out."

Sara nodded. "Got it."

Eleanor extended her hands. Sara frowned in confusion. "Prints, Sara. The prints."

"Oh, right. Here." She handed them over and then took a breath. "Eleanor?"

Eleanor stopped as she was about to open the door to her office. "Yes?"

"I was wondering if I could be in the room this time for the Peppy Cola meeting. I mean, I did a lot of work on the campaign you'll be pitching. I just thought maybe—"

"Stop," Eleanor chuckled, and the condescension in her tone made Sara's cheeks burn with embarrassment. "You'll come to the meetings when I say you can. Have someone send in my breakfast smoothie and get on those coffee orders for the 10 o'clock." She walked into her office, then paused. "Sara."

"Hm?" Sara managed, scavenging her memory for that one Bible verse she'd taped to her bathroom mirror. *Quick to listen, slow to speak, slow to anger...* how did it go again? If only that New Testament writer had known Eleanor, maybe he would have made an exception!

"We work well together."

Sara nodded tensely as Eleanor shut the door in her face.

What Eleanor neglected to say was that Sara did most of the work; yet Eleanor still excluded her from the important meetings, and Sara never got to enjoy any recognition for the exceptional work she'd done.

"Why, I ought to—" She considered barging into Eleanor's office to enlighten her of these facts but stopped herself and took a deep breath. *In everything... give thanks*, she muttered. Maybe if she repeated it often enough, she would genuinely be thankful, and maybe God would change her reality and help her find favor with Eleanor? And maybe she'd value the work Sara did? Presently, it was as if Eleanor was blind to the value Sara gave her. She checked the time: 9:15 a.m. Sara groaned. She had less than an hour to arrange all the coffee orders for the meeting. "Great," she muttered and rushed for the elevator.

* * *

Hours later, Sara was sitting at a Korean barbeque restaurant with Debra.

"Why don't you report her to HR?" Debra asked, sipping on her lemonade.

"Because," Sara paused to eat a slice of meat, "the whole firm will think I started trouble. Besides, Eleanor does know her stuff, and I can learn a lot from her. I've only been there three months. I have to be patient. I'll pray about it. I just... I get so busy with work, and I feel like I don't have as much time for God as I used to."

Debra nodded, then spoke around a mouthful of food. "It's so easy to do, to get too busy, and then time with God takes a back seat, but you need to make time."

"I so do. I remember the times I had with God when I was recovering from my injury, that peace I had, and His presence. It seems like a distant memory now." Sara sighed. She'd fallen so deeply into this mundane routine. She hadn't even taken time to really consider if she was happy or not. If she was being honest, life was a whirlwind, and the most important things were being ignored.

"What are your plans for Easter?" Debra asked, changing the subject and breaking Sara out of her thoughts.

"Mmm." Sara sipped her water. "I'm going home to Santa Monica. I'll spend a few days with my mom. Ezekiel's mom is hosting an Easter Sunday lunch, so I'll go to that."

"That's great that you'll get to see Ezekiel in person." Debra's tone didn't sound innocent though, and when Sara glanced at her, she could see an almost mischievous expression on her friend's face, confirming her suspicion.

"I know what you're thinking."

"Do you?"

"I don't want to talk about it."

"Fine." Debra raised her hands in mock surrender, and they ate in silence for a few minutes before Debra cleared her throat. "I got a promotion."

149

Sara's mouth fell open. "What?! Why didn't you say so?!"

Debra chuckled. "You looked so mopey when you came in. I didn't want to--"

"No, no. You should have said!" Sara felt guilty, being so self-absorbed that her friend hadn't felt she could tell her this great news. "Congratulations, Debra. I'm so happy for you, and the Marionette is so blessed to have you and your multiple talents!" She smiled at her friend. She really was happy for Debra.

"Thank you, Sara. I appreciate you."

An idea popped into Sara's head. "Oh!" She gasped and clapped her hands. "Let's get a cupcake and a candle and do a little celebration."

"You want to celebrate?"

"Yes, of course! This is great." Sara found Debra's humility cute.

"Okay, should we go for karaoke? Or I've always... " Debra trailed off when she noticed the look on Sara's face. "What is it?"

"I have that call with Ezekiel tonight, and I'm so sorry, but I have work tomorrow, too, and—"

"Okay. No, no. Don't be sorry. We'll do the cake thing and call it a night. I understand." Debra smiled.

"We can do something big during the weekend. We can invite other friends, too," Sara offered.

Debra chuckled. "That would be great, but it's fine." She sipped her lemonade.

Sara focused on her food for a moment, then realized she found Debra's silence suspicious. When she looked up, Debra was looking at her coyly while continuing to sip her drink.

"What?" Sara put down her chopsticks.

"I was just thinking, this friendship you have with Ezekiel can't be healthy. You realized you were in love with him months ago, but chickened out of asking him if he felt the same way, and now you guys are best friends talking on webcam every week," Debra blurted as if she had been waiting to say it all night.

"You know things were complicated, Debra," Sara dismissed her comment and rolled her eyes.

"Yeah, but you didn't fight for it," Debra persisted.

"There was too much going on, and seeing him with Miranda that day, I just couldn't ask him. I really don't know what happened, but something was off with me, and Ezekiel and I together just didn't feel right, once I saw him with her," Sara tried to explain. "Besides, I knew I needed to focus on my relationship with God, and I wanted nothing to get in the way of that, you know?"

Debra raised one eyebrow, "Hm, you mean like an all-consuming new job?" She shook her head, "Well, as long as you are okay, Sara? Your well-being matters to me, and you have been through so much...."

"It's completely fine. Okay? I'm fine. He's with Miranda now, and I'm over him. We're good friends because he was such an integral part of my salvation experience, and my childhood, and we understand each other in a way that no one else does."

"And this is your description of a platonic friendship? Has that kimchi gone to your head?" Debra cocked one eyebrow at her incredulously.

Sara snorted. "It's all totally platonic. Really. He gets me; I get him. We can really communicate and help each other out." Sara smiled and popped a ball of rice into her mouth. She knew Debra was going to bug her about it, as she did every time they saw each other, but she meant what she'd said. It was just platonic between them now. Their romance just wasn't meant to be. And clearly, Ezekiel had moved on since Miranda was back in his life.

"Are you sure that Ezekiel and Miranda are really together and serious, Sara? Have you even asked?"

"That is none of my business, Debra. I just know that we're not meant to be together," Sara shrugged, and Debra sighed in resignation, dropping the matter for the time being.

* * *

ON HER WAY home later that evening, Sara's thoughts were once again dragged back to the moment when she had thought she was ready to reveal her love for Ezekiel, and to find out whether he was still in love with her. She'd caught a taxi down to the set of the Wide-Open show where Miranda Twain was interviewing Ezekiel. Her previous short-term memory loss had come flooding back to her, and she remembered the all-encompassing feelings she'd experienced when she and Ezekiel kissed right before being shot. Every cell in her body had resonated with life and expectation as she had searched for Ezekiel after his interview—until she had seen him backstage with Miranda Twain. It was as if a bucket of ice-cold water was poured over her as she witnessed the obvious closeness between them. The entire scene played through her mind, and for probably the millionth time, she remembered every word and expression as if it had just happened....

"What is it?" Ezekiel had asked her.

"Ezekiel...." Sara started.

"Yes?" he'd replied, his eyes soft.

Sara looked behind him, where Miranda was talking to one of her crew.

Sara attempted to pull herself together as if her body had dissipated into the atmosphere and she had to somehow pull all the pieces back together.

"Ezekiel," Sara began again, willing herself to look at his face as she spoke, "I, um... I just couldn't leave things like that between us. I realize now that you wouldn't have put my name out there to the media. That you wouldn't betray me." She meant this. But her heart pounded in her chest, and she folded her arms awkwardly, then unfolded them again, hoping he wouldn't sense that she was holding back something more.

"Thank you for believing me, Sara," Ezekiel said, the genuine relief obvious on his face. "I didn't want to leave things between us that way either. I'm so grateful for you, and it's important to me that things are right between us," Ezekiel paused and turned to look back at where Miranda had last been standing. "Miranda and I are going out to get a bite to eat. Do you want to join us?"

Sara looked up into his eyes. "I don't quite understand, Ezekiel. Are you and Miranda... friends now? After all the harassment she has given you?"

"Miranda's apologized, Sara. She truly believed that I was taking advantage of you, but we've cleared things up about what actually happened. You're so welcome to join us, Sara. In fact, I insist. I know Miranda would love to hear your side of the story in person now." Ezekiel placed his hand gently on her arm. "Please?"

"I'm sorry, Ezekiel," Sara said, taking a step backward, the sensation of his hand scorching her arm. "I, uh, have a headache, and I don't feel up to it right at the moment. I have a flight to catch. Maybe another time."

Sara's stomach churned within her. Was this really happening, this whole 'happy family' thing with Miranda Twain? She felt sick.

"Let's catch up again soon, then, okay?" Ezekiel ventured. His eyes searched hers, but she glanced down to avoid him seeing any more than she could bear to reveal. "I'd better get going. Thanks for coming to see me, Sara. I really appreciate it."

"Sure," Sara nodded, and she turned and walked away. It was as if her stomach had risen to her throat, and she attempted to swallow over the lump there. She knew she would get a tongue-lashing from Debra later. She just couldn't take any rejection right now. Spending time with the Lord was her priority; Ezekiel was obviously just a distraction. She determined then and there that she needed to remain single and work on deepening her relationship with the Lord before diving into a serious relationship.

And now, months later, other than her weekly calls with Ezekiel, she'd kept that commitment. Well, except for spending more time with God. Somehow that had gotten crowded out lately. Sara shivered in the night breeze, shaking off the memories, and pushed in the door to her building. *Tonight,* she told herself, *I will definitely take some time to read my Bible and pray.*

* * *

LATER THAT NIGHT, Sara sat in front of her computer at the desk in her room, waiting for the man in question to answer her video call. She'd managed to overcome the grief of that moment months ago and settle for being his friend. Their weekly calls were one of the few things Sara looked forward to in her life these days.

"Hey there." Ezekiel's face popped up. He was smiling, his sandy hair slightly disheveled, probably because he'd had another long day.

"Hi," Sara smiled. "How was your Wednesday?"

"It was pretty much the same as always. We're so busy at the center." He pushed his hair back with his hand.

Sara nodded. "Any success with the funding appeals?"

He shook his head. "We're working on this fresh approach with it all. We hired that consulting company and are trying to follow their recommendations, but so far, it's not turning up any new major donors. That was supposed to be the results they promised, but...." He trailed off and let out a tired sigh. "Somehow, I feel like we're missing something, but I'm not sure what it is. So, I just keep trying."

Sara watched him for a moment. He looked like he always looked these past few weeks—neither happy nor sad, just tired.

"How's the ever-turbulent Miranda Twain?" Sara couldn't help asking. She was curious despite the pang she felt at the thought of Ezekiel dating Miranda.

Ezekiel tilted his head.

"I wouldn't say turbulent, Sara. You don't know her well enough yet. She's... dynamic," Ezekiel said, but Sara only rolled her eyes. There were other words she could use to describe Miranda just from watching Miranda's popular tell-all, the Wide-Open Show.

"Hm, guess I will have to take your word on that."

Ezekiel ignored her eye roll. "She's fine, though. She's overcome a lot in life, and I think we've both grown since we dated years ago. I wish you could get to know her a little better. You could see that she's full of passion and fights for justice. There's a lot behind the scenes that people don't know about her work."

Sara gave a half-hearted smile. "That's great she's doing well." She wasn't sure if she meant it. Miranda somehow just rubbed her the wrong way. "Have you told her about wanting to go on the mission trip?"

Ezekiel sighed, obviously exasperated. "Sara, I told you I'm not going. Too much is happening at the center right now."

"Yeah, but you said God had put it on your heart to go."

"I know, but maybe not right now. I have to follow through on these funding appeals. There's so much work to be done, a new year, and all that, and time is already flying! There are so many events to run, and the director can't just be missing in action. I can't just leave the work to the rest of the staff right now—it wouldn't be fair." He shrugged.

A flimsy excuse not to go if God really prompted you to do it, Sara decided, but kept it to herself.

"Where was it you'd go again?" she queried. She'd never even considered a mission trip herself, though she recalled listening to missionaries as a kid in church and envying their sense of adventure and boldness.

"It's a medical mission to Vanuatu," Ezekiel replied. "Now that I think about it, I don't know if I'd even be a good fit. They don't exactly need writers on a boat carrying doctors, dentists, and medical supplies. Maybe that sense of calling I felt was just a general pull toward some kind of international service in the future, you know? There are enormous needs all over the world, after all."

"True," Sara acknowledged. "But you said they needed support people on board the ship too, right? No special skills needed? But then again perhaps you'd be a hindrance. I seem to recall you're highly skilled at creating drama and then needing others to clean up your mess," she smirked and stifled a giggle.

"Hey! Watch it, there, Miss Ward! I see where you're going with this!" Ezekiel shot back with a wry grin. He held his hands up in protest. "I do know you're talented at sorting out other people's drama. Whereas my job was to reveal the truth. Perhaps the article helped to launch you into a whole new area of expertise?"

"I'm sure there would've been easier and less public ways of developing new skills," Sara smiled, thinking of the extensive travel they'd done as they travelled the country together trying to calm down a media storm.

"There's always a steep learning curve in learning something new," Ezekiel said. "I was just trying to help you."

Now Sara laughed loudly. "Yeah, yeah," she joked in return, "I'm sure it was totally selfless of you."

"Totally!" Ezekiel laughed.

Sara was so grateful to have her memories back of their brief time working together in New York and even the whirlwind media campaign after it all. That was when everything had changed. Years of pain, bitterness, and resentment had weighed her down for so long, but then Ezekiel had shown up—seemingly out of nowhere—and made it even worse. There he was again in all his perfect Christian goodness, and Sara felt more than ever that she was losing at life. Until she finally, desperately, opened her heart to God—and He had met her there. Jesus began restoring her broken soul and, at the same time, nudging her to take action on the investigation with which she'd agreed to help Ezekiel.

And then, along with all the other changes, her heart toward Ezekiel himself had done an about-face, too. His kindness had won her over. She smiled at the memory, although she had yet to tell Ezekiel exactly how much she remembered. Now he had a new relationship; it didn't seem so relevant, or if she was honest, it felt too vulnerable to tell him she remembered everything.

"But seriously," Sara continued, "Don't you think going on the trip would be like a sort of undercover investigation again? And all that you learn while you're there, you could then put into a story about—what are they called? Pacific Outreach Missions? I'm sure with someone of your caliber writing a story on their work; they'd attract a lot more support, right? So you'd multiply your impact."

Ezekiel tilted his head and raised his eyebrows, considering her words and studying her face on the screen. "Touché," he nodded, "You have got me there, Sara. I honestly hadn't even thought of that. I guess work here is so stressful that I haven't considered it enough." He paused, and she saw his jaw shift as he contemplated before speaking. "All right, all right. I promise I'll pray about it again, okay? What about you, though? At work. Did you ask for a new manager yet?"

Sara sighed; of course, he would turn the conversation on her. "I told you, Ezekiel, I don't want to stir things up at the office. I'm still too new."

"That's kind of a pathetic reason to keep letting Elizabeth walk all over you."

"Eleanor," Sara corrected drily, but she knew he knew that.

"The Sara I know used to sock hot-shot clients in the face." He raised an eyebrow sarcastically at her.

"Oh really?"

"I'm sorry, Sara, yes. But I realize, you may not remember all the details."

"It's okay, Ezekiel," Sara paused, "But are you saying I should punch my boss in the face?" she raised her eyebrows.

"I can just imagine it! Take *that*, Eleanor," Ezekiel threw a mock one-two punch into the air in front of the webcam and laughed.

Sara grinned and tried to ignore the warm rush that rose inside her chest at the sound of his deep laughter.

"No, of course not," he replied. "I'm saying, be you. The Sara I know doesn't sit back and just let a bully push her around. Your boss won't respect you any less if you show her what you're worth. You are a valuable member of that company, and she needs to recognize it."

Sara looked down at her hands soberly as she considered his words. "Wow, I guess you must know me better than I know myself these days." She smiled as she looked back up at him, then caught her breath at his somber expression. What was that look in his eyes? Sometimes she felt he could somehow see inside her, almost read her thoughts, but then—*no, we're good friends, that's all,* she reminded herself. She kept the smile plastered on her face. "Well," she chuckled awkwardly, "I—I should go. I should get to bed. I have to run after Eleanor all day tomorrow," she joked, ending whatever that moment was.

"Yeah. You should. Hey, I can't wait to see you at Easter, though."

"Yeah!" Sara was genuinely excited at the thought of seeing him again in the flesh and their mothers as well. "Me too."

"Great." He beamed. "Well, goodnight, Sara. Remember, I'm always praying for you."

"And me for you," Sara said quietly, a small smile on her face as he hung up. Her smile was still in place as she crawled into bed later. "Thank you, Lord, for friends like Ezekiel Cane."

CHAPTER 2

*E*zekiel stretched and was about to close his laptop when he noticed a new email at the top of his inbox: another reminder to apply for the Pacific Outreach Missions' upcoming medical mission trip he had inquired about a few weeks ago. His conversation with Sara fresh in his mind, he opened the email, then clicked on the video link it contained, and watched, emotion moistening his eyes, as a blind man saw for the first time in fifteen years after simple cataract surgery.

He knew Sara was right. He didn't have any medical skills that he could donate, but he could be a support person, and maybe through his newfound journalistic notoriety, he *could* help bring greater attention to these medical mission ships that operated all over the world, not just in the Pacific, and help raise more support for them. There was such an enormous need for the services they were offering—for the hope they were bringing. Ezekiel couldn't shake it; he still felt inexplicably drawn to this outreach. But—there was a need right here, too, at the center, and he was doing good work now—or so he hoped.

There was so much he didn't want to upset by going on a mission trip at a time like this. He was just getting settled in his current life... or was he? "Lord, lead me," Ezekiel whispered. "I want to do what is best, Lord, from YOUR standpoint, not mine."

Ezekiel closed his eyes and saw Sara's face in his mind's eye. The soft curve of her mouth as she smiled, her hand as she tucked her hair behind her ear. But he could see that she was tired, the dark shadows under her eyes almost a permanent feature these days.

"Lord, are you trying to tell me something about Sara? Or is it just my thinking? Please bless her and lead her." He prayed in his special language under his breath for a few minutes until he experienced a shift in his spirit.

He sighed, shook his head to move his thoughts away from Sara, and went online to categorize the entries on the bank statement that he needed to get loaded into the center's accounting software. It was late, but he had to get it done sometime. He needed to get everything up to date before his meeting with the board. He ran a hand down his face and tried to focus on the figures he was seeing, which seemed to run together on the screen. *I must be getting old, or maybe I need glasses*, he thought, blinking to bring it all into focus. "Lord, please provide for this shelter. I'm in over my head. Show me what to do," he prayed.

* * *

Ezekiel sat in his cramped office at the shelter late in the afternoon a few days later, his care-worn desk covered with paperwork and his laptop. He reviewed the replies from the many organizations they had reached out to for financial contributions, some by email and some in letters. He'd been so excited to send out these bids for support because he was using a new strategy based on the latest advice from the non-profit marketing consultancy company he'd employed, but so far, the replies were less than encouraging. Sitting back, Ezekiel sighed and ran his fingers through his hair. He'd felt so sure this would be a winning strategy.

"Keller," he called as he saw her walking past the office door and then waited before Keller walked in. She was a pleasant-featured, middle-aged woman whose job description was 'secretary,' but Ezekiel knew she wore at least half a dozen more hats, most of which had nothing to do with being a secretary, and yet she accepted her tasks and meager pay with a smile regardless. She came in smiling, just as Ezekiel had expected. "We're not doing so well," he said, getting straight to the point.

"No. We're not." She shook her head but didn't sound dejected. "I'm sure if we continue to plan the showcase for next month and trust God, some of these organizations will see how paramount the work we do at the shelter really is and be inspired by our vision for the future. And remember, we have the CEO from Above Board Construction company coming today."

"Oh, somehow that appointment had slipped my mind," Ezekiel said. He rubbed his hands over his face. This could be the opportunity they'd been waiting for. "I was just discouraged for a moment. So few people have responded to our requests."

"Well, the harder the problem is to solve, the bigger the miracle. Maybe you could use your journalistic fame to generate some interest?"

Ezekiel stood and stretched. "You are always so positive, Keller, and so capable as well. I can't thank you enough for all you do here."

"Don't mention it," Keller said. "I love what we do, and there is so much potential. Don't give up, Ezekiel. Things will turn around. Just wait and see."

Ezekiel sat down once again. "Thanks, Keller. I'd better get back to work, but I'm looking forward to this meeting. What was his name again?"

"Mateo Franco Bernal," Keller said.

"So he must be part of his family's business? They're pretty famous," Ezekiel said, "It will be intriguing to hear his story." He may not be working in journalism anymore, but a good story never failed to pique his interest.

"Yes, it will. I'll leave you to it," Keller turned and left the room.

Half an hour later, Ezekiel heard a soft knock at the door.

Keller walked in, followed by a man dressed in dark jeans and a polo shirt with an embroidered logo on the chest. He looked smart despite his casual attire. Ezekiel felt wrung out and underdressed after an early start in his jeans and plain white button-down with Hope Center stenciled over the pocket. "Ah, you must be Mr. Franco Bernal," Ezekiel stood and offered his hand to shake. "Welcome to the Hope Center. I'm Ezekiel Cane."

"Please, call me Mateo," the man said, reaching forward and grasping Ezekiel's hand with a hearty shake. "I've been looking forward to hearing about what you do here, and it's great to meet you, Mr. Cane."

"Ezekiel, please. We want you to feel at home here and relaxed."

"Thank you, Ezekiel," Mateo said.

"I was thinking of giving you a tour of the place, and on the way, I could share our vision, and answer any questions you have, if that's okay with you?"

"That would be great. Lead the way." Mateo turned and almost ran into Miranda Twain, who had entered the tiny office silently behind him.

Miranda, dressed elegantly in a floral knee-length dress, a wool coat, and long black boots, stood still momentarily, her dark eyes taking in the visitor.

Ezekiel watched as Mateo took a step back and banged into his desk. "And who do we have here?" Mateo asked, a smile lighting up his face.

Ezekiel came out from behind his desk and squeezed past Mateo and Miranda. He glanced at Keller, who was pushed up against the wall, and frowned.

"Miranda Twain, meet Mateo Franco Bernal," Ezekiel said. "Sorry, it's a tight squeeze in here for a meeting.

Keller squeezed past them and out into the hallway. "I'll catch up with you later," she said, and excused herself.

"Delighted to meet you, Miss Twain," Mateo said, taking Miranda's hand.

Ezekiel watched as Miranda's cheeks flushed. "Miranda, hey, it's great to see you."

"Hi, Ezekiel," she said, but her eyes remained fixed on Mateo's for a moment before she withdrew her hand and placed it on Ezekiel's arm, followed by a quick kiss on his cheek. "You never told me about your acquaintance with Mr. Bernal," she said accusingly.

Ezekiel faltered at seeing her fawn over the man, then quickly recovered. "Actually, we've just been introduced ourselves. We have a meeting about the center right now, and I'm about to give Mateo a tour. Do you want to meet me in the courtyard later, and we can have a late lunch together?" Ezekiel suddenly felt awkward standing between them, and he knew he didn't need Miranda making her usual negative comments about the center in front of this potentially very helpful donor.

"I'd be happy to join you for the tour," Miranda said, all smiles. "If that's alright with you, Mateo? I wouldn't want to intrude." *Yeah, right.* Ezekiel resisted the urge to roll his eyes.

Mateo smiled, and Ezekiel acquiesced, "Let's go." He led the way along the corridor to the main dining hall.

"This is where much of the work gets done; we serve meals to the homeless, and through here is the main kitchen."

"This is an excellent space," Mateo remarked, clearly impressed.

"If cooking is your thing?" Miranda said, wrinkling her nose.

"I personally find cooking relaxing," Mateo grinned.

"I would've thought you'd have a chef," Miranda said wryly, one eyebrow raised in scrutiny.

Mateo turned and stared at her. Miranda straightened a bit and lifted her chin with a sly grin. "Your fame precedes you, Mr. Bernal."

"Don't believe all you read in the tabloids," Mateo shrugged and looked away. "I'd much prefer my personal life to be private, honestly."

"But your company is one of the most successful Hispanic-American businesses in California, and your crossover into music is quite a sensation," Miranda said. Ezekiel was the one staring now, aware that he hadn't done so well with his research on Mateo—but clearly, she had. "You're an inspiration to a lot of people," she finished with genuine admiration.

"Thanks, that's very generous, Miranda," Mateo said, a smile taking over his face now.

"Maybe you'd like to do an interview for the Wide-Open Show?" Miranda asked. "We could do some promotion for you. People love success stories, and I'd love to hear more details about how your company started. If you'd like, you could even sing something for our studio audience, and we could talk about your music background?"

"Maybe I could?" Mateo's eyes lingered on her face. "It could be fun. As long as I can vet the questions first and keep the interview more about the business, rather than focusing on me? I'm sure your rise to fame at the Wide-Open Show would be more interesting, though."

"I can make your request happen, absolutely. But it would be good to include your love of music as well. My story... is a long and winding one, and there's not much to tell, really," Miranda finished as she looked at Ezekiel, their eyes locking before hers dropped toward the ground, then nonchalantly gazed out a nearby window. Ezekiel recognized her vulnerability at that moment, though he doubted anyone less acquainted with her would have detected it. He knew the scars she bore—and fiercely protected. A sudden urge to protect her as well rose within him. Those fierce dark eyes held so much pain behind them still. If only he'd done more back in college to prevent what had happened to her. He was determined not to make the same mistake twice with this fascinating and beautiful woman.

"A conversation for another time, Miranda, is that right?" Mateo asked, surprisingly intuitive.

Miranda looked up and nodded, her eyes wide. "Yes, another time, Mateo."

Ezekiel thought fast and sought a way out of the now awkward conversation for her. "Uh, Miranda, can you please see Keller about that... order?" Ezekiel suggested, hoping she would take his hint.

Miranda glanced quickly at Mateo, then turned to face Ezekiel. "Of course; nice to meet you, Mateo. I'll have my assistant contact you," she nodded back in his direction.

Mateo gave her a polite nod and a charming smile as she left the room. "I'll look forward to catching up with you another time, Miranda."

Ezekiel waited until she'd gone, then waved his arm around them and began again. "So, this main building is the area that is government-funded, and we have people who walk in off the street needing shelter, coming here. There are rooms in the main building to help house the homeless. Some of the other buildings have units that are great for small families, usually women in trouble and their children."

"There's a lot of potential here," Mateo pointed out, his hands on his hips as he surveyed their surroundings.

"We also have a rehab facility for those struggling with substance abuse issues."

"Yes, I had heard about that," Mateo nodded, smiling. "I'm interested in the facility. Is that also state-funded?"

"The rehab is private, giving us more freedom to help our clients. Rather than a twelve-step program, we have a one-way program: Jesus. We strive to introduce people to the 'Higher Power' Who actually works. Of course, we offer life skills development programs alongside discipleship as well."

"I am so excited to hear this! Jesus has helped me through a lot in my own life."

"Oh?" Ezekiel looked intrigued.

"It's quite a long story, so maybe we can talk more another day. Suffice it to say I have had some help from the recovery movement," Mateo said.

"Of course. I'd love to hear more of your story sometime. Let me show you some of the other buildings we have."

They walked outside and along to another one of the houses. "As you can see, it desperately needs an upgrade," Ezekiel commented as he pointed to one of the dilapidated structures, "and the demand for what we're offering here is so immense that we would love to build some new buildings in that area over there. Most people think the plight of the homeless is simply that they don't have a home to live in; but really, it is underpinned by so many interconnected issues: sometimes addiction, mental health, and also families in situations of abuse. We aim to help in all ways, and we have even collaborated with some lawyers who come and help people with legal advice."

Mateo was nodding enthusiastically. "This is fantastic," he said. "I really like what I'm hearing. You're not just giving homeless people a motel stay, but real hope."

Ezekiel nodded in reply, "Exactly. We are offering a comprehensive wrap-around program that helps people develop into functioning members of society who can stand on their own two feet. It's not an overnight transformation. It can take a few years to get people rehabilitated to being integrated, productive members of society who can support their families."

"I'm very impressed with what you are doing here," Mateo commented as he looked around. "I'm very interested in helping you. And I'm sure the company will agree with me."

"What do you have in mind, Mateo? We'd be grateful for any help," Ezekiel replied, unable to hold back a grin at Mateo's enthusiasm. "Would you like to stay for some lunch and discuss your ideas?"

"I'm sorry, I have another appointment to get to, Ezekiel, but thanks for the offer. I will definitely discuss your center with our board, though. My father would also be very interested in seeing what you do here. I think we can offer you some solid support."

"We'd love to see him anytime, and thank you so much for your time, Mateo." Ezekiel leaned forward to shake his hand.

Mateo returned his handshake heartily. "I'll be in touch."

They walked through the courtyard to where Miranda was sitting, scrolling through her phone, and she stood and followed them over to the gate.

"Lovely to meet you, Mateo," Miranda said.

"Likewise," he nodded as he pulled a card out of his pocket and handed it to her. He waved a final goodbye and climbed into his truck.

As Mateo drove away, Miranda looked down at the card, then turned to Ezekiel. "Well, if the Above Board Construction company gets involved, maybe you can finally focus on what you are actually best at, Ezekiel."

"What are you trying to say, Miranda? Specifically, please?" Ezekiel said.

She folded her arms and gave him a contemplative look for a moment before shaking her head.

"You are a Pulitzer Prize–winning journalist, Ezekiel; you could do any job that you want in the media. Why not join me on the Wide-Open Show? You haven't forgotten my offer, have you?"

Ezekiel's shoulders shrugged, and he tilted his head and looked at her wearily. "You know how much I hate the spotlight, Miranda. I never wanted to be on camera. Look at how bad I was in your interviews! You drove me off the set!"

She chuckled, and he was satisfied to see her blush slightly in response. "Well, I couldn't let you off the hook too easily, could I? I was convinced you were guilty of blackmail!"

"Ha!" he retorted. "Let me off easy? You crucified me on national TV! And now you think I will just hop back in front of that spotlight? You had better think again."

She snorted. "Oh, please! I had you back on and resurrected you from the media grave, didn't I? All is well now. America loves you again! And... I think we make a great team." She eyed him intently.

Her gaze unsettled him; beneath the obvious attraction and admiration he felt for her, something else nagged at the back of his mind, but he could never quite place it. He exhaled sharply and leaned against the gate. "Well, I have definitely enjoyed reconnecting with you since moving back to California. But I'm not ready to dive back into that industry yet. I wanted a break, remember? Besides, I have opportunities here to develop new skills and use some of my talents in other ways.”

“But you are in the prime of your life—the top of your field! Not to mention the fact that you’re throwing away the chance to earn a substantial income, Ezekiel. You’ve worked so hard. How can you just throw it all away? And for this...?” She gestured at the run-down buildings in front of them. The woman sure had a way of making a point.

Ezekiel sighed. “Look, there’s more to life than just money and professional achievements. What I do here *is* important.”

“Are you saying that what I do isn’t?” Miranda stared at him, an incredulous look on her face.

“Miranda, you know that’s not true. I support your work and your search for truth. All I ask is that right now, you support me in doing something different.”

"I just hate seeing you overwork yourself for *this*." Miranda swept her arm around, indicating the courtyard.

Ezekiel ignored the condescension in her tone; she just couldn’t catch his vision for the place. He looked around and tried to see it through her eyes. Too many weeds, cracked and pitted concrete, rusty folding chairs, and a faded picnic table cast a drab scene. It could definitely use some tidying up. He looked toward the bent basketball hoop. So many people enjoyed that hoop, and he himself had had many meaningful conversations with people struggling with the hardships of life here, despite the cracked concrete with weeds bursting through like sofa stuffing.

The court still worked. If only there wasn't so much else to do, brightening up the exterior of the place might take it from functional to inviting. If only she could see what he saw in it.

"I know this place needs a lot of work. That’s why I've been working a lot." He leaned down to pull one weed from a nearby crack. “Sara says I need a break," he muttered, almost to himself.

"Hmm," Miranda murmured. "She says a lot."

Ezekiel's eyes snapped up to Miranda's face. "Hey, don't do that."

"Do what?" She feigned ignorance.

"Pick on Sara. She’s been in my life a long time, and she’s a good friend."

"I know, but it doesn’t mean that *I* have to be friends with her," she smiled, even though the smile didn't reach her eyes. "Let's get lunch, I'm famished from missing it earlier," she said before he could say anything in reply, and she turned and walked toward the kitchen.

They carried their sandwiches back out to the courtyard and sat on the bench, the one that had the brass plaque acknowledging Ezekiel's father, Isaiah Cane. Miranda pressed down on her left leg as they sat, and the movement reminded Ezekiel of the tattoo that covered a self-inflicted scar, now hidden with thick woolen stockings. It was no doubt an unconscious habit of hers, but his heart suddenly sank at the memory of the deep wounds that had set off her destructive patterns years ago. How far she'd come since their days in college together—she was so successful in her career, almost a household name. But outward success couldn't erase the wounds on the inside that still needed healing, wounds he knew only God could heal.

Ezekiel chewed his food and prayed silently, *"Lord, please help me help Miranda. You know what's going on in her heart and that it needs to be healed. Only You can do that, Lord. I know she wants more from me. More than I'm willing to give right now. Help her turn to You, not me."*

"I was kind of surprised to see you here today, Miranda," Ezekiel ventured after a moment of silence. "I thought we'd catch up on our next beach run this Saturday?"

"Well, I wanted to see you, and I knew where you'd be," Miranda said simply.

"Even though you hate it here?" *She must have really needed to see me,* he thought.

"Yes."

"Well, tell me what's been happening with you," Ezekiel said and listened as Miranda shared the details of her latest exposé, the passion lighting up her face. He knew her dedication to her work was a worthwhile distraction from her past, and he also enjoyed the thrill of her work vicariously since his work at the center—although fulfilling—didn't always quite carry the same sense of excitement as hers seemed to.

"You know, you really are making an important difference in people's lives, Miranda," he said sincerely.

She beamed at his recognition. "Thanks," she replied.

Ezekiel was thankful Miranda's work was going well, and he determined to spend more quality time with her and share the keys he'd learned on his journey of connecting with the Lord. That way, he imagined, she could find her own healing; but he knew she also needed to do her part. Was her interest in God only superficial? Or even only to attract his interest? *It doesn't matter,* he decided. *God can reach her even if she's only half open to Him.* He would find more time for her, he assured himself, as soon as he could get the shelter on its feet again.

Ezekiel and Miranda walked back into the kitchen; she may be a famous TV personality, but Ezekiel appreciated that underneath her perfectly styled exterior, Miranda still had a hardworking down-to-earth approach to life. He rinsed their plates and handed them to Miranda, who put them in the dishwasher.

"I have some time off over Easter," Miranda announced. "I thought we could spend some time together if that works for you?" She glanced at him as she loaded the plates.

"Yeah, that would be great. Do you want to come to a special Easter service, and then lunch? My mom is hosting a lunch for a bunch of relatives and friends. It would be great to have you there." He smiled.

She nodded. "Sure, an Easter service and lunch sounds good. It's been too long since I went to church. Why not?"

Ezekiel could almost see the wheels turning in her mind. Miranda was so focused on her work that she sometimes seemed to forget the details of what was happening in her personal life. But under that layer of drivenness, he sensed something stirring in her.

"My sister is going to be out of town, anyway," she added as an afterthought.

"What about your aunt? What is she up to?" Ezekiel asked casually, glancing sideways to see her reaction.

She shook her head and frowned. "She's busy," Miranda said tersely.

Ezekiel raised his eyebrows. He wished she would open up about her aunt. During Miranda's struggles at the end of college, Ezekiel and her aunt, had joined forces to help her. Miranda had apparently forgiven him after everything that had happened; why could she not forgive her aunt? Was there something he could say or some leading question he could ask maybe, that would encourage her to consider reconciliation?

"I'd really love to see her again, Miranda, but no pressure. Another time."

Miranda looked at Ezekiel, an artery throbbing on her neck, but she spoke calmly. "I'm just not in the head space right now to see her, Ezekiel. But thanks for your concern."

He considered her thoughtfully, then spoke, barely above a whisper. "She was only trying to help, Miranda. We had to get you help."

"Yes, I know, but the help seemed... heavy-handed." Miranda ran a hand through her hair.

"You can't bury emotionally what isn't dead, Miranda. It will come back to bite you one day if you do."

"I just need some more time, and I'll contact her. I promise," Miranda's tone was audibly stressed.

"I'll hold you to that, Miranda," He smiled and leaned in to touch her arm, looking into her eyes with compassion. Miranda nodded slowly and then relaxed as he drew her into a hug.

CHAPTER 3

Sara rang the doorbell to the Cane residence. A basket of plastic Easter eggs was nearby on the veranda, a vase of Easter lilies on the outdoor table. Sara smiled. They were all too old for Easter egg hunts now, but Teresa Cane would disagree. She loved holiday traditions. Sara breathed in the heady scent of Teresa's gardenias growing profusely on a tidy bush next to the potted daffodils that lined the garden by the porch. She smiled at the memories of coming to this house as a child. Of course, her memories would have been much more pleasant if she hadn't been hell-bent on hating everything and everyone back then, especially Ezekiel.

"I hope Teresa doesn't serve this. Maybe if I'm lucky, the table will already be full," Mildred, Sara's mother, said from behind her as they waited for someone to answer the door.

Sara rolled her eyes at her mother and her existential crisis over her fresh strawberry pie. Sara thought it would be fabulous, and Mildred had kept it in a small cooler on the journey to Teresa's house, but she was convinced it would not be good enough. Mildred tended to be critical of herself; maybe she still hadn't forgiven herself for her part in allowing Darren, Sara's father, to be so hard on Sara as a child. Sara just wished she would move on; there was nothing she could do now that Darren had passed away. Sara had forgiven both of her parents and hated seeing her mother fret over the past.

"I said it before, and I'll say it again, Mom: your strawberry pie is always fine."

"Just *fine*?" Mildred looked genuinely horrified. The door swung open, and Sara was glad to drop the subject of the dessert. Now wasn't the time for yet another pep talk. Ezekiel stood before them, grinning widely.

Sara's heart leaped at the sight of him. He looked so good for someone as stressed as she knew he was. His hair, slightly longer was partially tucked behind his ears, but a few short strands fell over his forehead. His eyes had landed on her the second he opened the door.

"Ward!" He launched at her, hugging her so tightly that he lifted her off the ground. Sara giggled and wrapped her arms around his neck, pecking him on the cheek before he put her down.

"Ezekiel! I'm so happy to see you."

"Me too. Honestly, I know it's only been a couple of months, but it feels like I haven't seen you in forever. Webcam is not the same." He was smiling so hard that Sara soon matched his expression. Somehow, he seemed more relaxed, more himself, here at his family home. Sara found herself blushing, but he turned his attention to Mildred. "Mrs. Ward, you are looking so beautiful today."

Mildred squinted at him, then winked.

"Ezekiel Cane, are you flirting with my mother?" Sara rolled her eyes, and Ezekiel laughed before taking the dish from her mother.

"Never," he said. "My mom can't wait to see you two. Come in." He stepped aside.

Sara walked into the house, and Teresa Cane was standing in the entryway with her arms spread wide.

"Come here, you!"

Sara smiled, a warmth in her chest as she entered Teresa's embrace. Ever since Sara had given her life to the Lord, she'd become so grateful to God for Teresa. They'd had many conversations over the phone, and now, enveloped in her arms, it was as if she was coming home.

She knew Teresa had forgiven her for her bratty behavior as a teenager and, in fact, Sara was much loved.

"Teresa! You look as wonderful as ever."

"Oh, please. Stop the flattery," Teresa said, her tone stern but her blush betraying how much she appreciated the compliment.

"Come on. Let's let our mothers catch up while I put this in the fridge," Ezekiel suggested, motioning to the dish he had taken from her mother.

"Don't we need to get going? I don't want to be late for church." Sara glanced at the time on her phone.

"No, we don't," he answered. "Just one late service today." She followed him down the hallway as he launched into telling her about the people he worked with at the shelter.

As they walked, Sara was sure she overheard Teresa say to Mildred, "One would think they didn't talk online every week."

"I know. They are so good together," Mildred replied.

"Exactly. That's why they should be together."

"Tess, you read my mind," Mildred nodded knowingly, using the nickname she'd given Teresa years ago, when the "kids" were small.

Sara ignored their meddling mothers' comments and focused on listening to Ezekiel, hoping he hadn't heard them as well. She wanted to enjoy their time together with as little awkwardness as possible.

Another knock on the front door sounded, and Teresa moved to open the door as Sara and Ezekiel returned to the living room.

"Welcome, Miranda!" Teresa drew her inside. "I believe you know Sara, and this is her mother, Mildred."

Sara and Mildred both greeted her.

"Thank you for having me, Teresa," Miranda said politely, and she handed her a green salad.

"You didn't have any plans to see your own family today?" Teresa asked. "You would've been welcome to invite them here," she smiled brightly.

"Thanks, but I believe they have other plans," Miranda said. "My sister's on vacation up north and I'm sure my cousins will have lots going on. I'll catch up with them soon." She glanced at Ezekiel, who caught her eye and walked up to give her a hug then. Sara looked on and smiled, determined to be happy for them and to enjoy the weekend.

"I'm glad to hear that," Teresa said. "Well, now that everyone's here, let's get to church."

As they pulled over a few minutes later and parked in the church parking lot, Sara could hear the worship had already started. Sara and

Mildred exited the car and waited for Ezekiel, Teresa, and Miranda to catch up to them.

"Have you been to this church before, Miranda?" Sara asked.

"Not this one," Miranda said. "I used to go with Ezekiel to a New Life church when we were at Stanford, though." They walked into the church and were ushered to a row near the back, the sanctuary nearly full.

They stood and joined in with the congregation, singing a familiar melody and following along as the chorus rose, "My chains are gone, I've been set free…"

Sara looked toward Miranda, her eyes widening. Miranda's voice was amazing, a clear soprano, her notes ringing true; Sara closed her eyes and felt the presence of the Lord cover her, tingling and warmth from head to toe. When the worship ended, she sat down and whispered to Ezekiel. "Miranda has such a beautiful voice; it's a gift."

Ezekiel turned to her, smiled, and nodded.

Miranda must have heard Sara's compliment from the other side of Ezekiel as she turned to Sara and smiled tentatively.

After the service had finished, people stood and mingled. Sara looked around to see if she recognized anyone from their youth group days. Not seeing anyone familiar, she joined in the conversation with Teresa and her mother as they slowly made their way toward the door.

"Ezekiel, Sara, good to see you," a tall man said as they approached. Pastor Michaels, who'd given the sermon that day, was standing by the door shaking hands. "Congratulations on your article, both of you. You're both famous," he chuckled. "Who would have thought? And this is Miranda, I believe? From the Wide-Open Show?"

"Yes," Ezekiel replied. "Miranda and I went to college together and reconnected after our story went viral."

"Great to meet you, Miranda," Pastor Michaels said. "I watched your reporting on these two with great interest." He tilted his head at her.

"We got the truth out in the end," Miranda said, with a wry grin pointed at Ezekiel.

"Yes, she's a bit of a bulldog with a bone, this reporter," Ezekiel returned the tease as he put his arm around Miranda's shoulders. "Thankfully, I had a great PR team on my side," he winked and saluted at Sara.

"Well, it is good to see you all, and Happy Easter. He is risen!" the pastor declared with a smile.

"He is risen, indeed!" Sara and Ezekiel said together, looked at each other, and laughed. Miranda frowned, unfamiliar with the tradition.

"Come on, let's get going," Teresa urged. "We don't want the roast to be ruined."

Sara tapped her mother on the shoulder and tilted her head to indicate they were leaving.

A short time later, when they arrived at the house, Sara exited the car and ran to the porch. A tall young man dressed in a blue polo shirt and pressed khaki pants stood waiting near the front door. "Truman," she exclaimed. "I didn't know you'd be here!"

"Happy Easter, Sara. Yes, a surprise visit. I'm passing through on a business trip," Truman explained in his typical matter-of-fact manner.

Sara hugged him, but Truman kept his arms by his side. She giggled and took a step backward. "Sorry, Truman, I forgot you don't like hugs."

Mildred walked up onto the porch and introduced him to the others. "For everyone who doesn't know, this is my nephew, Truman. Thank you, Teresa, for inviting him today."

Greetings were said all around, introducing some of Teresa's other friends who had also arrived, and Teresa unlocked the door. "You're all welcome! The more the merrier! Now, let's see to that roast. Who's hungry?" A chorus of enthusiastic responses sounded.

Soon, everyone was seated at the long, decorated table piled with food, and Teresa said grace before they all started eating. Sara again sat next to Ezekiel, with Miranda on his other side.

"How's work, Miranda?" Sara asked. "Any scandals on the horizon?"

"There're always scandals," Miranda replied, cutting into a minuscule piece of meat. The tiny amount of food on her plate looked like starvation rations. Sara glanced at her own overflowing plate and shrugged. It was none of Sara's business if Miranda wanted to starve herself.

And money to be made at other people's expense, Sara thought, thinking back to how hard Miranda had been on Ezekiel after their story on the Wentworth corruption had exploded. Miranda had embarrassed Ezekiel on live television over details that weren't true, and what was the outcome? They'd gotten back together. It made no sense. Especially since Sara couldn't remember one instance of an actual public apology from Miranda. *Get it together, Sara*, she chided herself. *I must forgive her and be polite now.* After all, Sara and Ezekiel were good friends now, and if Miranda was important to him, Sara would honor that because her friendship with Ezekiel was worth preserving.

"It's a good way to make a living, revealing injustice," Miranda said.

As long as you get your facts straight, Sara thought.

"Yes, it must be very satisfying work," Teresa chimed in. "I know Ezekiel has always loved the intrigue and revealing truth when doing an exposé."

"Ezekiel, how are things at the shelter?" Mildred asked pointedly, changing the subject.

"Oh, um... Things could be better. It has lost a lot of funding in recent years and needs some refreshing, but I know things will start looking up soon." He smiled and stuffed a forkful of food into his mouth.

"But *do* you know that?" Miranda questioned pointedly, and all eyes turned to Ezekiel.

"Well, no, not for a fact." Ezekiel was still smiling, but Sara noticed his smile falter slightly then.

"So why say that you do?" Miranda asked. "I have seen how many hours you've put in at that place, and it is burying you alive. If we're being honest, its days are numbered unless something major changes soon, right?"

Ezekiel swallowed but seemed unable to think of a reply. He was caught off guard at Miranda's directness on the topic. Normally he appreciated her approach, but at the dinner table amongst family and friends, it jarred him. Suddenly he had a flashback to her grilling him on live TV and cleared his throat in an attempt to calm his nerves. This wasn't the impression he'd hoped she'd make.

"I know that Ezekiel's praying about it. I'm confident God will come through in the right way at the right time, and we'll all look back and be amazed," Sara interjected, attempting to sound light-hearted but aware of the slight edge in her own voice.

Ezekiel glanced at her, and the corner of his mouth curved in a half smile. She smiled back at him. *Another awkward conversation, oh joy,* she thought.

"We can't argue with that, now, can we? God is always good!" one of the other guests, Francine, Teresa's next-door neighbor, commented.

"Yes, but surely God isn't demanding that Ezekiel has to tether himself to a failing homeless shelter, especially when he could be doing so much good in the world through his journalism. He didn't win a Pulitzer Prize for nothing," Miranda said, so matter-of-factly that Sara almost choked on her water.

Teresa seemed to turn an unpleasant shade of gray, and Ezekiel went quiet. Sara could sense that Miranda didn't understand the importance of the shelter to their family. Maybe Ezekiel had never explained to her that his father, Isaiah, had been one of the shelter's founders. Either that, or Miranda honestly didn't care.

"Thanks, Miranda, I appreciate your belief in me, but... I think you're missing the point. You know I'm taking a break from journalism to do this," Ezekiel said softly, trying to end the conversation.

Sara cleared her throat, and for a moment, the only sound was the clinking of cutlery against plates, tension heavy in the room.

She glanced at Truman; she guessed his neurodivergent personality would find this conversation unpleasant. Truman appeared to be very focused on slicing his roast beef.

Miranda set her cutlery on her plate with a clink and raised her eyebrows. "I'm sorry. Is there something I should know?" She spoke calmly, but as she looked at Ezekiel, her eyes fierce, Sara could see the agitation on her face.

At that moment, Sara couldn't think of what Ezekiel saw in Miranda. She was certainly beautiful and intelligent but also hard, her physical features matching, her cheekbones angular, and her manner ultra direct. No doubt that personality was an advantage when reporting sensational stories on national TV, but at a dinner party, not so great. Ezekiel sat stiffly and opened his mouth as if to speak, and Sara just knew he was about to make an excuse for Miranda's tone-deaf comments like he always did. She couldn't take it this time.

"That shelter is something very special to his family, if you didn't already know that," Sara launched in earnestly, avoiding Ezekiel's gaze in case he tried to stop her. "Ezekiel's father was part of its founding committee and devoted much of his life to it before he died. His own father, Ezekiel's grandpa, actually lived through the Great Depression. When we were kids, he used to tell us stories of how he and thousands of others would never have lived through that time without the generosity of strangers. And so, both he and Ezekiel's father were passionate about showing that grace and generosity to others in times of need. Now that they're both gone, Ezekiel has stepped up to ensure it doesn't get shut down. And it won't," Sara finished emphatically, hoping she'd come off less like a scolding schoolmarm and more like an enthusiastic friend.

Miranda sat silent; her expression sober. Ezekiel turned to Sara, and she was relieved to see that grateful half-smile again, his eyes warm. Sara felt her heart go out to him and reached under the table to squeeze his hand. It was confronting to have someone close be so dismissive about the mission that had meant so much to his family for so many years.

When Sara's eyes left Ezekiel's and looked around again, she realized the entire table was looking at them with somber faces—except for Miranda, whose cheeks were flushed as she silently sipped from her glass of water and stared at the centerpiece.

"I'm so sorry, Miranda," Ezekiel whispered as he leaned toward her. "Somehow, I thought you knew the history." He thought she had seen his father's plaque on the bench seat in the courtyard at the shelter, but it occurred to him now—too late—that he must never have shared the story behind it. The table was still awkwardly silent.

"Excuse me," Miranda said, pushing her chair back from the table and throwing her napkin on the table with a flourish. "Where's the bathroom?"

"Let me show you," Ezekiel said. He stood up, and Miranda followed him as he walked down the hallway. Sara strained to hear the whispering between them but was unsuccessful. Gratefully she heard another guest changing the subject and joined the chatter.

A few minutes later, Sara cleared her throat as Miranda and Ezekiel returned and sat down once more. She picked up her glass and raised it.

"Let's have a toast! I'm so thankful for Jesus, His resurrection from the grave, and the new life He brings to all of us. I am so grateful for family and friends who never gave up on me, even when I made their lives miserable, like Isaiah Cane and you guys. And thank you Teresa for this wonderful food today."

"Hear, hear!" Most of the table echoed, and when Sara turned to Ezekiel, his eyes held so much emotion that Sara couldn't tell if it was gratitude or something else that resembled admiration. She felt heat rise to her cheeks as she quickly turned to face her food.

CHAPTER 4

Since Sara had stood up for him, Ezekiel found himself straining to hear everything she had to say, his eyes drawn to her as she interacted with everyone. There was something different about how she carried herself since the last time he had seen her, and Ezekiel was intrigued. But he was also highly aware of Miranda and eager to put her at ease, especially after the awkward conversation at the dinner table, for which he felt partly responsible. *I should have told her about Dad*, he thought with frustration at himself, determined to make it up to her.

Mildred and Teresa were organizing the desserts in the kitchen, and the rest of the party moved into the living room to sink into the comfortable chairs or lie on the floor. Ezekiel sat on the living room floor, and motioned for Miranda to join him. He put his arm around her, and although she didn't fully relax, at least she didn't stiffen or move away.

Sara sat across from them on a large ottoman. "Whew! I'm relieved we're having a break from the food," Sara said. "I feel like I'm about to burst!"

"Yes, you do have a rather healthy appetite," Ezekiel teased.

"Are you trying to say something?" Sara retorted, smiling and putting her hands on her hips.

"Not at all! It's great to see a woman enjoy her food." Ezekiel smiled widely at her.

"I'm blessed to have a good metabolism," Sara confessed.

"Lucky for some," Miranda scoffed as she scowled and adjusted her skirt. "I have to work hard to keep slim for my work. The camera always adds twenty pounds, you know."

Teresa's elderly neighbor, Jen, piped up from across the room, "I don't worry so much about my weight anymore. I know the pressure that's on you young ones, though. I remember it well."

Miranda cleared her throat. Ezekiel glanced at her, knowing of her battles with eating and image. *Time to change the subject again*, he decided. "Jen!" he chided with a grin, "Of course, you remember it well—I'm sure it wasn't more than a few short years ago that you were the local ballroom star! Would you like to show us some moves?"

Jen sniffed and waved a withered hand at Ezekiel. "Oh, go on, you young egg! But no, I'm happy to sit on the sidelines now." But her rosy-cheeked smile gave away her delight at his comment.

"Tell me more about the shelter, Ezekiel," Jen asked to take the focus off herself again. "What has happened since you took on your new role?"

"Well, he works too hard, and he's wasting his talents," Miranda cut in drily.

"I have to work hard because there's so much to do," Ezekiel retorted. However, he was relieved to see that the awkwardness from earlier seemed to have worn off somewhat.

"Couldn't you delegate some of your work, Ezekiel?" Jen asked.

"Not right now, because we need to do more fundraising, and lately, that hasn't been so successful."

"I am sorry to hear that," Jen said.

"You could ask for more help," Miranda pointed out.

Finally, we agree on something, Sara thought. "I agree," she said aloud and looked affirmingly at Miranda, who nodded in reply. "It's okay to feel overwhelmed and to ask for help," she directed at Ezekiel.

"I'd prefer if we could relax today instead of trying to fix my problems, please," Ezekiel sighed, exasperated now. "I feel I'm pretty capable of sorting things out. And it is a chance to develop new skills."

"Fine," Sara said, shaking her head in exasperation. *Miranda and I are actually on the same page, but he doesn't want us to talk about that! Typical*, she huffed to herself.

"That is just fine, Ezekiel. Maybe we can talk about something else. What is your profession, young lady?" Jen turned and raised her silver eyebrows at Sara.

"Yes, Sara. Tell us about your job. Why *do* you take all your boss's nonsense?"

"Ezekiel!" Jen scolded. Ezekiel shut his eyes the moment he heard himself. He could feel Sara's eyes boring into him.

"Excuse me," Sara coughed. She offered a tight smile, stood up, and walked out of the room as nonchalantly as she could manage.

Ezekiel sighed. He knew he shouldn't have said that, but he didn't understand why she was badgering him in front of everyone and taking sides with Miranda. *So much for pleasant conversation!* he thought with irritation. Now he'd have to apologize to a second woman today.

"Ezekiel, if you're feeling overwhelmed, you should take time off from the shelter," Miranda pointed out. Ezekiel shook his head. Somehow Miranda had missed the cue that they'd moved on from this topic. He gave her a sideways glance.

"I'm not overwhelmed." He stood up. "I'll be right back." He went to look for Sara, stopping by the kitchen to grab her a glass of iced tea. His mom's special iced herbal sun tea had been one of her favorite drinks for years.

He found her in his father's old library. Her back was turned to him, and she was looking at the books on a shelf opposite the door.

"Hey," he said quietly, and she turned around. She didn't look upset; instead, she offered a sheepish smile.

"Hi," she replied, shoving her hands in the pockets of her skirt.

"Hope you don't mind me following you here. Apology offering?" he joked as he walked up to her and gave her the glass. She took it from him, then smiled before taking a sip. They both fell quiet for a moment, just staring at the books in front of them. Ezekiel realized he hadn't actually apologized.

"I'm sorry," he said, and at the same time, she abruptly turned to him and said the same. They laughed, and Ezekiel felt a rush of warmth rise inside him as Sara's flushed and beaming face looked up at his.

"What... happened out there?" Ezekiel asked, genuinely concerned. She looked down, the color in her cheeks deepening, before looking up at him again, a strand of her hair coming loose from her signature bun. Ezekiel reached out instinctively and pushed it behind her ear. Sara's breath caught, then she suddenly seemed to discover the iced tea still in her hand and took a sip.

Ezekiel realized belatedly just how intimate such a gesture could be perceived. "Sorry," he chuckled again, his ears turning red.

Sara gulped and said, "No, I'm sorry. I was picking on you. I just feel like maybe you're not being totally honest with yourself about how you're doing. About the shelter, about wanting to go on that trip. About Miranda, too." She looked genuinely worried as she spoke, and Ezekiel felt his heart warm again.

"I keep telling you, I'm fine. I just need things at the shelter to look up before I focus on other things." He shrugged, trying to dispel her worry, even though he knew deep down that he had, in fact, been doing poorly at balancing all aspects of his life.

A knock on the door interrupted Ezekiel's thoughts. The door opened, and Truman stepped in.

"Hey, Truman," Ezekiel said. "I am so sorry you had to endure our awkward conversations out there."

Truman frowned, "Well, about that, Ezekiel. I believe I can be of some help to you at the shelter."

"Really?" Ezekiel's face registered his surprise. "What did you have in mind?"

"Well, part of my company has money allocated for charitable giving, so a donation for a start, and then maybe I can get some of my team to connect with you for ongoing fundraising?"

"That... sounds absolutely wonderful!" Ezekiel said, his eyes wide.

"Let's connect next week and make a plan. I'd prefer not to talk business on Easter Sunday," Truman said matter-of-factly.

"Sounds fantastic! Sara can share your details with me, and I'll call you," Ezekiel said. "Besides, I'm sure there will be an Easter egg hunt any minute. Can't keep Teresa waiting."

"Even with no children present?" Truman glanced around as if expecting a small child or two to pop out from behind a chair.

"We all have an inner child," Sara grinned and elbowed her cousin playfully. Ezekiel turned to her, watching the light in her eyes. She was so full of life these days.

"Let me check on dessert," Truman said. "I think I may have some more room now." He left the room.

"Well! There goes your excuse for not going on the mission trip, and no doubt other donors will be showing up as well," Sara said. She turned her body to face him fully. "God *does* provide, Ezekiel. It's not a selfish thing to do. Maybe... it will give you another perspective on your life?"

"Actually, you're more right than you know. We also have another expression of interest in regular support from a major donor." Ezekiel shook his head and looked out the window. "Sara, I have important work to do right where I am. I don't think I can leave."

"Ezekiel, surely you can see now that things are lining up for you so you *can* go. So why not go?"

"The shelter—"

"God will take care of the shelter while you're gone. And God has shown you that He is more than capable of doing that." She stepped closer to him and placed a hand on his arm.

Ezekiel watched her face thoughtfully, and the intensity in her eyes as she spoke struck him. "I know more than almost anyone what that shelter means to you. But so does God."

Ezekiel suddenly felt like a fool. Why was he putting up so many obstacles when it was something he really wanted to do, and with God's blessing, as he could see now? "You're right," he said quietly. She smiled again, the bright afternoon light from the nearby windows casting shadows on her face.

"Then go. Take a break and just go." She squeezed his arm a little and turned to leave the room.

"I will go," he said, stopping her in her tracks.

She turned around with a smile. "Good! That's great, Ezekiel."

"But you have to come with me."

Her smile seemed to freeze in place. "What?"

"Come on the mission trip! It would give you time to think, take a break from a toxic work environment, and do something specifically devoted to God. Plus... " He walked towards her. "It'll be one more of our many adventures in our friendship. From undercover investigators to media sensations, and now, arguably the most important adventure we've taken on yet—missionaries! Or missionary helpers, anyway."

She looked confused, and as if she was on the verge of refusing him, but she hesitated. Ezekiel grinned charmingly, seizing the opportunity to try to convince her. The thought had only just struck him, but already he was exhilarated by it. The thought of having a friend along on the journey made it even more appealing.

"Come on, think about it, Sara! I think it would be an awesome time to do something for the Kingdom of God. And to go somewhere in the Pacific Ocean—it's beautiful. Of course, everything in our lives should be building up His Kingdom, but, well, you know what I mean —this is all about serving! And wouldn't it be wonderful to get out of the city?"

"I've never thought about going on a mission trip, but I will pray about it," she said, her tone thoughtful. Ezekiel nodded, sensing a minor victory, and followed her out of the room.

* * *

Later in the evening, when everyone seemed to have eaten their fill of dessert, Ezekiel was sitting in the living room chatting with some of Teresa's guests. Suddenly feeling somewhat guilty, he stood and walked into the kitchen. His mother shouldn't have to do the majority of the cooking *and* all the dishes. What had he been thinking?

He found Miranda already standing by the sink, her gloved hands in soapy water. Ezekiel was impressed at her pluck, knowing it was outside her normal realm to step into the kitchen, let alone in someone else's home. Ezekiel came alongside her and touched her gently on the small of her back, intending to offer her a word of encouragement. Instead, he nearly had his head knocked off. Quick as a whip, she spun around, swinging her elbow in a wide arc so that he had to duck to avoid being slammed.

"Don't," Miranda hissed.

Ezekiel stood to one side and let out sharp breath as wet, soapy suds dripped to the floor from Miranda's shaking hands. He looked into her face, white and pinched with pain and fear. He took a step back, then softly ventured, "That's some reflex you have there, Miranda."

"I... I'm sorry," Miranda said shakily. She dropped her arms and pulled the kitchen gloves from her hands. "I can't do this right now."

"What happened, Miranda?" Ezekiel pressed; his voice gentle.

"A flashback. I—" Her jaw clenched, and tears ran down her face.

Ezekiel's heart sank. "You mean... that professor? Weber?" He reached out to touch her arm as she held her hand to her mouth and nodded, trembling.

Teresa, who was putting leftovers away, shut the fridge door and came toward them.

"I couldn't help but overhear, Miranda," Teresa offered softly. She pulled a tissue from a nearby tissue box and handed it to Miranda.

Miranda dabbed her eyes and blew her nose.

"Would you like to come sit down with me, Miranda?" Teresa asked, putting her arm around the younger woman's limp shoulders and turning her toward the comfortable window seat in the kitchen.

"Did Ezekiel tell you?" Miranda asked defensively, her eyes looking into Teresa's.

"No, he didn't," Teresa reassured her. "But it's easy to see that something terrible has happened to you." She wrapped her other arm around Miranda and pulled her into a motherly embrace. Miranda sobbed, her dark hair falling over Teresa's shoulders.

Ezekiel looked at them both, unsure of what to do. Teresa nodded at him and mouthed, "I've got this." Ezekiel looked questioningly into his mother's eyes. She lifted one hand off Miranda's shoulder to motion him away. He turned then and walked back into the living room; his hands shoved in his pockets. Sitting down on the couch, he distractedly watched the others laughing and joking. He felt a great sense of relief that Miranda had found a confidant in his mother; he knew she would be a positive influence and offer her wise counsel. But he was annoyed at his own sense of uselessness. Could he not get anything right?

CHAPTER 5

$\mathcal{S}$ara knocked on the door to Debra's apartment. She stood checking her emails on her phone as several minutes passed. She knocked on the door again, frowning. Debra had said she would be home when she connected with her the previous day via text. Where was she? Finally, the door opened, and Debra stood there, her eyes on the floor.

"Hi, Debra? Are you okay?" Sara's eyes took in Debra standing before her, her hair askew, greasy, her clothes rumpled, and her eyes red. "Have you been crying?"

"No," Debra said, quickly glancing up at her before turning and walking back into the apartment.

Sara followed her. The curtains were drawn in the living room, and the sink was full of dishes. "Debra, is it happening again—"

"No." Debra whipped around so fast that Sara had to step back. "I've just—I have, um... I've been sick. Yeah, that's all."

It sounded like a lie, but Sara went with it so as not to agitate Debra. She hoped it wasn't what she thought, and if Debra said it wasn't, she wanted to believe her.

'Why don't we clean up around here and get you into bed to rest?"

"No, I'm fine now. I don't want to be in bed."

"Are you sure? We—"

"I have work to do."

Sara frowned. "Already? I thought you were having the week off after the holiday weekend?"

Debra looked around the room as if she was seeing it through Sara's eyes. She pulled her mouth up into a semblance of a smile. "Yeah, I guess there's some work to do around here," she attempted a laugh and walked into her bedroom.

Sara stood in the middle of the room. She wasn't sure whether to push further or believe that Debra was fine. She'd been doing so well, although Sara knew Debra suffered from PTSD.

"Hey, I need your advice," she called out from the living room.

"Oh, yeah?" Debra called back. "What about?"

"I'll tell you once you've had a shower," Sara said. "I'll start on the dishes."

Debra stepped back into the lounge. "You know you don't have to," she said.

"I know," Sara smiled. "But that's what friends are for. Take your time."

"Thanks," Debra whispered, looking like the weight of the world was on her shoulders. She disappeared into the bathroom.

Sara began to collect dishes from the living room and the bedroom, rinsing and stacking them, then placing them in the dishwasher, all the while praying under her breath.

Fifteen minutes later, Debra reappeared wearing fresh clothes, the skin on her face shiny. "That feels better," she said. "Now, what were you wanting to talk about?"

"Don't you want to talk about what's going on with you, Debra?" Sara asked softly.

"No, not really. It will pass; it usually does," Debra said.

"But..." Sara began. Debra raised her hand in protest.

"Tell me what's going on Sara. Honestly, I could use the distraction."

"If you're sure...?" Sara searched Debra's face.

Debra nodded, "I'm sure, but let me get my makeup and you can tell me while I put it on." Sara frowned, watching her as she ran back into the bathroom and returned with her makeup bag. Debra flopped back onto the couch and started smearing some moisturizer on her face. She looked at Sara, "Come on then, spill."

Sara sighed and sat down next to her. "Ezekiel's asked me to go with him on one of the Pacific Outreach medical mission's trips in the Pacific. I'm wondering if I should go?"

"Wow, the Pacific?" Debra paused. "Sounds amazing! Palm trees, warm, blue water, snorkeling—not to mention helping people who really need it, unlike all these entitled clients we get paid far too little to 'serve' here in the city. I say go for it."

"Really?" Sara seemed genuinely surprised at Debra's instant enthusiasm. Immediately, however, her doubts clouded back over her thoughts. "But... it's so far away," Sara pointed out. "And expensive! And how would I ever convince Eleanor to let me go?"

"Take a break from slave-driver Eleanor; it would serve her right. You've been working your tail off for her. Maybe if you have some time off, she might appreciate you for a change. I know you've been saving. Take some time to have some fun; since you never have time for anything fun these days. "

Sara smiled. "It would be pretty amazing," she agreed, then sighed.

"What's the sigh for, Sara?"

"How would I cope with all that time with Ezekiel? I feel like I have just gotten over him and I'm finally sort of settled." Sara bit her lip.

"C'mon, there'll be plenty of other people there as well. It's not exactly a romantic getaway for two!" Debra teased. "And maybe, just maybe...."

"Maybe what?" Sara raised an eyebrow pointedly at her friend.

"Is Miranda going?"

"Not that I know of." Sara scrunched up her face. "Anyway, I hope not," she crossed her arms with a frown.

Debra laughed. "That's so kind of you, Sara."

"I'm not perfect, Debra. I know I need to forgive her, but seriously, she created so much drama for us both!"

"But Ezekiel has forgiven her, hasn't he?"

"Yes, but they have *history*," Sara mimed air quotes. "Secrets I am not allowed to know, and somehow that has helped him to forgive her. But I'll try, and I'll pray about it, I promise."

"Well, that sounds like progress, Sara, even wanting to be willing."

Sara shook her head, "Yeah, yeah."

"Hey, I'd better get going," Debra said, picking up papers and shoving them haphazardly into her tote bag.

Sara watched her. "Come here, Debra." Debra took a step toward her, and Sara pulled her in for a hug. "I love you, Debra, you know that, don't you?"

Debra nodded as she pulled back from the hug, her eyes glistening.

"And I'm here for you, too." Sara insisted, one hand on Debra's arm. "In fact... why don't you come with us, Debra? On the mission trip?!"

Debra looked into Sara's eyes. "Not right now. I'm not in the right space. It's supposed to be a trip to serve others. I'd rather have a vacation."

"Well, what about meeting us afterward for a vacation in the Pacific?" Sara suggested.

"Could you just let it go, please?" Debra huffed, barely hiding the edge in her voice.

"I'm sorry. Of course, I'll let it go. But, is it okay that I drop you off at work?"

Debra nodded. "Sure. That's fine."

"We'll go in my car," Sara said.

* * *

"I can't believe Miranda let you go this weekend," Sara said, pressing her lips into a fine line. "Doesn't she keep you on a tight schedule most weekends—running on the beach, brunch at that coffee shop, shopping downtown? I figured she'd consider a prayer meeting with our moms a colossal waste of time."

"Well, she's not...it's not like that, Sara," Ezekiel shook his head. He glanced at her; her old stubbornness, that cynicism from their youth, though a shadow of what it'd been in the past, was showing through. He knew she didn't like Miranda much after the way she'd grilled him on her television show the year before. "We do see each other most weekends, but she knew I was coming home today."

Sara nodded, but was clearly not satisfied. "So, what does she think about this trip?" she pressed.

"Well, I... we haven't actually talked about it yet," he admitted.

"What? Isn't this kind of an important thing to just forget to mention?" Sara was incredulous.

Ezekiel was silent as he considered his words. "I haven't forgotten to mention it." He sighed. "I just want to know whether I'm actually going before I bring it up with her, I guess. And I wanted to pray with you and our moms about it before deciding."

Sara was silent then, looking out the window as they drove from the airport toward his mother's home.

"Look, I know you still haven't gotten to know Miranda that well, but I hope in time you will, and you'll see, well, more of what I see in her." His voice softened when Sara didn't reply. "Sara, you of all people would know—we all have a story, we've all suffered in some way, and we all need to show each other grace. Hers isn't my story to tell, but I hope you two can eventually see each other more eye-to-eye. I hope in time you can relate to each other."

"Sure," Sara shrugged, and forced a smile. "I promise next time I see her, I'll make more of an effort, okay?"

Ezekiel smiled at her. "Thanks. Don't worry—her bark is worse than her bite!"

Sara snorted in reply as Ezekiel parked the SUV on the side of the road. She hopped out and immediately ran to embrace her mother and his, who were already on the porch, to greet them. His thoughts flashed back to the last time they'd been here on Easter weekend, when he'd stepped out on a limb and asked Sara to join him on the mission trip. Had he made a mistake? What would three weeks on a mission trip with Sara be like—and what *would* Miranda think? Ezekiel shook his head. If they did go, would Miranda support him? And if Sara knew what Miranda had actually lived through, he was sure her irritation would be replaced with sympathy.

Then again... His thoughts flashed back further, and the old familiar ghost of guilt gripped his insides. Would Sara think that he was partly responsible for Miranda's pain? He had always battled regrets over that weekend back in college. He told himself he should have been there to somehow protect Miranda, or at least should have tried harder to dissuade her from going on the trip alone with her professor. The trauma of that weekend was still, to this day, affecting her. He wasn't entirely sure yet how deep his feelings were for Miranda, but he knew one thing—he desperately wanted her to find true healing.

Teresa Cane waved, jolting Ezekiel back to the present, having almost reached the car now where he still sat with his hand on the open door. "What are you sitting out here for? Let's go inside. It's so lovely to have you *home!*" She hugged him as he stepped out of the car to wrap her in a bear hug, then turned to hug Mildred as well. Sara completed the happy circle, smiling as she watched. Her cynicism had melted away in the moments since arriving home.

"You two look so good together," Teresa remarked.

Sara's cheeks turned slightly purple, but she tried to hide her embarrassment with sarcasm. "Yeah, I'm sporting the jet-lagged look, and Ezekiel has definitely got the road-trip chic going with that old polo and yesterday's stubble." She poked his side playfully.

"Don't start, Mom," Ezekiel rolled his eyes. "We're here to pray for guidance about going on the Pacific Outreach ship and ask for your opinion too."

"Come on inside and let me get you some drinks," Teresa said. "Tea? coffee?"

"Just water," Ezekiel and Sara said simultaneously and then laughed. *Whew, that broke the tension,* Ezekiel thought.

Teresa disappeared into the kitchen as the others walked to the living room. She returned with a carafe of water and some glasses. They sat down, and Teresa poured them some water.

"Well, let's not delay. Let's pray, shall we?" Teresa asked. "Lord, thank You that You say to trust You with all our hearts and not to lean on our own understanding. And that You will direct our paths. Sara and Ezekiel want to know Your will, Lord, Your guidance, for Your glory. Lord, please make it plain if they're to go on this mission trip. Lord, we are all confident You'll make it clear."

After a pause, Ezekiel spoke next. "Lord, thank You for this opportunity, but it's a medical mission, and we don't have the relevant skills. Do You really want us to go on this particular trip? Please give us clarity. I have so much work to do at the shelter." Ezekiel finished earnestly.

The four sat there, their heads bowed, waiting on the Lord, each speaking quietly in a special language under their breaths. Long minutes passed in peaceful silence as each one sought to "be still and know the Lord."

"I see a picture of a beach," Teresa said then. "White sand, many palm trees, an inlet-type area. I see Jesus on the beach, surrounded by children. And a pile of planks of wood."

"I wonder what that means?" Ezekiel asked.

"I believe that not only children will be impacted on this trip but also others. Maybe through some sort of building project? I know it's supposed to be a medical mission but God knows the bigger picture. I guess we'll have to wait and see." Teresa shook her head slightly as she pondered what she'd seen in the spirit.

"What skills will be offered on this trip?" Mildred asked.

"Medical, dental, ophthalmology, and occupational therapy. I've been told there's a need for support staff, which is where we would come in, and that all people are welcome. I've offered to help with writing stories for promo, and Sara can help with advertising for the organization. And, of course, any manual labor or other admin tasks that might be needed. We just want to be a blessing if God is in this."

"I feel peaceful about this trip," Mildred said. "I believe in taking steps forward until God either closes the door or makes the path clear. He can always put a stop to it, if it's not the right timing."

"What about the shelter, Mom?" Ezekiel asked.

"A couple of weeks is not going to matter there. I think this would be a breath of fresh air for you, Ezekiel. It may even give you some new insight into how God wants to use you at the shelter when you return. Sometimes taking a step back is the most productive thing you can do. I'll keep in touch with Miranda as well." Ezekiel and Teresa caught each other's eye.

"Thanks, Mom," Ezekiel said. "You're amazing. I'm so grateful for you." He paused, then looked at Sara. "What about you, Sara? Is your boss okay with you taking time off? I know how demanding she can be."

"Yes, I've tentatively put in for time off. Believe it or not, Eleanor is actually away for most of that time, and as it turns out, she didn't want me working without her, so I think it will be fine. It seems incredible, to be honest, as I'm not due for vacation time right now, but I'll take it. I've been working so hard, and I really want to do this," Sara said, looking around at them.

"This trip isn't a vacation. You know that, though, don't you?" Teresa eyed Sara with a grin.

"Yes, but we can have a few days off afterward to explore the islands, and as you know, I've asked Debra if she'd like to come as well. She's been going through some really rough things lately, so I'd love her to come. But she said no. I'm praying she'll change her mind, though."

"Well, it certainly sounds like all is falling into line for you two to go," Mildred said.

"We still need to have our memorial service for Dad, too, Mom," Sara said gently.

Teresa placed her hand on Mildred's. "It took two years for me to feel anything like normal after Isaiah died," Teresa said.

"It's early yet," Mildred said, her voice catching. "With your injury, Sara, it's all been too much for me to really process."

"We don't need to do anything major, Mom. Just something simple for us."

"I'm not quite ready yet, Sara, but I promise we will do something." Mildred retracted her hand and rummaged in her bag to find a hand-kerchief to dab at the tears welling in her eyes.

"I think this trip would be really positive for us, Sara. I say we go," Ezekiel said.

"Well, that's certainly a change from the flip-flopping attitude you've been showing, Ezekiel," Sara said, turning to look at him.

"I feel peace about it, Sara," he continued, "Like... like we are actually meant to do this."

"Let's do it, then," Sara agreed with a grin. "But, can we pray for Debra now, please?"

They bowed their heads again and prayed for Debra, the shelter, and everyone and everything involved. Sara was so emotional and eloquent in her plea for Debra that Ezekiel opened his eyes to look at her. He was struck again by the sight of her as she prayed. He thought she was beautiful inside and out in spite of her stubbornness at times. He knew God could use that stubbornness to achieve His purposes if she'd allow Him to. He chuckled quietly at the thought of how that might play out.

CHAPTER 6

The following Saturday, Ezekiel breathed hard as sweat ran down his temples, grateful for the ocean breezes blowing up along the sand as he and Miranda ran. "Whew," he exclaimed, determined to keep pace with her. "One week off, and I'm already outta shape," he panted. "Good thing the water's not too cold for a swim this time of year. I'm going in as soon as we're done!"

"I was going to suggest we do another lap!" Miranda feigned seriousness, then laughed at his outraged reaction. She was hardly winded after 45 minutes of running up and down the beach. "Well, okay, lightweight. I guess we can call it a day when we reach the pier again. But no more skipping runs for you! I'm gonna leave you in the dust otherwise!"

They jogged to a stop near the pier and picked up their water bottles from where they'd left them. Taking a drink and waiting to catch his breath, Ezekiel looked at Miranda thoughtfully.

She swallowed and gave him a coy look. "What is it?" she asked him, one eyebrow raised.

"Just thinking. You definitely look good in running gear, but I would love to see you dressed up in something nice. Can I take you out to dinner tonight?" he asked with a grin.

She beamed back at him, her face flushed after their run and wisps of her long dark hair blowing around her face. He actually preferred this casual, natural look to the made-up fashionista version of Miranda that she wore most days. But he wanted to treat her to a night out so he could bring up the topic of the mission trip, and the fact that he'd be gone for three weeks—with Sara.

"Well, lucky for you, I just happen to be free this evening, so I'll take you up on that," she teased.

"Excellent! Now, want to join me for a swim?"

"I'll pass, thanks. Salt water makes my hair frizzy." She scrunched her nose up at the thought, and Ezekiel laughed.

"Okay, solo swim it is. Are we getting brunch at The Hive today?"

"Well, if we're going out tonight, maybe we should skip it?" she considered aloud. "I have some work I need to finish this weekend." She tapped on her phone. "Hm... yes, why don't we just enjoy a nice evening together tonight, okay?"

Ezekiel feigned a mournful frown. "I can take a hint; I know when I'm not wanted!"

She rolled her eyes and leaned against his chest. "Ugh, c'mon, Ezekiel. You know I have a really important interview coming up next week. I just need to be sure I'm well prepared."

"Kidding! It's fine," he said, and wrapped a sweaty arm around her shoulders. "How about you just get ready tonight, and I'll pick you up in my car around 7 and we can go from there?"

"That's good. Just remember—I need plant-based and organic, okay?"

"Right. Carl's Junior, not an option. Subway has salads—would that work?" he joked.

She laughed and punched him playfully in the stomach. "Go on. I'll see you tonight."

"Awesome. I'm looking forward to it. See you then," he said, and kissed her on the cheek before turning and jogging into the surf.

* * *

"I'll have the plant bowl, please, and..." Miranda paused as she turned to the beverage menu. "And the pomegranate mocktail as well, thanks." She passed the menu back to the young man in a white shirt and pants, long black apron, and black Vans.

"No problem," he said with a casual smile. "And for you, sir?" He looked at Ezekiel.

"Can I get an order of that sourdough bread and then the lamb kabobs, please?"

"Of course," replied the server. "Anything to drink?"

"Hm," Ezekiel mused over the menu. "How about an iced tea? Do you have that?"

"Yes, iced tea it is." He took Ezekiel's menu and smiled again. "I'll be right back with your drinks."

Ezekiel nodded as the server left the table, then turned and smiled at Miranda. Her hair was elegantly arranged in long, wavy chunks around her face, and her long earrings sparkled as they caught reflections from the strings of fairy lights that decorated the patio section of the restaurant.

"Nice dress," he nodded, with a teasing understatement. Miranda wore an ankle-length deep pink wrap dress with flowing ruffles that fell flatteringly around her slender shoulders and draped over her tanned knees. She was stunning, no less so as the color of her dress contrasted with the pale marble table-top, black napkins, and white sofas on the patio.

"This old thing?" She waved her hand dismissively, but grinned at him, her eyes sparkling. "It's obviously last season, but I thought the color was still acceptable, and I haven't had a chance to shop the new season sales yet."

"I give it a 10/10. Definitely a keeper," he said, keeping his eyes on hers.

"Well, you clean up pretty well yourself," she lifted her chin pertly as she spoke, eyeing the deep blue suit jacket that nearly matched his eyes over crisp white button-down shirt and pale trousers. "Not bad for a guy who spends most of his time helping the homeless."

"Thanks," he said. "Can't take a gorgeous girl out on the town in my work clothes."

Their server returned and set down their drinks and a plate of crusty bread with a large dollop of butter and some fresh herbs. "Please let me know if I can get you anything else. Otherwise, your orders should be ready in about fifteen minutes," he said with a smile before leaving them alone.

They continued to talk and enjoy the warm late summer evening together. Ezekiel couldn't help noticing the admiring glances of others at tables nearby; he was definitely dining with the most attractive woman in the restaurant, and despite it being an upscale LA spot, people still stared at the two minor celebrities as they ate and laughed. Miranda's dark eyes flashed whenever she spoke about her work, and she listened intently when he told her stories of his past work during the years they'd spent apart.

As Ezekiel paused to sip his iced tea, Miranda suddenly noticed the song playing from the restaurant sound system. "Wow, I haven't heard this song in years! It must be 90s night," she remarked, then sang along effortlessly with the chorus. "Just call my na-a-a-a-ame and I'll be there!"

"Oh wow, is that Mariah Carey?" Ezekiel chuckled. "Yeah, that brings back some memories. I'm picturing you, a karaoke restaurant, and me, the designated driver."

She laughed. "Of course. Weren't you the default designated driver in those days?"

"Yeah, I guess I was 'the boring one,' huh?" he shrugged.

"I never thought of you as boring, Ezekiel," she said, her face serious. "You've always been one of the truest, kindest, most interesting friends I've ever had." She looked down at her plate thoughtfully, then back at his face. "I think that's why I was so intent on knowing the truth about your job in New York with Sara. I didn't want to think of you as having sunk to become some sleazy, selfish, blackmailing womanizer. I had to know what really happened. And I'm glad to know now that you never changed. You're still the same great guy." She looked at him meaningfully.

Ezekiel smiled, grateful. "You know, hearing you sing again reminds me, you have a real gift. Whatever happened with you and music? We haven't really talked about it, but do you ever sing anymore?"

She shrugged. "Ha, only if you count singing in the shower or in the car on my way to work. I'm just far too busy. But I do love singing. It was really nice singing in church with you at Easter," she admitted, "Although I didn't know most of the songs."

"You know I'd love it if you came with me to church more often, Miranda. My offer is always open. I think you'd find it really welcoming at Real Life LA; they're so down-to-earth, and most of them are in TV and film, like you. You'd probably end up knowing a few people there, in fact."

"That's my hesitation," she retorted. "I probably would, and you know me. I like to keep my private life *private*. I'm more into doing things solo or behind the scenes. It's why I love volunteering at the crisis center, because I can just answer the phone and be anonymous, and talk those women through things without even revealing who I am."

He nodded. "I get it. But don't you feel that sense of longing sometimes? For something... more?"

She gazed at him a moment before answering. "Yes," she said simply. "But I guess I don't often stop long enough to pay attention to it."

"Tell me about it," he teased. "You're not one to sit still for long. Well, as I've said, I would really love to have you join me one Sunday, or maybe a Wednesday night Bible study if you'd like a smaller group better? Either way, the invitation stands."

"Thanks," she said sincerely. "I'll keep it in mind."

Ezekiel took a deep breath. "Hey, on that topic... of feeling like there's something more? I wanted to tell you something kind of big, actually."

"Oh?" She eyed him with a raised eyebrow, her cheeks coloring. She put her glass down and laid her hands in her lap expectantly.

"A few months ago, I heard about this organization called Pacific Outreach Missions, and the work they do sailing around to remote islands offering free medical, dental, and other services to the people who live there and who usually don't have access to that level of care. Most are either very poor or live too far from anywhere with the skills and equipment needed to meet their needs, but often simple procedures that we take for granted can actually save their lives." His face lit up as he spoke.

"Okay?" Miranda questioned, clearly taken aback at the unexpected topic, and not knowing what any of this had to do with Ezekiel.

"Well... I can't exactly explain it, but I felt somehow that God was calling me, or maybe prompting me, to look into going on one of their ships to help serve those people."

Miranda responded with another raised eyebrow. "But, you're not a dentist or a doctor. What would you do?"

"Exactly. I was a little surprised at the prompting to get involved, too, what could I possibly offer? But the reality is that they need all kinds of people on these ships to help support the work of the medical and dental volunteers. Basically, they need grunt workers who are willing to serve in any capacity. I can do that!"

Miranda frowned. "So... you're leaving the shelter now? But not to go back to journalism? Instead, you're planning to become a deck swabber on some sailing hospital in the Pacific? I'm sorry," she shook her head, "I don't get it."

"No, no—I'm not leaving the shelter. It's just a three-week trip. At first, it felt like an impossibility to be gone for even that long, but I went home last weekend to pray with my mom about it, and I also prayed with my pastor about it. I have to say; I am pretty excited about it now. I am really looking forward to—well, whatever it is they give me to do. I just feel drawn to go."

Miranda seemed unruffled by his enthusiasm, but he was relieved that she didn't seem upset either. She sighed and picked up her glass again. "Okay. So, when do you sail?"

"It's still a few months away. We have to raise some financial support to help cover our airfare costs and contribute to the operating costs of the ship and everything. Plus, they time the trip for the best time of the year in terms of the weather—it wouldn't do us much good to get caught in a cyclone." He smiled, clearly excited to share this with her. "I'd wanted to talk with you about it before now, but we've both been so busy, and I didn't know until this past weekend that it was actually a real possibility. It's great to be able to share it with you now."

"Well, it sounds... fascinating. Right up your alley, I guess." She took a sip of her drink and then tilted her head at him. "Wait, you said 'we' need to raise funds? Who is 'we?' Are there a lot of people from your church going, too?"

"No, just me from my church. But that's the other thing I wanted you to know about. You know Sara Ward, obviously. She has decided to go on the outreach as well."

Miranda spluttered and nearly choked at that moment; she grabbed her napkin and carefully dabbed at her nose and eyes, coughing to clear her airway.

"Are you okay?" Ezekiel asked, reaching across the table to touch her arm.

"Fine," she replied. She looked at him with a level gaze. "I'm sorry, did you just say that you're planning to spend three weeks on a Pacific island cruise with Sara Ward? Did she plan this, or did you?"

Ezekiel sat back and looked at Miranda for a moment, unsure of how to respond. The edge in her voice made it clear this part of the plan didn't please her. He had expected it would annoy her, but her reaction seemed to exceed mere annoyance. *Honesty is the best policy*, he told himself.

"Well, first of all, it is definitely not a 'cruise.' It's a service ship full of dentists and doctors and other support staff who are going to help the poorest people in the Pacific with life-saving treatments and anything else we can offer them over the course of a couple of weeks. We won't be sitting around in swimsuits sipping cocktails under the palm trees."

Miranda didn't answer, but crossed her arms, as if she dared him to continue.

"And I told Sara about it during one of our regular calls a while ago, and she's been encouraging me to go. And then at Easter, the subject came up again, and I sort of challenged her to go, too. She has this high-powered PR job in New York with a brutal boss and no time off, and...."

Miranda put her hands up and said, "Enough."

Ezekiel frowned, but waited for her to speak.

Folding her hands on the table in front of her and pursing her lips, she looked at him with those dark brown eyes, moments ago full of admiration, and now—was it disapproval? "For a man as insightful and experienced as you are in the world of undercover investigation and exposing deep, dark secrets, Ezekiel Cane, you seem to have some rather large blinders applied when it comes to your own personal life," she said shrewdly.

"What exactly do you mean by that, Miranda?" he responded softly. He felt somewhat cornered now, but knew that staying calm and listening to her couldn't hurt.

She rolled her eyes and gave him a pitying look. "Look, I know you and I have been taking things slowly. I'm busy, you're ridiculously busy, and we wanted to give ourselves a chance to get to know one another again in our new lives. It's been wonderful." She paused.

Ezekiel could tell she was sincere, so he ventured a response. "I agree, Miranda. It's been—exhilarating reconnecting with you over the past few months."

She looked into his eyes again, almost as if she were searching for something there. "But all along, I've had to ask myself: can I *really* trust this man? Yes, you are an honest man, Ezekiel. A good man. I know, from everything in the past and over the last year as well; you are an honorable man. God knows I need that kind of person in my life."

He smiled at her, and reached across the table to grasp her hand.

"But Ezekiel, I don't know if you are really being honest with *your-self*. You tell me you're attracted to me and want to spend time with me, I am important to you, and so on... but you can't let go of Sara Ward. And now you tell me you've asked her to fly off into the Pacific sunset to serve the poor with you? Seriously, Ezekiel, can you *not* see how mixed up this is?"

Ezekiel frowned and released Miranda's hand. He leaned back in his chair, looking around them and suddenly realizing they were the only diners still seated on the patio. He inhaled sharply and suddenly felt tired. What could he say that would convince her?

"I don't know, Ezekiel," she shook her head. "If you can't see this clearly yourself, maybe I just need to help make things plain for you." She took a deep breath and leveled her gaze at him. "Look, if you really want to be with me, I am on board. I think we have the potential of a great future together. And I don't see a problem with you serving the poor on some boat in the Pacific. In fact, if it helps you extract yourself from the shelter to any degree, I say that's a fantastic thing. But know this: you can't have me *and* Sara Ward. You have to choose." In a rare moment of vulnerability, Miranda's eyes fluttered down to rest on the table between them as she spoke again. "I hope you choose us. But I won't hang around if your heart belongs to someone else, Ezekiel. I just can't do that. I'm sorry."

Ezekiel was silent at the weight of Miranda's confession, his heart heavy with emotion. He reached out then to take both of Miranda's hands in his, the familiar sense of protectiveness welling up in him. "Miranda, I'm here—with you. Sara Ward is an old friend, a fellow Christian who prays with me about things, and yes, a one-time romantic interest of mine. But that was in the past. She made it clear that she only wanted to be friends when we were traveling together, and we have both long since moved on. She knows, and I know, that you and I are together now, and I agree with you: I want to find out what our future might hold." He reached up and gently cupped her chin in his hand, searching her eyes.

Miranda's eyes glistened, and she smiled at him then, relaxing into his touch. "Me too," she said quietly.

CHAPTER 7

Sara removed the seatbelt from her middle, and shuffled uncomfortably in the hard, narrow economy class seat. She breathed in and out slowly as the exhaustion threatened to overwhelm her. "Why did we not have a stopover?" Sara asked again, rubbing her face in her hands, her eyes gritty, as her feet twitched, ready to walk.

"To save money, remember?" Ezekiel replied sleepily. "It'll all be worth it."

"I hope you're right," Sara yawned.

At last, she was able to stand up and move towards the front of the plane. As they walked down the stairwell into the Port Vila airport, a wave of heat hit them. *And this is winter?* Sara thought. It was a long way to come and it involved considerable expense but she believed it would be worth every penny. Sara still wanted Debra to come, although she knew it was a long way for a short vacation. Debra had said no, more than once, but Sara hoped she would change her mind at the last minute. It was a long shot, of course, especially because airfares were so much higher for last-minute trips.

Sara and Ezekiel had managed to get reasonable airfares, although both of their savings took quite a hit. They were also massively encouraged by the enthusiastic sponsorship their old church provided after their mothers decided to do a fundraising effort for them both. With only a day to spare before the final portion of the funds was due, every last penny had seemed to materialize out of nowhere in the form of many unexpected and random gifts. Even Miranda had chosen to contribute, and rather generously, to Sara's surprise.

As they made their way through customs, they saw a couple waiting on the other side, holding a handwritten sign with their names on it.

They walked over, carrying their backpacks.

"Hi, we're Sara and Ezekiel," Ezekiel began, extending his hand.

"Welcome," a tall slim man with an American accent said, "I'm Jarryn. Great to have you with us. And this is Annie. We're on the Pacific Outreach permanent staff. Let's get going. You must be exhausted."

Sara nodded, and Ezekiel sighed, "You've got that right."

"Don't worry, you'll have time to get over the jetlag before we sail."

"Let's go," Annie said. Sara couldn't quite place Annie's accent. Australian? New Zealand? British? She assumed they'd all share their stories once they'd settled in.

They walked outside and along to a van parked under a palm tree. Jarryn pulled open the rear door, took their packs, and placed them inside.

"So good to have you with us. We were needing extra support people. Have you thought about what you'd like to help out with? We need people for the dental team, assistants, and help with getting people to and from the boat. We also need support for the medical team." Jarryn chuckled as both Ezekiel and Sara stifled yawns at the same time. "Don't worry, we can discuss it later, as we have a few more volunteers to come. I am excited to say that we have a full team of medical personnel lined up: doctors, two dentists, a hygienist, a physiotherapist, and an occupational therapist, as well as an optometrist."

Sara rubbed her eyes. Good thing she'd made the decision to forego makeup while on the trip. She'd be looking something like a raccoon about now had she applied it. Ezekiel leaned back and rested his head against the headrest as he struggled to keep his eyes open.

"Please excuse Jarryn; he talks too much. Let's get you fed, and then you can rest if you like. He's just so glad that you're here. We've been following your work, Ezekiel, and have seen some of your more recent interviews on YouTube."

"Oh no," Ezekiel moaned. "I'm so bad at interviews."

"At least he'll have kept you entertained," Sara said with a grin.

Ezekiel punched her softly. "Thanks very much." He shook his head. Sara laughed.

"So sorry, I am too tired to have a sense of humor right now," Ezekiel yawned again.

They drove into town, and Sara found her eyes kept closing against her will. Annie was providing a running commentary as they drove along the main road into the city front, her voice almost too soothing. They passed a group of men without shoes working in concrete. Sara poked Ezekiel in the ribs and pointed out the window.

"What, really?" his eyes widened at the sight. "Surely that can't be good for you." They bumped over some large potholes as they pulled into a parking lot and stopped.

"This is us," Jarryn announced.

Sara nodded, then looked around and followed Ezekiel as he exited the van. Jarryn opened the rear door and they grabbed their packs. "This is sort of like a bus stop, but instead it's where we catch the tender boat that will transport us to the ship."

They sat down on a bench seat and watched people milling around. A stench hit Sara's nose and she held her breath, then stood and moved away. As she turned around, she realized the source of the putrid odor was from a pile of trash overflowing from the rusty bin stationed nearby.

It wasn't long before a small runabout boat arrived and Jarryn indicated that this was their ride. They stood and walked towards the edge of the concrete, passing their packs over to the man inside, who was introduced as Andy. Once they had all seated themselves carefully in the boat, Andy turned the throttle, and the boat rushed over the sea out to the old white fishing vessel they could see anchored in the bay. Angling the boat so it was close to a ladder positioned on the side of the ship, Andy began hoisting the bags up first. Sara watched as her pack was passed up to someone standing on the deck. She could just imagine the pack splashing into the sea below with all her belongings soaked, or even disappearing completely into the depths of the harbor. Suddenly before she knew it, she was on board with the others and listening as yet another crew member explained the protocol of signing in and out of the boat, so they knew where everyone on the team was at all times.

Everyone was all smiles as they welcomed them both onto the boat. Sara followed a young woman, Hayley, who chattily pointed out where everything was located as they walked: dining area, toilets and showers, cabins. She led Sara below deck to her cabin, and as Sara pushed her backpack into a cupboard inside the tiny cabin, Hayley finished off her orientation speech with an invitation.

"Dinner's at 6pm, so you can do whatever you like until then. We may be allowed to swim off the boat soon if you feel like a dip?"

"That sounds amazing, but as tired as I am, it might not be safe just yet. I think I'll read my book for a while, assuming I can stay awake to do so," Sara smiled back and stifled yet another yawn.

Hayley nodded. "They'll ring a bell for dinner, so if I don't see you before that, I'll catch up with you at dinner time."

Sara smiled again. "Thanks, see you then." She wondered where Ezekiel would be right now, somewhere else in a cabin exclusively for men. She knew that much. She'd see him later.

As Sara lay down to read, her eyelids would not stay open, and she gave in, knowing that it may not be the best thing to sleep as she wouldn't adjust to the time zone change as quickly. It'd be better if she stayed awake, but the urge to rest overwhelmed her.

A couple of hours later, she was awakened by the dinner bell and made her way back to the main area set up with dining tables. She joined the food line and started up a conversation with a dentist who was from California, who in turn introduced her to a dentist from New Zealand and an assistant also, from Malaysia. Sara sat down with her food on a bench seat and began to eat as she listened to their stories and what had brought them to Vanuatu. She was in awe of some of the people's commitment to be here, such as the cook who'd been on the ship for many months now, and others who would stay on longer term at the Pacific Outreach center based in Port Vila.

The volume of conversation was high, and Sara rubbed her temples, which she suddenly realized were throbbing in pain. The excitement of arriving and meeting everyone and discovering the new location had distracted her till now, but she knew she'd need to go back to sleep soon with a headache like this. She saw a familiar hand touch her arm and turned to look at Ezekiel, who had stopped by her table.

"Do you want to have your dessert on the deck with me, Sara? I saw a table at the stern of the boat where we could go?"

"Sounds good to me," Sara agreed, and they stood and lined up to get their dessert before walking around the side of the boat, watching as the waves lapped gently against the ship.

They set their plates on the wooden round table and sat down. "Are you okay, Sara? I know that plane flight was grueling," he asked.

Sara inhaled the salty air, grateful for the relative peace on deck, and thought for a moment. "There are so many amazing people here. I feel as if I'm part of a special moment in time."

Ezekiel nodded. "Yeah... I'm sure you're right, although..." his voice trailed off as he looked at the water.

"What is it? Are you having second thoughts about coming?" She chuckled softly. "Not that you have much choice in the matter now, unless you know someone with a private yacht?"

He snorted in reply. "No, I didn't come all this way to back out now. It's not about this trip, but I guess after coming all this way and seeing all these amazing dedicated people here—I just feel like I'm... waiting. Waiting for my life to really start."

Sara frowned and tilted her head quizzically. "Waiting for what, exactly?"

"For God to show me what my purpose is... or rather, what *His* purpose for my life is. I almost feel like I'm getting in His way sometimes."

"Yeah, I think I know what you mean. I haven't been enjoying my job as much as I thought I would. But I know that God led me back to New York and provided that job, so if I just keep doing my best and trusting Him, then He will promote me at the right time, or take me somewhere else. Then again, I sometimes struggle with this stage of my life—it *is* kind of like a waiting period as you said, but I'm not exactly sure what I'm waiting *for*. I'm not where I want to be forever, but it's not like I'm in a horrible place either, so I guess I'll just wait it out. You know?"

"I know. Trust me, I do. I'm waiting for God to show me the next steps in my life, too. Sometimes I think that everything should be perfectly lined up, but it is never that way."

"Exactly. And it's not just about work. It's wanting to deepen my relationship with God, and also trying to know His peace in my life. I feel like I have no time for anything extra. And I'm always too tired. So, I tell myself *tomorrow I'll start eating healthily. Tomorrow I'll pray more. Tomorrow I'll ask God for direction. Tomorrow I'll really think about my career*. And before I know it, another week has passed and 'tomorrow' never happened."

Sara had been looking out over the waves and gesturing with her hands as she spoke. As she finished, she turned to face Ezekiel once more, and found him gazing at her intently. The deep sense of longing she felt seemed to be mirrored in his expression, and their eyes locked briefly before he spoke again.

"I don't know what to say, except that I totally get it. It's hard. When I decide that today is going to be the day to start whatever I believe I should be doing, but then nothing changes—man, the guilt can be intense. It's not a good experience. You know?" he said.

Sara nodded. Something in her questioned her next move, but in the moment, she felt such a strong connection that she ignored it and laid her hand on top of his with a smile. She was sure he tensed at her touch, but then he relaxed and smiled back at her naturally.

"So, what does one do? With that struggle?" she asked.

"I don't know what *one* does, but I know what a believer, someone who's a 'Jesus disciple' does."

His voice was quieter now, and in spite of herself, Sara relished the sense of intimacy they shared. It also occurred to her that maybe he was just quiet because he was exhausted from their journey too. She nodded for him to continue.

"A believer prays, and gets up again, tries again as he or she receives ability and strength from God. More and more, our lives will model Jesus's life as we follow Him. And as we commit our way to Him today, I believe that He'll help us with whatever the next steps are. So, yeah... we keep waiting, but keep working, too."

Sara pondered his words for a moment, then she sighed, and looked up at him.

"You are very good for me," she said, as her shoulders slumped and she leaned lightly against his arm, grateful for a close friend who was also someone she could share her faith with.

"And you for me," he responded, nudging her arm in return. "And I know on this trip we're going to experience some amazing times. God will speak to us."

She squeezed his hand, then pulled hers away and took a deep breath as they sat silently looking across the sea. Everything would be okay, no matter how challenging. She looked at the ocean surrounding them and the beauty of Ifira Island nearby with its quaint little thatch huts. She thought of the people they were here to serve and wondered what they would be like, hoping that they would get to see the depth of their real lives, rather than just a tourist's view. *Thanks again, God. For Ezekiel, and for this.*

CHAPTER 8

For the next two days, they remained anchored in Port Vila and had the chance to get to know their fellow volunteers. A constant hum of conversation filled the main living area, as people shared their life stories and journeys to date. There were people from all walks of life as although it was a Christian missionary organization; anyone who had a heart to serve people freely was welcome to volunteer. More and more people arrived on the ship and settled into cabins, and Jarryn led discussions about where each person would help out.

They also learned more about the local Ni-Van people. The native people of Vanuatu were ninety percent Christian, and although they had virtually nothing in the way of material things, they were a people filled with joy and gratitude. The team learned their destination was a village on the west side of Santo Island, where a conference would be held, and there'd be many people gathering who needed help of various kinds. Scouts had gone out beforehand to let the people know that the Pacific Outreach ship was arriving with the offer of free services to anyone who had a medical, visual, occupational rehab or dental need.

On the afternoon of the third day, Ezekiel and Sara caught the tender back to the Port Vila harbor with a couple of the other volunteers and wandered through the local market as well as along the shorefront. A local man showed them his pet iguana and asked for money as Sara took a photo. "Debra won't believe this," she laughed and showed the man the image on her pocket-sized digital camera.

Walking further along, Ezekiel suddenly touched Sara's elbow and pointed toward a group of children playing soccer on the sand. "Look at their ball. Can you see what it is?"

She looked for several seconds before it dawned on her that the cluster of boys wasn't actually kicking around a real soccer ball, but instead, a tightly-wound wad of strips of cloth and plastic material, held together with strings. Her mouth dropped open, amazed at their ingenuity and skill with even such basic resources. "I'm pretty sure we had at least a couple of deflated soccer balls in our stash, right?" she asked. Ezekiel nodded with a grin.

Sara's cousin Truman had donated a suitcase full of toys, and they had the privilege of dividing them up among the teams, who would distribute them to the children when they started their outreach. Ezekiel couldn't wait to start. Only two more days to go.

Later on the ship, Ezekiel lay on his bunk bed in his room below the deck. Holding his Bible, he read through 1 Timothy. After his conversation with Sara the night before, he was determined to spend more time reading the word and focusing on the Holy Spirit within. He wanted to know a connection with God in a tangible way. He needed His strength and grace. Paul was always a great example of that in the Bible. Ezekiel marveled as Paul encouraged Timothy, who was a free man, from his jail cell—a cell that would be unrecognizable by today's standards, yet Paul was at peace and able to worship and praise the Lord in spite of his circumstances. Timothy was the one who needed reminding not to be fearful, with the familiar words, "God has not given us a Spirit of fear but of power, love and a sound mind." Something definitely to aspire to. The bell that rang for dinner took him away from his imaginings of the challenges of the early church, and back to present reality.

He met Sara on his way to the main dining area, and smiled. Her long, thick, auburn hair was down, and she looked refreshed and free, her green eyes sparkling. Ezekiel was so grateful they had found a semblance of peace after all they had been through together.

"Hungry?" Sara asked.

"Yes. And I feel pretty spoiled; here we are to serve people in poverty, and we're still being served ourselves all this amazing food?"

Ezekiel inhaled the scent of a hot cooked meal wafting out from the galley.

"Yes, we're very spoiled, although apparently, even with the wonderful food here, Andy ended up with some sort of intestinal bug. He has lost a lot of weight, unfortunately."

"I'm amazed at the long-term mission workers here, their sacrifice, and that they've managed to get funding for such a lengthy term. I salute them."

"Yeah, totally. I feel like what we offer just being here for such a short time is like a drop of water in the ocean. But hopefully, it will still help, even if just a little?" Sara replied.

"Hey," Abbie, the American dentist, interjected from her place behind them in the food line. "Sorry to jump in, but I hear what you're saying, and I want to encourage you: what you do here has great value. Remember, Jesus came for the *one* person, and making a difference to just *one* person is invaluable. The need here is so massive, and some of the infections we help with here, actually save people's lives. You don't tend to see the same problems in the West. I heard you two are going to support the dental team?"

"Yes, we'll be on the dental team. I feel a little nervous because it's not something I've done before. Will I be a help or a hindrance?" Sara wondered with a nervous chuckle.

"A dentist can't work without an assistant, Sara, and your help will be most appreciated," Abbie insisted. "Without an assistant, the dentist can't see. The suction units on this ship aren't the most... *ideal*, so you will definitely be busy suctioning." She laughed.

"Even if I'm slow?" Sara persisted.

"It doesn't matter," Abbie continued. "We do what we can with what we have."

Ezekiel frowned. He wasn't convinced. "Surely anyone can take blood pressure and medical histories, right? I think that's what I was signed up to do?"

"Just you wait, Ezekiel. The job of taking blood pressure and medical histories all helps and saves me time, so I can get to the real work, and you can check on their well-being after any procedures. Plus, it's a chance for you to connect with the patients, help them feel at ease, and most importantly, maybe get a sense of how to pray for each one. You'll see, it's going to be great. Plus, one bonus! In the dental room, we have air conditioning. The doctors will be so jealous. They get so hot on the shore."

They carried their plates into the dining room, and Jarryn smiled at them. "You're both looking better today, Sara and Ezekiel. I hope you've had a restful day."

"Yeah, it was wonderful, thanks," Sara replied.

"Time for grace," Jarryn said and raised his voice. "Lord, I thank you for our wonderful volunteers who have traveled from all around the world. Thank you, Lord, that they arrived here safely. Lord, I ask that on this trip that You keep us and the people we serve safe. Help us to be Your hands and feet, and to minister to those in need. Lead us to make the right decisions for the health of these people. Give us special discernment in any confusing situations. Lord, thank You for the sailing tonight. We ask that Your hand be on all things and that the preparation we've done will have been all we need to have a successful sailing. Thank you for Your provision. Bless those hands that prepared this food and bless it to our bodies, in Jesus' name I pray, Amen."

"Amen," echoed from around the room.

"After dinner, as we get ready to sail, no one will be allowed on deck. We'll sound the bell again when we're leaving."

After dinner, as promised, the bell sounded, and the hatches that opened to the decks were shut. The ship began the long sail to Santo Island, and the rolling began. Many of the volunteers went to their cabins to attempt to sleep. Whereas Ezekiel seemed to thrive on the motion, and he stayed out in the lounge chatting to the few that remained, Sara said goodnight and retired to her cabin.

"Goodnight, Sara. Hey, God bless you as you sleep!" Ezekiel smiled up at her as she stood to leave.

Sara frowned, her face pale, and nodded weakly.

Ezekiel smiled then at Abbie, who sat beside him. "I love experiencing the sea like this!" He walked over to look out to the waves through one of the portholes.

"Yeah, I do, too," Abbie said. "I feel fully alive."

"Ugh... me, not so much," Sara said. "Goodnight, guys!"

CHAPTER 9

Two mornings later, they were anchored and ready to go. The team sat in the living area, dressed in green scrubs and green Pacific Outreach t-shirts. A sense of anticipation and excitement was palpable in the room.

Sara watched the others sing as she sang quietly. She wasn't overly confident in her voice, although she knew that the Lord accepted her worship, even if she did sound a little like a croaking frog. She watched as Abbie played her guitar and sang, her voice strong and clear. *Is there nothing this woman can't do?* she thought with a twinge of envy. Abbie, as it turned out, was the head of the dental team. Sara watched Ezekiel smile at Abbie as the song finished, and fought to ignore the envious thoughts nagging her.

"Thank you, Abbie," Jarryn said as he moved to the front of the group. "Such an anointed song." He smiled. "Thanks, once again, to everyone who has come to join us on this trip. If you have any concerns today, Anthea, the chef, is available to answer questions. She has the first aid gear, and we have the defibrillator in position here for any heart emergencies." Jarryn pointed to the box on the wall.

"I hope you all have a wonderful day!" Jarryn continued. "Let's pray. Lord, thank you for this day, and help us to be like You today in every way. Help us to meet the most important needs of the people here, which may not even be physical needs. We know there is so much need, but Lord, like You multiplied the loaves and the fishes, may You multiply the works we do here to help more than just what we can see. May we start a change in the community to help improve their overall health. And Lord, we ask for Your miracles too, while we are here in Jesus' name. Amen."

Jarryn then held a hand up for attention. "I'll take the first of the medical team to the shore and then return to the boat with patients for the dental team. See you soon! First people for the boat, follow me." He walked outside to the deck with a group following him.

"Dental team!" Abbie raised her voice, commanding their attention. "Let's all head to the dental room and go over our protocols. See you there."

In the dental room, Abbie showed Sara through the drawers and the materials, rattling off the names of the instruments she'd be using. Sara's mind whirred with so much information. "I hope I can remember all of this," she said, eyes wide in disbelief.

"Don't worry. Trust me, you'll have it down in no time, and I'll be right here coaching you all the way," Abbie smiled reassuringly.

Half an hour later, Ivy, a local woman from the nearby village, was interpreting as a man with sparse gray hair and bowed legs, introduced as John, walked into the room. Sara hovered nearby, waiting for instructions as John took a seat in the camp-style dental chair. Abbie scooted around on her swiveling chair and shook his hand. Ivy asked him what he would like help with today. He opened his mouth and pointed to some teeth that Sara couldn't quite see. Sara leaned over, attempting to peer into his mouth from her spot. Abbie nodded and advised him that those teeth would need to be extracted. Sara watched carefully as Abbie pointed out to her what she would need in order to get the teeth out. Sara placed the instruments and the local anesthetic syringe on the tray and then stood aside as Abbie injected some local anesthetic into the man's mouth.

In the meantime, two other patients entered the room. Sara watched as one patient sat down in the chair with the other dentist, and the conversation began again, one that she couldn't understand, but thanks to Ivy, the patient's needs would be met. The third patient sat in a chair next to the hygienist, and soon the buzzing of a high-pitched instrument filled the air. Sara watched as water and chunks of something brown clouded the man's mouth. *I hope I'm not squeamish,* she thought.

Sara turned back then to watch as Abbie started to move the tooth in John's jaw, and Sara hovered over his mouth with the suction tip waiting for instructions. She felt Abbie's eyes on her, and moved the suction tip to where Abbie indicated, reminding herself to breathe at the same time. It wouldn't be much good to the poor man if she fainted in the middle of his tooth extraction! She took another deep breath to stifle a nervous giggle at the hilarious but horrifying thought, and focused again on her task.

In no time, Abbie had swiftly removed the first tooth and was on to the next one. Sara watched as John released the side of the chair that he had been gripping, his hands almost white. Abbie placed some gauze in his mouth and mimed that he should bite together. Then, eyes smiling over her mask, she nodded that Sara could clean up. Helping John to his feet, Sara led him to the side of the room where Ivy would go through follow-up instructions with him. Sara then cleaned the area and took the instruments to be sterilized.

As Sara moved back next to the dental chair, Abbie asked, "Are you all right, Sara?"

Sara nodded and let out a breath she hadn't realized she'd been holding. "Yes," she smiled. "There's just a lot to remember!"

"You'll get the hang of it! I can already see you're going to be great at this," Abbie encouraged her. "Don't you worry. I'll get my next patient." Abbie stood and left the room, and moments later returned, Ezekiel not far behind her at the elbow of an elderly woman. As he helped the woman up the stairs, Sara could see him speaking to Abbie, but the noise of the dental instruments in the room prevented Sara from hearing his words. Abbie threw her head back and laughed, obviously enjoying whatever private joke they had just shared. The woman, now seated on the chair, was smiling. Ivy came over, and the conversation began again.

At the end of the day, as Abbie left the room to see if there were any more patients, Sara stretched up tall and rubbed the side of her neck.

"That was the last one," Abbie reported as she reentered the room. "I just have some notes to write up, but you are free to go. We may be able to go to the shore soon and have a swim. Thanks for your help, Sara. You did very well here today."

"Really?" Sara asked, relieved to hear Abbie's praise. "I felt so clumsy most of the time."

"Yes, really," Abbie said with a smile, turning to begin writing her notes.

Sara walked out the door and into the sunshine, smiling as the warmth of the sun fell on her face. She closed her eyes and breathed in the sea air.

The sound of laughter floated up from downstairs. She listened, and could hear Ezekiel and Ivy chattering and then laughing again. Sara frowned. *Hmph, he certainly has no trouble making friends with the women around here.* She immediately felt a pang of guilt at her critical spirit... or was it jealousy? She shuddered at the thought. *God, I'm pretty sure both of those attitudes are wrong! Help me? I want to see Ezekiel with Your eyes.*

"Hey, Sara." She jumped, realizing Ezekiel was standing beside her on the deck. "I'm going to go to the shore with Jarryn when he returns the last of the patients to the village. Do you want to come?"

"Yes, absolutely," Sara said, determined to put away any negative thoughts. "I'll go get changed."

As the boat bumped over the waves to the shore, Sara noticed Ezekiel whisper something in Ivy's ear and felt the familiar pang of envy rise. *Give thanks*, came a surprising thought to her mind. *That has to be You, God!* she thought, *as it definitely wasn't MY first instinct*, but she looked back toward the ship and thanked the Lord under her breath for all they'd achieved that day as part of the dental team. She knew there would be a few sore people in the village that night, but that it would be such a blessing for them in the long term. What if their teeth had just been left in such a rotted state? She couldn't even imagine, as personally, she had only ever had minimal dental work herself.

Minutes later the boat lightly bumped up to the shore, and Sara noticed her annoyance at Ezekiel's gregariousness had vanished with her thoughts of gratitude. *Wow, thanks again, God*, she prayed silently. She wanted to be focused on the purpose of this outreach, on having a great time, and on deepening her walk with God—not on distracting thoughts of a guy who was never going to be more than a good friend.

Sara noticed some of the medical team swimming in the surf, and others standing around chatting with some of the Ni-Van people. As people left the boat, Ezekiel, now standing on the wet sand, offered her a hand. *I can get out myself,* she thought, until the boat moved in the gentle waves, and she lost her balance. She grabbed Ezekiel's hand, and suddenly, it was all she could feel, the gentle pressure of his hand like the warmth from the sunshine. Sara inhaled sharply and pulled her hand back, her feet now planted in the sand beneath the lapping tide. "Thanks," she chirped, a little too sharply she worried. She hoped he hadn't noticed her awkward reaction, and with her bag and her shoes in hand, she splashed past him onto the hot sand and found a spot to leave them while she went for a swim.

Wading back into the lazy surf, she dove under the water. It was lukewarm and clear, like a bath, inviting and refreshing. She swam along the beach doing some freestyle strokes, relishing the sensation of moving her body after being in a cramped, fixed posture most of the day. After swimming up and down the beach a few yards, she relaxed into a floating posture and allowed her thoughts to drift, moved by the swaying tide.

This is nothing like the frigid waves back home! came her first thought, and again she lifted prayers of thanks for such an amazing opportunity to experience this beautiful place. *But I AM getting seasick, Lord—from all the crazy emotions over Ezekiel! I know you brought me here to serve, NOT to get distracted by attraction to a handsome, friendly, godly... UGH! See?! There I go again!* Now she was treading water, and could see Ezekiel back on the shore, tossing a frisbee with another volunteer, his ruffled blonde hair flopping in the breeze, those blue eyes like the sea that she could sink into... At that moment, one of the other female volunteers crashed playfully into Ezekiel as she dove for the frisbee, and Sara rolled her eyes at the all-too-familiar move. The guy certainly wasn't hurting for attention, even on a remote Pacific island. She suddenly wondered what Miranda would think of all the attention he drew here. Sara shivered, despite the warm temperature of the water. Time to get out of the water and soak up some sun.

Sara swam back toward the others, then stood and watched as she saw Jarryn waving for those who wanted to return to the boat. She walked up the shore as he called out.

"I'll be doing another trip, so you're welcome to stay here for a while if you want?" Jarryn offered.

"Do you want to stay on the beach a little longer?" Ezekiel asked as he walked over to her.

"Yeah, that sounds great," Sara nodded. She walked over to her bag, pulled out her towel, and began to dry herself off.

"We haven't really talked about how your day went," Ezekiel said as he followed her. "How did it go for you?" Sara looked around. The others from the dental team must have returned to the boat while she was enjoying her time in the water.

Sara sat down on the sand, and Ezekiel sat next to her.

"It was fine," Sara shrugged her shoulders.

"Just fine?" Ezekiel laughed. "Come on, you must have more to say than that, Sara. Remember, you now possess keen investigative journalism skills." Ezekiel raised his eyebrows at her.

Sara laughed now. "Okay, okay! Well, at first, watching the extractions, I have to say that I actually did feel a bit faint—and I rarely get squeamish. But the pressure of keeping up with Abbie's instructions and everything that was happening kept me focused, I guess, and as long as I reminded myself to breathe, I found I could get through just fine."

"Wow, Sara, way to go. You're a natural," Ezekiel said. He chuckled. "However, I may have had a bit more of a struggle. I get a little queasy at the sight of plaque," he quipped.

Sara snorted and rolled her eyes.

"But I am really glad for you; I was kind of worried you might not cope too well with all the gory stuff."

Sara punched his arm lightly. "Your concern is touching. Thankfully, I got used to the procedures," Sara said. "It was definitely a unique experience. I loved the people; they seemed to radiate happiness, in spite of so many of them being in obvious pain."

"Yeah, exactly; here the people are so grateful," Ezekiel said. "We can really learn from them. Some of the clothes the people were wearing were so worn out; one lady actually had a moldy t-shirt on."

"I'm pretty sure that Ivy gave that lady a clean t-shirt. There's a bag of clothes to give away upstairs in the clinic room."

"That's great. Oh, I brought some of Truman's toys to the shore this afternoon. I can't wait to give them to some of the kids here."

"Yeah, let's do that for sure," she agreed. Sara looked at Ezekiel's beaming face. She hadn't seen him lit up like this for a long time.

"Missing the shelter?" Sara asked, watching him as his smile dropped a fraction.

"To be honest. No, not really. It feels like such an adventure here that I haven't given it much thought. It's kind of a nice change for me."

"What about Miranda?" Sara asked. "Have you talked to her since we left?" Sara tried to ignore the nagging thought that he couldn't really be missing Miranda with all the flirting he seemed to be enjoying.

"No," Ezekiel answered. "The phone coverage here is pretty bad. So no, I haven't been able to talk to her yet."

"You don't exactly seem to be missing her," Sara observed as casually as she could, nearly clapping her hand over her mouth after she'd said it. *Way to sound nosy*, she chided herself.

Ezekiel eyed her with a puzzled frown. "Missing Miranda? Well, she and I don't exactly get to see each other every day in LA, so... I guess I haven't had a chance to miss her yet. Should I?"

"Well, if I was in a relationship with you and you were away, I'd hope you would miss me," Sara pointed out.

"Sure, but that's different, when we were together, we saw each other every day," Ezekiel pointed out. "So of course I would miss you if we were together, but apart for a trip. I would definitely miss you," he grinned, completely unaware of the effect he had on her. "Miranda and I are taking things slowly."

Sara felt heat rise to her cheeks, and was thankful for the blazing sunshine, hoping it disguised her blush. She coughed and fished in her bag for her sunglasses, avoiding his gaze. *He is clueless*, she thought, *and it's a good thing, too!*

"Anyway, Miranda was glad for me to get some time off from the shelter, and I told her we probably wouldn't get to talk much while I'm here. So, I don't think she's worried." He shrugged, then stood up and moved over to a grassy area nearby. Some children were playing with a familiar wadded-up ball of scrap materials, and before he had watched for long, Ezekiel ran further up the beach to his bag and took out one of the soccer balls Truman had donated.

Returning to the group of laughing children with it under his arm, he stood until they noticed him. As their ball came towards him, he stopped it with his foot. "Okay if I play?" Ezekiel held up the brand new ball in his hands to communicate his intention. As the children nodded and cheered in approval, Ezekiel dropped the new ball and kicked it into their midst before running to follow along with their play. They were clearly delighted and shouted enthusiastically, crowding around him and each clamoring for a turn with the shiny new ball.

Sara watched him as he ran around with the children, running her hand through her wet hair like a rake in an attempt to comb it. She sighed as she flopped down on her towel to warm up in the sunshine. This was going to be a long two weeks unless she could keep her thoughts focused, and *away* from Ezekiel and Miranda.

CHAPTER 10

That night at dinner, the dental team sat together around the round wooden outdoor table at the stern of the boat. Jarryn had given them instructions about an upcoming concert later in the week that everyone was expected to participate in, and the team discussed ideas. As Ezekiel finished the last bite of his meal, he leaned backward. He glanced at Sara, who was distractedly looking out to the sea.

"Are you alright, Sara? You need an early night?" Ezekiel asked her.

"I'm fine. You're not my keeper, Ezekiel," she added, a bit too sharply she realized belatedly. *Ugh! What is my problem?* Sara thought. *I'm the one who insisted on being 'just friends.'* She smiled to lighten the mood again. "I'm just tired after a long day."

"Sorry, I know I'm not responsible for you, but I do care about you, and you did have a serious head injury not so long ago."

"Really?" Abbie jumped into the conversation. "What happened?"

"Oh—really, it's not a problem. I'd rather not go over it tonight, actually," Sara replied politely, "But I am tired, so I think I'll turn in early tonight." She stood and began to collect the empty plates around the table.

"Leave them," Abbie reassured. "I'll get them."

"No, I'm fine, really," Sara shook her head and continued picking up and stacking the plates.

"Let me help you at least," Abbie insisted.

Sara nodded slightly, smiling briefly. Ezekiel grabbed the last remaining plates and brought up the rear.

As they walked around the deck of the ship, Abbie said, "As a member of my team, your well-being is my responsibility during this outreach, Sara, so please do let me know if you need a rest or anything. And when you feel more like talking, I really would like to know what happened, if you don't mind. Anything medical or dental is always intriguing to me."

"Well, I was in the hospital after the injury, so it was a serious event, I'll tell you that much. And it was pretty traumatic for me emotionally. After the accident, though, I had the most wonderful times with the Lord. I attribute my recovery to Him. I don't think I'd be here without Him."

"You're a miracle, Sara! You don't need to downplay it," Ezekiel said.

"I didn't think I was," Sara said. She pressed her lips together. "I know we were all over national TV and everything, but after all that, I guess I just don't feel like everyone needs to know my business, Ezekiel."

"Fair enough," Ezekiel raised his hands in surrender as he set his plates on a counter in the kitchen.

"Hey, so about the concert, would you be interested in doing a song for it, Sara?" Abbie asked, tactfully changing the subject. "I actually was thinking maybe we could write a song."

"Count me out," Sara laughed. "Much as I enjoy music, it is definitely not my forte. But you guys go ahead. Ezekiel has more musical experience than I do." They walked back through the dining area toward the emptying tables as others began to clear away their dishes.

"I could help with words?" Ezekiel offered.

"The investigative journalist writing a few poetic verses instead of long, complicated paragraphs. That should be amusing," Abbie joked.

Sara rubbed her eyes and yawned, "I'll leave you to it. Good night, guys."

Ezekiel watched her walk away, and suddenly felt disappointed. Why did it seem like she was putting up walls? Hadn't they agreed to support each other as friends? Suddenly Miranda's words floated into his mind, "*You can't have me and Sara Ward...*" He bristled at the thought. *Sara has been my friend since we were kids*, he reasoned, *and my feelings for Miranda have nothing to do with that*. But he hadn't counted on Sara pulling away from their friendship. How would he deal with that? Surely that wasn't what she wanted? He shook his head in frustration.

"Hey," Abbie tugged on his shirt playfully, jerking him back to the present. "We've got work to do. Let's find Ivy. She's brilliant on the guitar."

* * *

EARLY THE NEXT MORNING, Ezekiel walked up the steps to the dental surgery.

"You ready to practice?" he asked Abbie. "Where's Ivy?"

"She won't be far away," Abbie answered. "Come on. We need to work this out."

Ezekiel had come up with a few lines the night before, and Ivy had worked out a chord progression to go along with them.

"It's pretty basic," Abbie said, "so I can have a go at it until Ivy gets here."

"I've taken a few ideas from Psalm 135," Ezekiel said. "Here's what I've got so far:

"Your name, O Lord, endures,

Forever through generations,

You vindicate your people...." his voice trailed off as he seemed lost in thought for a moment.

Abbie cocked her head up at him as he paused. "Is that all you've got?" She gave him a teasing look. "All that time, and it was already in the Bible?" She started chuckling, then broke down laughing until tears ran down her cheeks.

"Easily amused, are we?" Ezekiel remarked dryly, one eyebrow cocked, but he was stifling a laugh as well. "In my defense, it *is* my first time writing a song, and there are a few more lines than that," he pointed out, attempting to look offended.

Abbie snatched the piece of paper he'd been holding up, dabbing at her eyes to stem the tears. "Let me see this," she said, and burst into laughter again after one glance. "Okay—um, 'Praise the Lord' repeated four times in a row doesn't *exactly* count as 'a few more lines, Shakespeare!"

Ezekiel couldn't hold back now, either, and his laughter rose as he playfully tried to retrieve the paper from her hands. "Okay! Okay! I'll put more effort into it!" he exclaimed.

Just then, the door opened, and Sara stepped in, glanced between the two of them, and placed her hands on her hips.

"Can I please talk to you outside for a minute, Ezekiel?" Sara said with a stern look.

Ezekiel shrugged as he wiped the tears from his eyes. He walked over to Sara, who turned and walked down the stairs to the seating area at the stern of the boat.

"Sorry, but this is really bugging me now. Doesn't Miranda matter to you? I know I'm not her biggest fan, but seriously, if I were her and knew how much all these women were flirting with you constantly, I'd be—*not* impressed." Sara glared at him.

Ezekiel stood still and stared blankly at her. His mind was racing to make sense of what she'd just said, but before he could think of a response, Sara continued her interrogation.

"She certainly shouldn't trust you, should she?" Sara turned and stalked away.

"What—what do you mean?" Ezekiel asked, following her. "Why are you so upset, Sara? There's nothing going on at all with Abbie, if that's what you're thinking. We were just having a laugh over my semi-pathetic songwriting attempts."

"Would Miranda see it that way?" Sara insisted, turning back to him.

"Since when do you worry so much about Miranda?" Ezekiel was truly flummoxed.

"Every woman deserves a faithful man."

"Yes, absolutely," Ezekiel agreed. "But...."

"But what? Why can't you be honest about what is going on?"

Ezekiel sighed and looked at her reflectively for a moment. "I think this is more about you, Sara. What *is* really going on?"

"Ugh! That is just like you, Ezekiel, to use my words to turn it back on me," Sara snapped.

"Look, can we please talk about this later, Sara?" Ezekiel felt cornered, and knew he needed time to think, before he said too much.

"I think you've got it all wrong. But we're here to serve the Lord and these people, which I'm pretty sure we *do* agree on, so maybe we could have this conversation at a more appropriate time?"

Sara glared at him, then turned and strode away. Ezekiel watched her disappear around the side of the ship. His shoulders sagged and he slumped onto a bench nearby.

Abbie came out of the dental room and touched Ezekiel gently on the shoulder. He started.

"Is everything okay, Ezekiel?" Abbie said.

"So, you heard that?" Ezekiel turned to look at her.

"That I did," Abbie said, "Maybe I should tell Sara about my boyfriend back home. Would that help?"

"Honestly, Abbie, it's not your problem, but thanks for offering," Ezekiel said. "We'll work through it, I'm sure."

"Well, as long as you two can keep it together today. We are here to work as a team and to serve the people, you know?" Abbie said.

"Sure, absolutely," Ezekiel said. He rubbed his hands on the front of his shorts and then stood. Sighing, he followed Abbie along the side of the ship and into the dining room, anything but certain about the day ahead.

* * *

LATER, as the working portion of the day came to an end, Abbie came down the stairs and stood in front of Ezekiel's workstation, frowning. "Okay. You two need to sort out whatever is going on between you. It's affecting the whole team today."

"I'm so sorry." Ezekiel knew it hadn't gone well. He thought back to each time that day when he'd entered the dental surgery, and how Sara had refused to look at him. "I'll go find Sara, right now." He stood and walked up the stairs into the surgery. Sara was handing the last of the instruments to be sterilized to Mary, the lady working as a scrubs nurse.

"Hi there, good to have the day over," he said, smiling.

"Yes, I can't wait for a swim," Mary said. "And we're the ones with the air conditioning" Mary shook her head, "But I need to get these instruments done first."

"What about you, Sara?" Ezekiel asked. "You want to head in for a swim again this afternoon?"

"No, thanks," she said tersely.

"Hey, can we talk, please?" Ezekiel pleaded.

"Not right now," Sara said, shaking her head before she left the room.

Well, then... space it is.

CHAPTER 11

The following morning as Ezekiel walked into the dining area, he saw Sara chatting with one of the medical team. He walked over to see her.

"Morning, Ezekiel," Sara said, "Have you met Nathan?"

"No," Ezekiel said, holding out his hand to shake Nathan's, and silently grateful that whatever walls Sara seemed to have put up the day before seemed to have been forgotten for the moment. "But I think I overheard that you're a physical therapist, is that right?"

Nathan responded and shook his hand, "Yes, Sara was filling me in on things with the dental team. How's it going for you?"

"I'm having a terrific time meeting the people, and it isn't hard work for me. Of course, Ivy is our translator, and she does a fabulous job. We're having a lot of laughs, hopefully putting people at ease, even praying with a few, although some people didn't look that keen to be there."

"You should come to shore sometime and check out what we're up to," Nathan invited.

"Yeah, Ezekiel, you should go," Sara agreed quickly, and Ezekiel wondered if Nathan could see that her smile looked a tad forced. "Anyone can take over your role easily, after all, right?"

Ezekiel started to laugh, but then stopped, suddenly unsure whether Sara was teasing or serious. "Uh, yeah, well, that is, I could talk to Jarryn, and see if someone could fill in for me today. It's pretty easy to take someone's blood pressure once you know how."

"Let's find him," Sara said. "See you later, Nathan." She smiled at him.

Sara marched off, so Ezekiel nodded at Nathan and then took some long strides to catch up with her. As she moved out onto the deck, Ezekiel touched her arm gently, "Hey, can we please talk?"

Sara turned from his touch as if it was a hot fire and crossed her arms. "I'm not ready to talk to you, Ezekiel. Please give me some space. I think I just need a little more time to pray and figure out what I want to say. Anyway, you wanted to see what they do on shore, right? You should really go for it while you can."

"Okay, I get that. But, can I just ask, is it Miranda you're worried about?" He spoke softly, not wanting to offend her but hoping to open up the topic.

Sara sighed, her arms still crossed, as she looked out to sea. She pursed her lips, but didn't respond.

"Right, I can see you're not ready to talk, like you said. But, can I just say... if it *is* Miranda you're thinking of, while I am sure she'd appreciate that, there's nothing to worry about? She and I have had some really great talks before I came on this trip, and she knows I'm committed to her."

"Thanks, but you said it, I'm not ready to talk. Let's try again later, okay?" Ezekiel sighed, "Let's find Jarryn then." They walked around to the back of the ship, hoping to find Jarryn. He was sitting at the table at the stern of the ship, his Bible open in front of him and a cup of coffee in his hand.

He looked up, and his eyes moved between them both. "Is there something I can do for you two?" Jarryn asked. Sara stood there, clearly wanting Ezekiel to do the talking.

"Nathan has invited me to shore today," Ezekiel said. "I was wondering if someone could fill in for me? I would love to hear more about your overall vision for the mission here."

"Yeah, there's another young guy with us, Karl, who's quite proficient in Bislama, and he'd love to help on the dental team today, I'm sure. I'll find him."

"Thanks, Jarryn, I appreciate that," Ezekiel said.

"Meet me on the deck after breakfast. Bring some decent shoes as well. Are you any good with a hammer?" Jarryn asked.

"I can try," Ezekiel replied with a bit of trepidation. He was immensely curious about what hammers had to do with medical procedures, though he wasn't entirely sure he wanted to find out.

"That's the spirit," Jarryn said.

* * *

As Ezekiel walked up the beach he marveled at the beauty around him, savoring the warmth of the sun on his skin. He was grateful to have a change of pace from the past few days, as well as some space apart from Sara to think and pray. Her snarky treatment caught him off guard, and he couldn't shake the feeling of heaviness at her accusation that he wasn't trustworthy. *Ironic,* he thought, *Miranda thinks she'll lose me to Sara, while Sara's busy making sure I'm faithful to Miranda!* Maybe he'd been too naive about coming on this trip with Sara, after all? He'd thought their friendship had reached a great place of mutual trust and respect, but now he questioned his judgment. *Search me, God, know my anxious thoughts...* he prayed.

He looked up then at the medical team walking toward some buildings further up a slight incline at the end of a grassy slope, small thatched homes dotting either side of the field. Jarryn, who waved in his direction, brought him out of his reverie. "This way, Ezekiel," Jarryn called, and began to walk along the right side of the field.

Ezekiel ran to catch up. "On my way!"

"We're here to help some of the local guys make an alteration to the entrance of that house, to help a man who's had a stroke. Nathan is going to help him with exercises, and hopefully, we can get him plugged back into his community again. After his stroke, he's been pretty isolated. He used to be a skilled craftsman working as a builder, but now he's been very limited in what he's been able to do, even in his own home. We hope the new entrance and a new wheelchair will allow him to get around better. Our medical staff think that with a little encouragement and the right tools, maybe he can even work part-time again."

Ah, now the hammer made sense. Relieved, Ezekiel followed the instructions of what he was supposed to do and began moving timber and helping to frame the entrance. Suddenly he remembered his mother's vision during their prayer time. She'd seen a pile of lumber. He looked down at the pile in front of him and was overcome with joy and peace, in spite of the conflicts with Sara at the moment.

As the sun rose higher in the sky, he could feel his muscles ache, and his sweaty clothes clinging to him. He hadn't done this type of physical work for a long time, even at the shelter, and it was catching up with him. When he stopped to take a long pull at his drink bottle, Jarryn called out that they would have lunch.

"Time for a break and a swim if you want," Jarryn said. "Let's go and catch up with the medical team."

Ezekiel followed the crowd toward where the medical team was seated under a large tree at the side of the field.

"How was the morning?" Ezekiel asked one of the doctors, Sam Murphy.

"Productive. Then again, there's not as much we can do about some of the most serious issues. Elana and Mary are performing skits this afternoon to educate the people about diet. They love sugar and often add far too much to cups of tea, among other things."

"Yeah... I did notice that the people don't seem to be starving," Ezekiel agreed.

"There is an abundance of food," Dr. Murphy continued, "however, not always the right sort. We will be encouraging them to eat what they produce rather than the food the Westerners bring in. 'Cargo food,' we call it. Far too much sugar and carbohydrates. That's why their teeth, in particular, are bad. Add to that the fact that there'll be many people with undiagnosed diabetes, or at the very least blood sugar issues, which can lead to all sorts of physical problems in the long term."

"Yeah, my aunt had diabetes," Ezekiel remarked. "She told me all about the complications that can occur with it. Not that I remember them all."

"Exactly," Dr. Murphy nodded and fanned his face with a large palm frond. "Whew! It's so good to be out in the fresh air," he said. "It's stifling in there."

"Hot working outside as well," Ezekiel said. "I can't imagine what it is like in the summer."

"I think it would be very oppressive, with extreme heat and

humidity and then, of course, the potential of cyclones. Not good to be around in the ship then," Dr. Murphy said.

Ezekiel laughed, "Yeah, I think the heat this time of year will be just fine."

As Ezekiel was just finishing the last bite of his sandwich, Jarryn walked over to him. "Up for a walk, Ezekiel, and maybe a swim?"

Ezekiel nodded and stood up, waving a farewell to Dr. Murphy.

"There's a great little trail we can check out here that takes us through some bush to the next bay. Let's go," Jarryn pointed out. They followed a worn footpath that wound around the outskirts of the village through native bush and undergrowth and into a shady grove of trees.

Ezekiel welcomed the green coolness of the surrounding ferns and flowering bushes. "This is different, but great! Can we hang out here in the shade for a bit?" he suggested.

"Absolutely," Jarryn replied. "It's a nice spot." They found a log lying on the ground and sat down.

"Hey, I just wanted you to know that while you're on this trip, Ezekiel, I'm always available for prayer and counsel," Jarryn said. "I could see that things looked pretty intense between you and Sara today. You feel like talking about it? I have noticed you two seem to have a pretty strong connection."

Ezekiel looked at Jarryn with interest. "How can you tell?" Jarryn smiled and gave Ezekiel a friendly clap on the shoulder.

"Eh... I've been around a while, and I pay attention to people," he explained. "And as one of the staff responsible for pastoral care on this trip, I try to be tuned in to how everyone's doing, you know?"

Ezekiel nodded. "That's great. I actually was hoping to pray about this whole... thing with Sara today, so I appreciate you asking."

"No problem," Jarryn assured him. They looked into the trees, listening to the unfamiliar birdsong of the native birds for a few moments before Jarryn spoke again. "So, what's the story? What's going on with you and Sara?"

"Well, we have a long history, right back to childhood; we sort of grew up together, same church, same school, our parents were friends. We weren't actually friends back then, but we reconnected a couple of years ago, sort of through my work. Actually, we ended up all over national news last year because of that. It was a wild ride; one I wouldn't want to go through again. But I get the feeling you haven't heard that story?" Ezekiel looked at Jarryn for a reaction but was relieved to see a blank expression on his face.

"Sorry, man, I've been working out here for the past several years, and I have to say, I'm pretty out of the loop on a lot of what happens back home. I wouldn't have heard about it unless my family fills me in on something. But I gather you and Sara managed to weather that storm since here you are?" He smiled.

Ezekiel nodded. "Let's just say we've had more than our share of adventure as friends." He looked out through the trees toward where the ship was moored in the bay before speaking again. "It's been so great over the past few months, though, just having Sara as a friend I know is always praying for me, and who knows me better than most people in my life. She's actually the one who encouraged me to come on this trip. I probably wouldn't be here if it weren't for her."

"But you two are just friends, nothing more?" Jarryn asked pointedly.

"We are now," Ezekiel replied. He rested his elbows on his knees and stared thoughtfully at the ground in front of him. "At different times we have each felt something more for each other, but... well, we never seemed to be on the same page at the right time. And she finally said she only wanted to be friends, so I've respected her wishes. And over the past several months I've reconnected with another woman from my college days, Miranda, and that's been going pretty well. In fact, that's what seems to have caused the friction with Sara here."

"Sara... disapproves of your relationship with Miranda?" Jarryn guessed.

"Well, no... I'm not sure, really. I think she's worried that I'm somehow being unfaithful to Miranda by spending too much time enjoying the company of the women on my team. But I can't quite figure out why all of a sudden Sara seems so concerned about Miranda. She's never gotten to know her very well and they aren't exactly best friends, put it that way," Ezekiel smirked.

Jarryn thought for a moment, then tilted his head and looked at Ezekiel again. "It sounds like maybe Sara could use another woman to talk to about some of this, too. I'll have a talk with Abbie later on today."

"Sounds great," Ezekiel said. "You guys sure come prepared! Here we are ready to serve, and instead we're *being* served so much by all of you."

Jarryn chuckled. "Nah, it's all of us serving together. You guys have contributed more than you realize, bringing a lot of encouragement and enthusiasm to the work you're doing, not to mention just good old elbow grease!"

Ezekiel smiled. "I'll take your word on that!"

Jarryn sat silently for a moment, but then his hands were moving, grasping a large orange-flowered plant that grew close by the log on which they sat. Ezekiel watched him with curiosity as he broke the plant's stem near its base, then held it up for Ezekiel to see.

"Pretty sure this is one of the plants they consider a weed here!" he explained. "'Invasive species,' they call them." He dropped the plant in a heap behind their log.

"You're a jack of all trades," Ezekiel chuckled. "Builder, pastor, gardener."

Jarryn smiled at him. "Just like to keep busy, I guess. You know, Ezekiel, the thing about close relationships, the kind that go deep over a long period of time, like you and Sara have, is that they put down roots, down into the soil of our lives, of *us*."

As he spoke, Jarryn used the heel of his boot to rough up the soil around the spot where he'd snapped the bush at its stem. In just a few strokes the root system of the missing plant was revealed; Jarryn reached down to grasp part of it, and pulled. With some difficulty, he managed to extract a portion of the roots, which he held up for Ezekiel to see.

"So, you might think the plant is removed, and you've made way for a new plant to take its place, right? But if the roots are still there in the ground, whatever you plant is now is going to have to compete with the existing roots, for space, water, nutrients from the soil. If you really want to give new plants a fair chance to grow, you're going to have to take those roots into consideration." Jarryn looked Ezekiel in the eye.

Ezekiel stared at him. "Wait, are you saying I...I can't be friends with Sara if I'm in a relationship with Miranda? I don't know about that," he shook his head doubtfully.

"No, not exactly," Jarryn explained. "There's room in a garden for a variety of plants. And let's be real, we aren't plants. It's just a loose analogy, a sort of object lesson. But the basic idea is that if you still have some strong feelings for Sara buried beneath the surface, maybe even some old hurts that weren't really properly addressed, then I would say you might want to take those things to God in prayer soon. Because Sara may have a point there. For you and Miranda to really flourish you need to make sure you have the right conditions, which means no competition for your focus."

Ezekiel's thoughts were whirling. He had not expected at all to be confronted by this subject while on the mission trip.

"We have some time free now, Ezekiel, if you want to pray. I'm happy to pray with you if you'd like. Or you're welcome to spend some time in prayer by yourself. There's a track around the beach edge to the next bay."

"Some time on my own would be good. But aren't we supposed to be working on the house?" Ezekiel said.

"It's too hot in the heat of the day. We usually wait a while to begin again, so you have some time," Jarryn said.

"Thanks, I'll go for a walk." He walked down to the water's edge and watched some of the team in the water splashing around. He removed his boots and walked in up to his knees, dunked himself in the water to wash off the grime of the morning, before walking out again and continuing barefoot around to the next bay, his boots dangling from one hand. He knew his clothes would be dry before he was expected back at work, and the dampness helped refresh his body.

As he prayed, going through each situation that came to mind, it was as if a layer was lifted before he moved to the next situation. Walking and praying, he felt the light of God radiate through him, and his heart began to bubble with laughter, which then spilled out of his mouth. *Why do I have to make things so complicated,* he thought. *Who made me the savior of every situation...oh, wait, I did,* he realized, and he laughed at the lunacy of that thought. As he released it to the Lord, the rightful Savior of every situation, along with the joy of the Lord, filled him to overflowing. Between the confirmation that he was truly here by God's order via the 'pile of lumber' in his mother's vision, and now finally realizing the many burdens he'd taken upon himself instead of allowing the Lord to carry them, he felt freer than he'd felt in, well, ever. It was an incredible sensation.

Ezekiel piled his plate up high at dinner that evening, having worked up quite an appetite between the physical labor in the hot sun and his refreshing and freeing conversation with the Lord. He sank down into one of the comfortable seats and after grace, began to enjoy his food as he listened to conversations around him.

Sara walked over to him, "May I sit with you?" she asked.

Ezekiel looked into her face, searching for hints of her emotions. Her face was usually so expressive. Presently she was smiling. *There's hope, after all*, Ezekiel thought.

"Sure," Ezekiel said, shuffling over to make room for her. "How was your day today, Sara?"

" So many extractions today. I am honestly amazed at Abbie's skill. She seems to be very quick, and so capable at what she does. So many teeth out today." She shook her head. "Abbie had given some dietary advice for the medical team to share. It would be great to be able to be more proactive with people's health rather than just cleaning up the mess of poor diets."

"I guess, as always, the less healthy food is easy to get, cheap, and addictive. Just like in the West," Ezekiel said.

"True that," Sara said, "How was your day, Ezekiel?"

"I think every muscle in my body aches, so I will be happy to be back on the dental team tomorrow," Ezekiel looked at her. "I had some time to pray today, and feel more at peace. And Sara, I need to apologize..."

"No need, Ezekiel," Sara interrupted him, "You were right. I need to spend some time praying, too. After all, that's part of why we're here as well. To spend time seeking the Lord."

"But we obviously have some things to discuss, Sara," Ezekiel said.

"Yes," Sara said, "But not right now, Ezekiel."

Ezekiel frowned. Just as he was ready to talk to her about deeper issues, she backed off again. *In your time, Lord*, he prayed. *Help me to continue to release these burdens to You. How easy it is to want to pick them back up and 'help' You.* The mere reminder that it wasn't his job to make everyone 'better' caused an immediate relaxation in his spirit and his frown faded away.

* * *

THAT WEEKEND the villagers invited the volunteers from the Pacific Outreach to a shared meal on the shore. Sara, Abbie, and Ezekiel walked around the village, and Ivy spoke to some of the villagers. A single woman from the village invited them into her home, a thatched hut. There was a slat bed with no mattress and a fire well dug into the dirt floor.

"Remind me never to complain again," Sara whispered in Ezekiel's ear as Ivy was translating for the woman.

Lunch was served under a large tree, and Jarryn gave a speech for the villagers that Ivy translated. Some of the villagers performed a dance after the meal.

As they clapped for the performance, Ezekiel was filled with gratitude for what they could help with and the blessing of being part of the whole experience. He thought of what Jarryn had said and about how they were wanting to empower the people with skills to help with healthy food production and also building skills. Maybe that could also be something that they could develop at the shelter. Particularly now that Mateo and the building company were interested in collaborating with them. He rubbed his jaw as the thoughts began to flow.

When the festivities were over, the party walked back to the beach, waiting to catch the tender back to the ship.

Not paying close attention, Sara was walking and joking with Abbie when she tripped and went sprawling next to Ezekiel. Quick as a whip, he grabbed her, stopping her fall.

"Ezekiel," Sara said as he held her. "You can let go now. I'm okay."

Ezekiel pulled his hands back as if in surrender. "Sara, I'm sorry! I just... I was worried, after your..."

"I'm okay, Ezekiel, really. I simply wasn't paying attention to where I was walking. Just distraction, not a side effect of my injury," Sara said. "It's not your job to save me, or the world. Thanks, though."

Abruptly, she hugged him, wrapping her hands around his waist. Ezekiel hesitated for a moment, the warmth of her pressed against him, startling him. He felt himself melt into the moment, slowly wrapping his arms around her and hugging her back. After a moment, she leaned back, her arms still around his waist, looking him in the eyes.

"It's sweet of you to worry, Ezekiel." She hesitated. "I like you a lot more for it. But God has got me."

"I'm sorry I freaked out."

"It's fine. I may have, too, if it were you." She smiled as she released him, and they began to walk towards the water's edge. "Or maybe I wouldn't," she joked.

"Stop it." He nudged her softly, and she laughed.

The next morning, Ezekiel got up earlier than usual and sat at the back of the ship to pray, starting with his father's charity. He had more ideas now to make it more impactful and productive, but he wanted God's ideas. Clearly, man's ideas had been very much less than successful. Maybe he'd been doing it in his own strength. Employing the company with the suggested marketing ideas had seemed like a wise investment at the time, but now he wasn't so sure. He just wanted things to work out, he wanted it to succeed and expand and grow in so many ways, but he needed guidance.

He had been there for nearly an hour, when suddenly he was sure he heard quiet sobbing, so he stood up to investigate, heading up the stairs toward the sound. It was Sara, seated on the upper level of the ship.

"What's the matter? Are you okay?" he asked, startling her.

She looked up and wiped the tears from her cheeks with her fingers.

"I'm fine," she smiled. "I was having a moment with God. You know?" She looked out at the sea, its vastness stretched out in front of them.

"It's beautiful." Ezekiel smiled in return, feeling a sense of awe at the beauty around them.

She looked up at him. "Do you want to sit?"

"With you? Always." He sat down beside her. There was a moment of silence while they breathlessly took in the scene before them.

Then Sara took a deep breath. "Sometimes I think about how far we've come. From childhood enemies...."

"I'm pretty sure that was an 'only you' thing," he interjected.

"....to undercover investigative journalists," she continued, completely ignoring his jibe. "To the whole PR scandal, and now, missionaries. But really, mostly, just great friends."

Ezekiel nodded, watching the wind blow her hair back from her face.

"I think those are some of the highlights of my life." He smiled.

"What are friends for, if not to be part of moments you will always remember?"

"Moments that are the most special to you," she said, her expression wistful as she stared at the beach. Ezekiel felt a strange sense of contentment.

Sara's smile was tentative. "But I'm not sure what's next, and I feel anxious. I didn't expect my life to turn out this way,....the accident, the career change."

Ezekiel watched her for a moment, the sun hitting her face, her hair scattered around her, no bun this early in the morning. She looked angelic in that moment of laughter. He felt his pulse pick up. He couldn't imagine her, headstrong and obstinate, ever being afraid as a child. Yet he knew better than to put faith in appearances. Her childhood had been marred by the absence of her father's love. She had experienced a great deal of fear and pain that had marked those younger years. He let out a soft breath as his eyes roved over her face.

"Why are you looking at me like that?" She stopped laughing, a light blush on her cheeks.

"You're just...." He stopped, unsure if he should be saying this. He shook his head. "I'm sorry."

He sat up. She sat up too, all of a sudden sober.

"Ezekiel...."

"There you two are. Come on! We're having a special breakfast this morning for Abbie's birthday, " Ivy said. "You're not going to want to miss it."

Ezekiel decided it was best that they were interrupted. He didn't want any feelings to resurface. He pushed down the feeling that not only was she beautiful, but she was his best friend, plus they were on the same spiritual journey. Yet he was very aware that he was dating Miranda. He couldn't afford to have feelings like this. Maybe Miranda was right; what *was* he doing pursuing a friendship with Sara? Was it even possible for him to have a platonic friendship with Sara after all they'd been through together? He could ruin everything: the incredible friendship he had developed with Sara, and his new romantic relationship with Miranda. *Needing You, Lord. Thanks for leading me....*

* * *

Ezekiel spent the afternoon trying to keep some of the patients calm; a bit of a wind had kicked up, causing the boat to rock, and some of the patients waiting seemed anxious to go back to the island. One of them even threw up over the side of the ship. An elderly woman appeared to be shaking in fear. Ezekiel marveled as Ivy spoke softly to her, resulting in the woman visibly relaxing. Apparently, not all of the island residents were comfortable in choppy waters. Ezekiel took one of the young men upstairs for his dental treatment.

In the surgery, the other dentist nodded at him. "I'm ready for the next patient," she said.

Ezekiel walked back downstairs and nodded to Ivy. "They're ready for her now." Ivy stood and walked the lady up the stairs, her arm supporting the older woman's elbow.

Half an hour later, Ivy came back down with the lady, who was now smiling shyly, "Not as bad as I thought," Ivy translated for her.

"I'm so glad," Ezekiel replied, returning her smile.

Once the dinner was over, Ezekiel went to the bow of the ship, attempting to find some private space. He shut his eyes and felt the sea breeze blow over him.

He had so many thoughts and questions about his future, and his friendship with Sara, although right now he didn't want to ask in case he got a reply that he didn't want. It was dark when he headed back to his room, and even though he hadn't heard anything specific from God, he had sensed a nudging in his spirit to keep asking with a willing heart. God would reveal all in His own time. The important thing was to seek Him.

"Jeremiah 29:13 And you shall seek Me, and find Me, when you shall search for Me with all your heart," he recited quietly to himself.

CHAPTER 12

Sara shuffled into her room after a long day and plopped down on her bed. She was thankful that, at that moment, she was the only one in her room. She'd come to enjoy everyone's company, but she needed some respite now and then.

She picked up her Kindle and clicked on her latest book and began to read, although it seemed she couldn't get past the first paragraph. Sara sighed and put it down. Just then, there was a knock at the door, and Abbie poked her head around the door.

"Hey Sara, I was wondering if we could hang out for a bit?"

"Sure," Sara replied. *So much for some quiet time,* she thought with resignation, *not that I could focus anyway.*

"Let's go somewhere where there's a breeze," Abbie suggested, fanning her face with her hand. Sara nodded and followed Abbie to the top of the ship. They sat down on a bench that was bolted into the floor.

Abbie turned to Sara. "I wanted to say how much I appreciate your help in the surgery and how lovely you are with the people, Sara."

Sara turned to her and smiled, a rush of relief filling her, "Thanks, Abbie, that means a lot coming from you. You're so good at what you do. I'm amazed at how much you achieve for the patients."

Abbie smiled back. "And as team leader and I hope now a friend, I just wanted to check on how you're doing overall. Your health? Energy levels? And also... you had a glitch with Ezekiel the other day? Would you like to talk about it?"

Sara nodded and blew out a breath, "Going back to my head injury," she paused.

"Hmmm?"

"Before my injury, Ezekiel and I almost got together, romantically, and then after I was shot...."

"Shot? Wow, Sara, I'm so sorry, that's massive!" Abbie leaned over to touch Sara's hand gently.

Sara lifted her hand and shook it in a wave. "No, it's fine. It's in the past now, and being here, I am finally beginning to let it go. But look it up online when you can if you want to hear all the details. There's plenty about it on YouTube, unfortunately. The main issue is that after the accident I lost my memory, and so Ezekiel and I had to deal with the fallout from the incident as well as the fact that for a while, I didn't remember anything."

"That must have been so tough for you, Sara," Abbie said.

"For us both. Ezekiel was heartbroken, and I couldn't empathize with him. Until my memory returned."

Abbie tilted her head and looked questioningly at Sara. "How come you aren't together then? Didn't Ezekiel say he has a new girl-friend now?"

"I... never actually told him I recovered *all* my memory," Sara leaned forward and put her face in her hands.

"But, why not?" Abbie frowned.

"Well, I went to talk to him after his final TV interview after the whole thing, and I couldn't wait to tell him. But then I got to the TV studio, and I saw him with Miranda—she was the one interviewing him. It seemed...intimate somehow, and I knew they'd reconnected. And I just decided then that, as a new Christian, I needed to put God first, not Ezekiel."

"Of course, it's always right to put God first in our lives, but does that have to exclude a relationship? Not always," Abbie answered her own question.

"True," Sara acknowledged. "But there's so much complicated history between us, and I couldn't face it, if you want the honest truth. And now he's with Miranda."

"Do you want my advice, Sara? I know I don't know all your history but..."

"Yes Abbie," Sara turned to look at her as Abbie stood.

"I think you need to be honest with him. He's a good guy, Sara. If you want him to be free to move on with Miranda fully, it would be best to tell him. Or perhaps, there may be another outcome?"

Sara sighed. "Yeah, you're right. It's like we have unfinished business," Sara said.

"You think?" Abbie grinned.

"There's just been so much going on with my new demanding job, still struggling with headaches at times after the injury. Trying to let Ezekiel go and just be friends. Worrying about my friend Debra. So much, including being a new Christian; but I don't think I've been honest with myself either."

Abbie walked over and sat back down on the seat. "You'll do the right thing, Sara, I know you will. You're a great person. A person with integrity and a good heart." Sara held her temples in one hand. Abbie tentatively placed an arm around her shoulders and hugged her. Sara turned to her and suddenly felt safe to let the tears flow as she rested on her shoulder.

"Okay if I pray?" Abbie whispered. Sara nodded. "Lord, thank you that you know all of this, and you are with Sara and for her. Lord, continue to bring healing to her heart. May she know your love and peace."

Sara lifted her head and looked at Abbie. "Thanks, Abbie."

Abbie nodded, "You've got this."

After they'd parted ways, Sara returned to her cabin. So much to think about. As she opened the cabin door, her phone was ringing. It was Debra.

"Hey." Sara smiled as she answered. "I feel like we haven't talked in forever." Just then, Debra's voice cut out, and Sara stood and made her way back to the top of the ship.

"Debra? Can you hear me now?"

"Yes, Sara. That's better." The connection was now clear, which Sara was thankful for, considering the miles that separated them.

"Yeah. I...." Debra paused, then sighed. "I'm sorry. I just missed you."

Debra didn't sound like her usual perky self. There was something like defeat in her voice.

"Are you okay? Deb?"

Debra was silent for a moment.

"Yes, I...." She stopped again.

"Debra?" Sara frowned. "Did something happen?"

"No." She cleared her throat. "I'm sorry. Don't worry about it."

"Are you sure? You don't sound so good.'

"I'm sure. I just wanted to see how the trip was going. I miss you.'

"I miss you too, and I want to know what's happening for you. I'm sorry I haven't called you. I should've called," Sara said. "The coverage has been erratic, and we have been so busy."

"How is it all going?"

"I wish you were here," Sara sighed. "It's been a big learning curve. I'm working as a dental assistant. Can you believe it? Me. Thankfully I'm not usually squeamish, but I never imagined myself doing this kind of work. Some drama," Sara paused, "of my own making, of course."

Debra chuckled, but it didn't sound as merry as Sara was used to hearing from her best friend. Was she just tired, or was something else going on? Something Debra wasn't willing to talk about yet. "I'm glad, Sara. Let's talk more soon. I think I should go. I need to, ugh... I need to go."

Sara frowned.

"Okay. I guess I'll call you soon." Sara wished that Debra had come with them, although in her heart, she knew the timing was not right.

The line went dead. She went back to her room and sat back, and pulled her journal out of the cupboard. She'd brought it with her even though she hadn't used it in months. It was time to start journaling again. She opened it to the last entry. It was from when she'd gotten her job at Mode PR. She couldn't help but feel a bit downcast as she read her hopes and aspirations for her job at Mode. In hindsight, they seemed so foolish.

If only the Sara that wrote those things could see her now. She laughed at herself mockingly, and there was a ring of spite to it. She closed her journal and placed it back in the cupboard. She needed to cool off, she decided, as she got up and gathered her things for a shower.

She had to walk a bit, as the shower rooms were down the hallway. When she was done, she put on her shorts and t-shirt, grabbed her stuff, and started heading back to her room. However, she changed her mind and decided to go to the stern of the boat and be still, with only the stars bringing light to the area. As she relaxed, she began to hear Ezekiel talking. He must be on the upper level where they'd been sitting earlier.

She meant to return to her room, but then she heard her name from whomever he was talking to on the speakerphone.

"...with Sara. It hasn't felt right with you being there together." Sara didn't need anyone to tell her it was Miranda on the phone.

"Miranda, we talked about this; I've told you; Sara and I are just friends." Miranda sounded upset, and Sara felt a pang of sadness for her.

"Well, it hasn't felt right that you've gone halfway around the world with her. And... I've been talking to your mother,"

"What? You've been talking to my mother about our relationship?" Ezekiel said aghast.

"No, Ezekiel, not everything is about you. I've been talking to your mom about Jesus and what he did for me. Somehow, it's finally made sense, and I've asked Jesus into my heart."

"That's awesome news, Miranda!" Ezekiel enthused.

"I've experienced God's peace, Ezekiel. Now I know what you've been talking about all this time, finally."

"I'm so thrilled for you, Miranda," Ezekiel said. "I have prayed for this for so long; this is awesome!"

"And so, I'm breaking up with you."

"Wait, what?"

"I need some space, Ezekiel. I've had this feeling that you've been with me for the wrong reasons. That somehow you were... wanting to fix me? Heal me? It's not your job, Ezekiel, and I want you to know that I am not your responsibility anymore," Miranda said.

"I... don't know what to say," Ezekiel faltered.

"I wanted you to know, as Sara has always come first with you, and now, you're free to pursue her."

"It's not like that, Miranda," Ezekiel said, sounding weary.

"If you say so," Miranda said. "Let's move on as friends, Ezekiel. And I have a surprise for you at the shelter," Miranda said.

"Really?" Ezekiel's tiredness suddenly disappeared. "Tell me more about this surprise? What is that about?"

"There's plenty of time for that, Ezekiel. If I tell you, it won't be a surprise, then, will it? Have fun on the rest of your trip. I'll look forward to catching up and sharing with you as my friend when you get home. Us breaking up is for the best, I'm sure you'll see that soon."

Not wanting to intrude, Sara started to sneak away slowly.

Ezekiel turned around and began walking down the staircase, just now noticing her. Sara froze. She wasn't sure what to say.

"I'm guessing you heard that?"

Sara nodded, her cheeks red. "I wasn't trying to eavesdrop... I was just having a moment on the deck below, and, um...."

"So, you heard that things are over between Miranda and me," Ezekiel said.

Sara could feel her heart beating faster. Should she tell him her truth now? She swallowed and took a deep breath. "I'm sorry, Ezekiel. I know you really cared for Miranda." She wondered what more she could say.

"Thanks, Sara," Ezekiel pulled his hand through his hair like a rake. "To be honest, maybe things weren't quite right between Miranda and me. I guess I didn't see it very clearly before, but there was someone in between us. My best friend. You, Sara. And you are so important to me."

"You're important to me, too." She felt like her heart was racing as he stood in front of her. "In fact, I have a confession to make."

"A confession?" he said softly.

"I remember, Ezekiel."

"You remember? What exactly?"

"*Everything*, Ezekiel. I'm sorry that I haven't said anything before now." Sara looked into his eyes.

She could see his chest rise and fall more rapidly then. She wondered if the air around him had suddenly grown still or if he felt the sudden pull she did. She needed to step away; she'd told her truth, but she couldn't be his rebound. There was still much that they needed to discuss before anything could happen.

Yes, she should step away; she shouldn't be alone with him when he was vulnerable. Right now. Immediately... Instead, she closed her eyes, leaned up on her toes, and took his face in both hands before kissing him. At first, he didn't respond. He was still, but then his hands came around her waist, and the kiss grew from sweet to fervent. His lips were soft as he nudged hers open gently. It felt like they'd both been waiting for this. Hadn't she, at least? She could barely think, her thoughts muddled in the intensity of the moment as he pulled her closer.

Abruptly, Ezekiel pulled back. It took Sara a moment to recover, but then she did. *Oh no.* She wanted to slap herself. What had she just done? She blinked at him. He shut his eyes tightly and ran a hand down his face.

"Ezekiel, I'm so sorry. I... I don't...."

"No. No. Don't...."

She didn't let him finish before she fled down the stairs.

"Sara," she heard him call, but she was running towards her room. She couldn't shake the dread in her chest. Had she just ruined their friendship? That night, Sara tossed and turned on her bed, her thoughts more oppressive than the heat.

CHAPTER 13

*E*zekiel would deny it if anyone asked, but he knew deep down that he'd been waiting for Sara to arrive. It was the final party, the celebration dinner mainly for the volunteers, but for the rest of them, too. The mission trip was coming to an end, and Jarryn and the team wanted to show their appreciation.

"Hey." Ezekiel caught Jarryn quickly as he was getting another drink. "I was wondering if you'd seen Sara?"

Jarryn frowned. "No. I hope she'll be here soon. We want to thank all of you for all your hard work."

Ezekiel nodded. He looked around, taking in the especially made-up tables with starched white coverings and fresh tropical flowers.

"She'll appreciate this," he said, forcing himself to be calm. She had been avoiding him for almost two days, as much as that was possible on a small ship. He turned as he heard her voice.

"This is beautiful," Sara said.

Ezekiel sucked in a quick breath. Sara was dressed in an elegant satin dress with shoestring straps, the azure blue of the fabric enhancing her eyes.

"I never thought you would be lost for words, Ezekiel."

Ezekiel swallowed over the lump in his throat, "Will you sit with me Sara?"

She nodded shyly, and they turned to watch Jarryn who was standing in front of the tables.

"This has been a very special mission, and I appreciate you all. I thought tonight would be a great time to go over the achievements of the trip. Four hundred and something teeth removed, was it, Abbie?

"Three hundred and ninety-eight," Abbie laughed, "but who's counting?"

"And how many would you usually do when you are at home?"

"Usually in the single figures, each week," Abbie said.

"I want to thank you for not only what you have achieved that will make a difference in these people's lives like you could not believe, but for the training that you have given them, health education, gardening, and building. All these things will have a lasting impact. And to thank you all for sharing your talents with us at the concert. I know that took some of you out of your comfort zones."

Ezekiel smiled. It had been such a special time, but as usual with Sara, somewhat tumultuous. He sat still, the awareness of her presence distracting him from the words spoken.

"Over to you, Abbie," Jarryn said.

The different specialty leaders said their thank yous to their team and shared about what they had experienced on the trip, making sure to highlight not only what they felt God had done through them, but several of the lighter, funnier moments, leaving everyone chuckling.

As the last leader sat down, Jarryn stood again, "I just want to encourage you all to put Jesus first in your lives. Know that with Jesus 'at the helm', He will help grow you into the person you were meant to be. No matter where you have come from, there is always His grace, kindness, and healing. Being on the mission here has taught me to trust Him and that there is no hurt or pain or past that God cannot heal and even redeem. He is the God of making things new. I encourage you all to strive to keep Him central in the everyday aspects of your life, no matter how big, no matter how seemingly insignificant, and to ask for His help in everything. So, keep God close. Pursue Him daily, hourly. Let Him be the very center of your life. He will not disappoint. And you'll never regret it. As in 2 Corinthians 5:17, 'If any man is in Christ he is a new creature; old things are passed away; and all things become new.' And please know that the leaders on the teams are available to talk and pray with anyone if they would like it."

With the speeches over, the hum of conversation rose in the room. Ezekiel leaned toward Sara and whispered close to her ear. "Sara. I'm sorry about the other day."

Sara turned to him and looked into his eyes. "Let's go up on the deck, Ezekiel." Ezekiel nodded and followed her outside onto the deck. They walked up to the bow and leaned over the railing. Ezekiel watched Sara as she looked below into the water; the waves lapping gently against the ship.

At last, she looked up at him, "I'm the one who is sorry. I shouldn't have kissed you. It was late, I was tired, and I don't know what came over me, such bad timing. I'm sorry," she said.

Ezekiel nodded, but he could feel the disappointment in his heart as she spoke. "Yeah. It's fine. It's probably best that we don't go there again."

She smiled and nodded, but it looked strained to Ezekiel, "I've decided to stay with the outreach, Ezekiel, and travel the world," Sara said.

"What?" Ezekiel said. "What about our friendship?"

"Our friendship will still be no matter what. Let's let it be."

"How can we be friends if I never see you?" Ezekiel's mind was racing, and he felt blindsided by her announcement.

"Can't you trust me to do the right thing, Ezekiel? That I have to find out what is right for me and my journey in life? Can't you accept me as I am and who I want to be?"

"I think you're being selfish," Ezekiel said.

"Selfish?" Sara said, "You're the one being selfish. You just want to feel good about fixing everyone. I'm an adult, and I can live life as I choose to."

"I'd hoped that maybe we could consider... But never mind, you're running away again," Ezekiel said, "You're good at that."

"We want different things, Ezekiel," Sara said. "And I'd like you to accept that."

"You're right, Sara. Excuse me."

Ezekiel could feel how awkward it was between them now; they spent the rest of the evening apart, and when they bumped into each other, they spoke silly polite pleasantries. Ezekiel hoped they would get past this eventually.

After the party had ended, Ezekiel was cleaning up the dining room. The hall was empty: some were in the lounge nearby, and some were enjoying the balmy tropical air outside. Ezekiel cleared the last of the decorations from the tables. Jarryn was returning drinks to the kitchen.

"Did you enjoy yourself? And your time here?" Jarryn asked.

Ezekiel thought about it for a moment, then nodded.

"Yes. I did," he said, but his tone was apprehensive. Jarryn put the bottles down he was holding and leaned against one of the benches.

"What's with that tone?" Jarryn asked.

Ezekiel sighed.

"I enjoyed being here and helping the Ni-Van people immensely, in fact," He paused. "I just think I've been a bit foolish."

Jarryn frowned. "How so?"

Ezekiel felt he needed to admit this to himself, anyway.

"Miranda and I broke up, and then in the next moment, Sara and I kissed. We should've talked, not rushed into kissing. I know now, I've still been kidding myself about my feelings for Sara, and everything in me wants to be with her, but now Sara wants to be a full-time missionary. And I am once again on the out.

"Our history is so rocky, and after dating Miranda, which to be honest never did feel quite right; I wonder if my motives with Sara were also wrong. Maybe our friendship hinders both of us from living our best lives. Maybe I'd let her down as well. It seems obvious we need to move forward apart from each other. We both have roads to travel that we can't travel together. Especially now we are going to be in separate parts of the world."

Ezekiel felt so torn as he said this. The thought of not speaking to Sara, of not seeing her, broke his heart.

"Why are you obsessed with this notion that you're not supposed to be together?"

Ezekiel shut his eyes. "I don't know anymore. I just want to be sure. I don't want to hurt her, and I don't know if she meant it when she said we should just be friends."

Jarryn watched him for a moment, then nodded slowly.

"You're scared because you don't know. You don't want to start and end badly. You care about her too much."

Ezekiel nodded. That about summed it up.

"Ezekiel, the good thing about being a Christian is that we don't have to be scared of uncertainty. We can pray and ask God to guide us. One of my favorite verses is Proverbs 16.3, in the Amplified Classic version. It reads, 'Roll your works upon the Lord [commit and trust them wholly to Him; *He* will cause your thoughts to become agreeable to His will, and] so shall your plans be established *and* succeed."

"But what if God's guidance is to not be with her?" Ezekiel's head dropped. He didn't want to hear God tell him or cause his thoughts to be 'disagreeable' that Sara wasn't the one for him. He didn't want to hear that. Jarryn was looking at him with pity.

"I believe that God *will* lead you. To me, He is already leading you. You are already growing in that you see where you've been in error. I think God is most interested in our character; as we put aside the things of the flesh, then we will be more like Christ. The more we are like Christ, the better our relationships will be. To love a woman as Christ loves the church in that you would lay your life down for her; now that is amazing love. Something to aspire to. Remember, though, that in all things, God works together for the good of those that love Him, including our love lives. Also, remember Paul's words about how it can be easier to devote yourself to the Lord as a single person, but challenges always come with relationships. Still, if the relationship is of the Lord and ordained by Him, there's another scripture that says, "One can put to flight a thousand, but two can put to flight ten thousand. With a relationship blessed of the Lord, the impact is multiplied, not added. I find that very exciting."

Ezekiel laughed. "Yes, I already know plenty about challenges! But you've given me some things to ponder and pray about that I hadn't considered before."

"I'm going on a hike tomorrow. There's a very beautiful mountain not far from the village which one of the villagers has offered to take us up. I like to hike and pray. It makes me feel closer to God when I'm in nature. You should come."

Ezekiel thought about it for a moment. It would help him clear his head.

"Okay," he accepted. "Thanks, Jarryn."

Jarryn smiled and the two went back to tidying up.

CHAPTER 14

Sara sat down on the upper deck looking out to sea. Although she had made a tentative decision about doing more volunteer work, she felt like she wasn't doing right by the people in her life right now. Still more disturbingly, she felt like she wasn't doing right by either herself and, most importantly, her Heavenly Father.

She needed to trust God and ask Him for guidance. She needed His guidance on what to do about the next steps for work. Should she do paid or volunteer? Was she being selfish, like Ezekiel said? Was she just running away again? What were her feelings for Ezekiel? At least she'd been honest with Ezekiel now, but they still hadn't had a proper conversation about her revelation.

Her mind landed on Debra. She wished she had been just a little less self-absorbed and taken more time to care for her friend. She knew she wasn't doing well. Should she have even come on this trip when Debra needed her? How could she go traveling when Debra was obviously not well? Her mind was spinning in a hundred different directions at once, yet she felt like she was getting nowhere. Just then, Sara heard footsteps coming up the stairs.

"Jarryn?"

"Hey, Sara, a few of us are heading to shore tomorrow and going for a hike. There's a beautiful mountain a bit further in the bush and I like to go there to pray and talk to God. You look like you could use some time with God in nature."

Sara watched Jarryn for a moment then smiled.

"I do, don't I? I'm in."

It would probably help her clear her head and pray about all the stuff she was thinking about. It would give her a chance to really surrender to the One Who knew and loved her most.

* * *

SARA WOKE up bright and early the next day for the hike. At breakfast she learned of the various activities that would be happening that day. The last day before they sailed out. Some would visit a local craft market; some would go snorkeling. She felt like today could be the day something changed. She got dressed in her hiking gear and left her room with a smile. That didn't last long, because her smile faltered as she laid eyes on Ezekiel, standing with Jarryn, Abbie and Ivy.

"Ezekiel." She couldn't keep the surprise out of her voice. "I didn't know you'd be coming."

"I didn't realize *you* would be either. I'm glad you are. We all could use some time in nature." He smiled. Sara just nodded, too uncomfortable to return his smile.

"Alright. Let's head off folks," Jarryn led the way as they climbed down the side of the ship and into the tender. Sara and the others filled the boat and then sat watching the wake as the motor roared while they traveled to the shore. When they arrived on dry land, Ivy chatted to a fellow Ni- Van man, who was introduced as Joseph. They shook hands, and followed him along a flat path past the village, and then they came to where the real hiking was to start.

Sara had to admit to herself that she didn't enjoy the walk through the bush. She felt sticky and it was hard to breathe in the heat. She was sure she would enjoy the open air of the mountain, and tried to reassure herself just as her foot got stuck in a vine.

"Ugh." She fell, catching herself with her hands before she hit the ground.

"Are you okay?" Abbie rushed to her, but the men had already gone too far ahead to notice.

"We can't lose them," Sara said, breathing rapidly as Abbie helped her to her feet.

"Oh, don't worry. Ivy knows this path as well. We'll find them along the way or at the top. Are you okay?" Abbie asked again.

Sara dusted off her clothes. "Okay then. Thank you. I'm fine. So, which way?"

Abbie looked around for a bit. "Uhm... This way. There's bound to be markers."

Sara didn't feel entirely confident, but she followed anyway. A couple of hours later, they reached a plateau with a wonderful view. If the guys were up here, she couldn't see them. They agreed to take a little while to sit and recover, just enjoying the scenery.

Sara laid back against a rock and closed her eyes. Her body was weary from the hike and the heat; she hadn't been doing enough exercise lately. She thanked God for the breeze. Sara took a deep breath as she felt tears well up in her eyes and overflow. "Lord, thank You, that You promise to give rest to all who are weary. Lord, I need Your rest and guidance. Please lead me." She moved onto her knees and bent forward, her face in her hands.

She stayed there whispering her prayers, until peace flowed over her. *Thank You Holy Spirit,* she whispered.

She sat back on the ground as she heard Him speak.

Beloved.

Sara realized it had been too long since she'd really connected with Him. For too long she had simply been going through the motions, only focused on asking Him for things instead of cultivating a true relationship with Him. She had cheated both of them out of so much joy. The peace and just the feeling of gloriousness was so beautiful. She felt fresh tears come from her eyes, but this time, they were joyful.

"What about Ezekiel?" she asked, her voice small. "Lord, what about *him*?"

Delight yourself in the Lord, and I will give you the desires of your heart.

Sara's eyes flew open, and she felt her heart begin to beat faster. She could only blink. *What did her heart really want?*

* * *

THEY HAD LOST SARA, Abbie, and Ivy, but Joseph assured Ezekiel in his limited English that Ivy knew her way around. Ezekiel found a spot, sat down, and began to pray. He started with thanksgiving and some worship, and then he asked God's forgiveness for anything he had done. Then he prayed for his family, the homeless shelter, Miranda and hew new faith, the advancement of the gospel, and guidance for his career.

There was just one thing he hadn't mentioned.

You do not have because you do not ask, My son.

He heard God clearly in his spirit, even as he sat there, his eyes closed. He only kept hearing that reference from scripture.

"Lord, I want You to be my everything. But I'd still like to be a part of Sara's life, even if we can't be together. And now she wants to be on the other side of the world. Help me, Lord; I can't fool You. You know how much I care about her."

He stayed quiet, his eyes closed, his hands in his lap.

You can and you will, beloved. Trust My heart for you, Ezekiel, I am with you, your desires are MY desires because I've placed them there.

Ezekiel felt like fireworks were going off in his head at this revelation. He took several deep breaths of relief and then focused on listening to God again.

He wasn't sure how much time had passed, but he felt truly happy when they began the hike down the mountain. God had even helped him put aside this need to somehow fulfill his father's purpose at the shelter. God wanted Ezekiel to be like his father, and impact people's lives, but he didn't have to be a carbon copy. That was what ministry was about, touching lives. Ezekiel had so many ideas for the shelter now to expand the impact the program would have on people's lives. And the programs he was thinking of would need other skills. He would be free to delegate. He could still be involved in some way, but it wouldn't consume him.

"Hey!"

Ezekiel and Jarryn looked up at the same time. They were near the ground when Abbie called out, from a path across the mountain from the one he and Jarryn were hiking.

"Where have you guys been?" Abbie yelled out again.

Jarryn replied to her, but Ezekiel wasn't paying attention. They were saying something about meeting on the ground. Ezekiel's eyes locked with Sara's when hers locked with his. He stilled, and so did she.

Her hair was loose, and blowing all around her face. She looked simply divine. Maybe it was from spending a longer time in God's presence than either of them had in a while or maybe it was just that he knew she was his, but she looked otherworldly and exquisite in that moment.

She looked like she was afraid to breathe and Ezekiel felt much the same. "Hey." Jarryn touched his shoulder, breaking him out of his thoughts. "Let's get back down to the village."

Ezekiel slowly dragged his gaze from Sara to Jarryn. "Yes, we should."

He could feel his heart pounding as he reached the bottom of the mountain. He took off in Sara's direction, walking as fast as his legs could safely carry him. He stopped at the base of a shortcut. Abbie had already climbed down, and Sara would arrive momentarily and waited. He felt giddy, just waiting for her to get down.

"I'm sorry. I'm not very fit at the moment," she called down to him. She was only a few feet from level ground by now.

"That's fine. Take your time," he called back. *We have a lifetime*, he wanted to add, but stopped himself, a silly grin on his face.

The grin was replaced by a terrified expression in an instant when he heard Ivy screech Sara's name, and then he saw her slip. His heart stopped as he watched Sara lose her grip and collapse down the hill face.

"Sara!" Without thinking, he leaped to the right a few inches just in time to catch her, and they both fell to the ground with a thud, she on top of him.

Both of them were breathing frantically. His heart was beating a million miles per minute, as he was sure hers was. He was holding her the way he had caught her, firmly around the waist, and he wasn't sure he wanted to let go.

"Are you alright?" he managed to ask between heavy breaths. He pushed some hair out of her face, trying to ensure she was okay.

She coughed and rolled off him, sitting on the ground. Ezekiel sat up, a bit of panic rising in his chest as he watched her cough and clutch at her chest, her head down.

"Sara, are you...."

"I'm fine," she said finally, looking up, with a shaky smile and nodding. "I'm fine. Just got the wind knocked out of me for a minute is all."

Ezekiel let out a breath he hadn't realized he was even holding. They sat there for a moment breathing heavily as Joseph, and Jarryn rushed over to them. Ivy made her way safely down the last part of the shortcut. He knew such a fall was frightening and she would need a few minutes to recover. He stood up, and waited until Sara extended her hand before helping her up.

"Thank you for breaking my fall. I hope you're alright." She smiled.

Jarryn, seeing that they were all right, smiled and winked at Ezekiel before leading the others back towards the village.

Ezekiel chuckled and nodded back at Jarryn, almost not believing how much at peace he felt. His life was far from perfect, but he knew that one thing was true.

"I'm in love with you," he whispered.

Sara's eyes widened. She looked into his eyes. "Really?" Sara whispered back.

Ezekiel nodded gently and took her hand in his. It felt so right.

"I don't want to just be your friend, but if that is still what you want, I don't know that I can do it. I don't mean to say this to press you with an ultimatum, only to tell you that it is how I feel. And I want to support you in whatever you do. If that means leaving the US and volunteering in the Pacific, I'm with you."

His heart was in his throat. Sara's eyes welled up, and Ezekiel wasn't sure what that meant.

"I don't...." She looked away and laughed, but it was more of a small sob than a laugh. Ezekiel felt like his heart would fly away soon, it was beating so fast.

"I don't want to just be your friend either. I think I've been in love with you longer than I've admitted. And you were right, I was running away again. I want to do more of this work in the future, but the timing is not right, not now. I want to be with you, Ezekiel," she replied.

Ezekiel froze, emotion overcoming him at her words. He blinked at her and then shook his head.

"Sara Ward."

"Ezekiel Cane."

He wrapped his arms around her waist and pulled her to him,

taking in her scent, feeling her against him. They fit. It felt right. She looked up at him, and, this time, *he* kissed *her*. Ezekiel could feel fireworks in his heart, taste the sweetness of her. She put her hand on his face as the kiss deepened. And then they broke apart for air.

"Good trip?" Ezekiel joked, still emotional.

"Great trip," she laughed and linked her arm with his. "But I think I'm ready to go back to the ship now."

* * *

FOUR MONTHS LATER, Ezekiel was seated next to Sara. She looked like a vision in the new dress she had purchased, especially for Christmas Day. It was a day to celebrate, as at long last Sara had moved to LA so they were no longer doing a long-distance relationship.

"Hey," he murmured. She turned to him. *Beautiful*, Ezekiel thought. Her hair was slicked back in a low bun. Her earrings were trendy, a green art deco enamel design bringing out the color of her eyes. "You're beautiful," he said, barely a whisper.

"Don't you think we should get ready to serve dinner?" Sara asked pointedly, looking at the crowd of people gathering in the dining hall.

"Yes," Ezekiel said. He stood, pulled her chair back, took her hand and kissed it as she stood up. She smiled and looked back to her hand where her engagement ring was, the diamonds in the unique setting surrounding an oval aquamarine gem twinkling in the light. They walked over to trestle tables laden with food.

"May I have your attention, please," Ezekiel raised his voice over the hubbub of conversation and paused as the conversation ceased. "For those who don't know me, I'm Ezekiel Cane, and I have been helping here at the shelter for a while now. But I've a special announcement to make tonight. However, first things first. I'm sure you're all hungry and looking forward to your Christmas dinner, so announcements can wait. Over to my mother, the wonderful Teresa Cane."

"Thank you, Ezekiel," Teresa said, "I welcome you all here for this meal, and may we all reflect on the reason for the season, the birth of our Lord and Savior Jesus Christ. Lord, I thank You for the provision of this wonderful food. May you bless it to our bodies Lord, and may Your peace and favor be with us all today and in the coming year.

Amen. Please line up for the food and don't rush away as we have some surprises after the meal."

Ezekiel and Sara lined up with Debra alongside as well, serving turkey, ham, mashed potatoes, gravy, and hot green vegetables.

Before the first course was finished, Teresa stood up.

"Now you are no longer ravenous," Teresa smiled, "or so I hope. Please be assured there will be seconds, but we have some announcements to make here at the shelter. Firstly, many of you know that Ezekiel and Sara are engaged, and I want us all to congratulate them! Please stand, Ezekiel and Sara." They stood up, and everyone clapped. Ezekiel only had eyes for Sara.

"About time," Debra said, and then laughed. Sara fake punched her in the arm. "Your turn next, Debra." Debra turned to Sara, her expression one of faux mortification.

"If only I was as blessed," Debra said.

"And because I am going to be busy soon with a new wife," Ezekiel said, and the crowd cooed, "I am going to take some time out for other things. But not before we get some new programs up and running. I am excited to announce that we are starting a building program, teaching people the basics, and we'll be building some tiny homes. The bonus will be that we will also get the maintenance done that is long overdue, which will mean the buildings will be much more attractive and homier and we'll be able to cater to more people. Also, we are going to grow a community garden and have a chef come to teach lessons for healthy, affordable eating. We hope that these initiatives will inspire, as well as enable, those who are involved to find employment in the community. And I am delighted to announce that Teresa Cane, my mother, and wife of the late Isaiah Cane, will be setting up a team of people to get this all started. Please stand and give her a round of applause."

"Thank you, so much," Teresa said, "I helped Isaiah so much during his time here and I'm looking forward to being more involved once again. Today I am happy to introduce to you our very own choir that has been working hard behind the scenes, just for a special performance today. Over to you, Mateo and Miranda."

Miranda stood and walked over to the side of the hall; others joined her and they stood in a group. Ezekiel caught her eye and smiled. Mateo walked over and stood in front of the choir, then turned and began to conduct them as they started the Christmas carol "O Come All Ye Faithful."

Ezekiel and Sara glanced at each other as Miranda sang a high harmony in the second verse and then the rest of the crowd joined in as Mateo turned to them and waved his hands in encouragement for the others to sing. Ezekiel had to shake his head in amazement. This was the surprise that Miranda had been working on, a choir. Not only had Mateo come on board to collaborate with the shelter in the building project, but he was sharing with them his musical gifts.

Later on in the afternoon, Ezekiel and Sara sat in the courtyard and watched as children ran around playing with their toys that Truman, as Santa, had given out. He did manage to accept an awkward hug from an especially enthusiastic child now and then.

"What an amazing Christmas," Sara whispered. "It seems everything is coming together here. And I'm so glad we finally figured *us* out."

"Me too." He kissed the top of her head.

"Mm. This is my favorite place. In your arms." She looked up at him, and he pecked her lips.

"Mine too." He smiled.

EPILOGUE

Two months later, Sara and Ezekiel drove their car into the driveway at the beach house in Santa Cruz, where their families had holidayed when they were teenagers.

Sara stepped out of the car and breathed in the sea air. Ezekiel popped the trunk and grabbed their bags, walking toward the house. Sara carried some smaller bags up onto the veranda.

"So many memories," Sara mused. Her eyes were moist.

Ezekiel unlocked the door and placed the bags inside.

"Come here, you," he said. She walked to Ezekiel and gave him her hand. He pulled her into his arms and kissed her softly on her lips.

"How does it feel to be here, Sara?" Ezekiel said. "Are you okay?

Sara took her father's urn and gently placed it on the mantelpiece. She nodded.

"One more night, Dad, and you'll be in one of your favorite places," Sara said.

The following morning, Mildred arrived, and they walked along the beach to find the small dinghy that would take them out to the launch they had hired. The sun was beating down, and the cry of seagulls filled the air. When they found the dinghy, the captain held out his hand so Mildred could step from the sand into the boat. Sara and Ezekiel clambered over as well and settled in their seats, donning their life jackets. Sara raised her face to the sun as the captain turned the motor on and the boat roared out to the launch. Once settled into the launch the captain motored out into the open sea. Eventually, the captain cut the engine and retreated below deck into the cabin.

"I didn't get to say goodbye, Dad," Sara said. "But I thank you for all the good things that you were and gave me. Thank you that you helped me to be determined and never give up. Things are good now, Dad. You'd be so proud, I'm sure. I'm with your adopted son, the one you loved, who I love now as well, and we are so happy."

"Thanks, Darren," Ezekiel said, "For everything. And for your beautiful daughter."

Mildred's lips quivered as the tears came, and they each took a turn in scattering Darren's ashes into the sea. "Until we meet again, Darren," Mildred said.

Sara unpacked the food they had brought, and they had a picnic up on the top deck, reminiscing about the good times they had had as a family.

"It's so wonderful to have you here, Ezekiel," Mildred said. "And Darren would be so happy that you two are together. But what's next for you? Now you are not so busy at the shelter?"

"Did Sara tell you I'm working on a book?" Ezekiel asked. "Which I will work on in between helping Sara at her new company, and being an ear for any issues at the shelter."

"You will be fabulous in your new role, Sara," Mildred leaned over and patted her hand.

"But what about the shelter? Will Teresa be able to manage all her responsibilities?" Mildred said.

"Keller will help her. The two of them are very capable. Keller has always been way more than a secretary, and Truman was so thrilled about giving the toys for the mission trip, that he is taking on a major role there as well, with fundraising. Between them all, the shelter will be in excellent hands. Truman has many contacts in the business world, which will help with the ongoing projects. There is a plan moving forward for funding. Keller organized a fair recently with a primary emphasis on toys as well as music and fabulous food. It put the shelter on the map with other smaller local investors wanting to make a difference. And then the support from Mateo and the Above Board Construction company. I couldn't ask for more," Ezekiel shook his head. "All that worry for nothing." he laughed. "I've learned to trust." After all, his dream of being with Sara had come true, and he could trust the One who cared more than he did for the next step as well.

They moved around to their seats again as the captain turned the engine back on, and the boat bounced over the sea and the rolling waves back to the dinghy. Soon they were once again on the shore.

"Thank You, God, for a new life and new memories," Ezekiel whispered. In spite of near tragedy, many obstacles that seemed to indicate a dead end, and even some incredible miracles, Ezekiel realized he had a much greater understanding now of a verse that even he had, many times, blithely quoted, without truly believing it - '*all* things work together for good to those who love God and are called according to His purpose'. Now he could vouch for its truth and redemptive promise like never before.

Sara leaned over and kissed him. Gazing into her emerald green eyes, Ezekiel knew he couldn't be happier. He couldn't wait to see what God had in store for the rest of their lives!

FREE EXCERPT FROM "LOVE AFTER TRAUMA"

Debra hadn't been feeling her best for the past few weeks. The episodes of panic attacks and nightmares, regular events since she was a child, had resurfaced. Her life was perfect when they weren't happening, but the moment they started; and she didn't even know what triggered them anymore; her whole world was thrown upside down.

She forced a smile and looked up at her best friend, Sara Ward, well, Sara Cane now. Sara looked like a vision in her wedding dress. "Ready for the first dance? Just come on a minute after me and Ezekiel," Sara smiled.

Debra found her smile feeling more genuine as she stood up from her seat and watched as Sara linked her arm with Ezekiel's. How could she not be happy at her best friend's wedding? She needed to not think about anything and just be present.

Debra watched as the two of them made their way to the dance floor, the spotlight finding them. "And now, welcome the bride and groom to the floor for their first dance," The host announced. "And Ezekiel and Sara insist that you join in with them on the floor; Debra will let you know when to join in."

Sara giggled. "Ready?" Her smile was radiant.

Debra nodded, and stood back-to-back as they lifted their arms in a ballroom dancing position. Debra swayed to the soft music playing.

She couldn't help the emotion beginning to rise in her chest. Sara was so special to her; they had been best friends for over four years.

"I'm going to miss you." She turned and whispered, fighting tears.

Sara pulled Ezekiel sideways so she could talk to Debra more easily, a frown on her face. "Deb, I'm always going to be available for you. Anytime you need me. Don't worry."

Debra gave her best friend a sad smile. She could tell that Sara was getting emotional too, and she didn't want to make the bride cry, so she nodded, even though the words did nothing to reassure her. Debra had been alone for a long time before she had met Sara, then they had done everything together, even worked and lived together. Although Debra was happy for Sara that she was getting married, Debra felt alone again. It had been a lonely and terrible few weeks for her, and she felt afraid for her future. The music began and the married couple took the first steps, followed by Debra and the best man.

Debra felt her stomach begin to turn, and in a moment, she felt cold. She pulled back. As she caught Sara's eye, Sara somehow managed to maneuver Ezekiel over towards her.

"Deb?" Sara asked, drawing her eyebrows together. "Are you okay?"

Debra recognized the feeling that was beginning to creep up her chest, but for the life of her, she couldn't understand why it was happening now. She stepped back and placed a hand on her stomach. "I...." Debra looked up at Sara's worried face. "Yes." Except that she wasn't okay. It was getting hard to breathe, and she could feel her hands shaking.

"Deb." Sara took a step towards her. The crowd was beginning to murmur.

"Thank you. For the dance. I think that.... that uhm, everyone should join us now." She turned pointedly to the host, and thankfully he seemed to take the hint and invited the guests to the dance floor.

"Debra, you don't...." Sara began to say.

"I need to go; I'll be back." She said quickly and rushed through the crowd, each breath coming in shorter and shorter. She was beginning to panic, a sense of dread creeping down her back. Oh God, she couldn't breathe. She couldn't even see where she was going.

She felt like something was going to overtake her, something terrible. The pressure in her lungs seemed to be mounting, and she was beginning to feel dizzy.

"Hey, steady."

She stopped short as she collided with someone's chest. As she touched him, he caught her around the waist. His voice cut through her daze, and she looked up, blinking to clear her vision. She was still struggling to breathe and could feel herself shaking, but she felt more present than a moment ago.

The stranger dropped his head so that his mouth was by her ear. "I need you to trust me."

She wasn't sure what he'd said, but she nodded. Her lungs were beginning to burn, and she felt his hand move up and down on her back in a soothing motion. His other hand found her shaking one.

"I... I can't... I can't breathe." She managed to say through gasps of short breaths. She wasn't sure why she was telling this to a stranger, but she had an intuition he could help, even more so, like he was *supposed* to help her.

***Love After Trauma* coming in 2024**

ABOUT THE AUTHOR

Elizabeth Marie lives in the Northern part of the South Island of New Zealand on a farm with her husband. She loves all things related to stories and devours books and movies. She loves to walk in the hills and hang out with her dog and her friends. She also loves music, singing, and playing the guitar. She attends the local New Life church.

Find out more about Elizabeth Marie at:
www.elizabethmarieromance.com
www.facebook.com/elizabethmarieromance

Also, be sure to visit the website to receive this FREE subscriber-only copy of Love: A Summer Prelude as well as to be notified of any new releases, giveaways, contests, cover reveals and so much more.

Also by Elizabeth Marie:

Love After Trauma
Love In Hiding
Love Comes Around
The Reluctant Billionaire

***P.S.** It means the world to me that you bought my book. Writing is my passion, and I look forward to YOUR feedback.*

So if you liked this book, I'd like to ask for a small favor. Would you be so kind as to leave a review on Amazon? It'd be very much appreciated!

From your friend, Elizabeth Marie

www.ingramcontent.com/pod-product-compliance
Lightning Source LLC
Chambersburg PA
CBHW050231110726
47898CB00007B/2110